Oddly, though, I heard voices. I crept to the bedroom door, stealthily twisted the knob and peered out. Although the table lamp was on, Mama faced the front door blocking my view, so I couldn't tell who else was there. Obviously a person Mama chose not to invite in. Only phrases escaped from their low-pitched conversation. The stranger sounded like a woman. ". . .should know."

"Appreciate. . . Cora Lee."

Mumble. Mumble. When Mama stepped forward, they hugged. The arms that encircled Mama's back were white. I bit my bottom lip to keep from crying out. The woman, whose face I never saw, left, but Mama stayed by that front door. Cold, I retreated to bed. Her footsteps, deadened against the homemade rag rugs, beat louder on the bare floor. In the kitchen the water faucet shuddered; the teakettle clanged against the burner. Full of questions, I fought sleep.

NOTES WHEN SUMMER ENDS

BEVERLY LAUDERDALE

Genesis Press, Inc.

Black Coral

An imprint of Genesis Press, Inc.
Publishing Company

Genesis Press, Inc.
P.O. Box 101
Columbus, MS 39703

ISBN: 1-58571-180-2
Manufactured in the United States of America

First Edition

Visit us at www.genesis-press.com
or call at 1-888-Indigo-1

DEDICATION

To my mother, Margaret

CHRIS

At last I've found a ball point in my purse under a flaking saltine cracker and two outdated store coupons. Guess I'll write the first thing that pops into my mind.

Friday, 10:08 P.M.

Well, book, you lie on my lap, accusing me just as those composition books did years ago in Miss Simmons' English class—full of blank pages and straight lines that ran on forever. And I feel just as I did in Miss Simmons' class each fall—unsure what to write, where to begin. All Cammy said when she handed this to me was, "It's a memory book." Memory? Of my actual days with Emily Jane? An accounting of what I might be asked to say at the tribute? Might I have to pass the book to those two other women Cammy invited?

I have met one of them before, Savannah, but I don't *know* her. And this Ann flying in from San Francisco is totally unknown. She's supposed to come sometime tonight. Savannah arrived about thirty minutes ago. When I heard the click of a door, I carefully turned the bedroom doorknob and peeked out to see Cammy usher Savannah into her bedroom. Strange that Cammy would give up her own room. I've only been in there, what? Four? Five times in my life?

Gently I closed the door and returned to the overstuffed chair, one that Emily Jane had bought in high school at a garage sale. We carried it for eight blocks. Had a hard time with the stairs until Cammy finally helped us. Emily Jane knew right where it would go, in this corner where she, and sometimes I, could stare out over the rooftops of Centerville. On summer nights like this one, we'd respond to "moon fever." That's what Emily Jane called it. We'd exchange secrets and weird dreams. But right now, I'll not think about them.

Instead, I'll look around her room. It hasn't changed much. The double bed where I slept beside her—on the right side away from the window—is the same. Once I told my daughter about our sleepovers, and Heather paled. "The same bed! God, Mom, how lesbo."

"Hardly," I said and offered nothing more. While there was an innocence in our growing up, and we didn't experiment with the same sex, neither of us was sexually naïve. This I didn't care to get into with my daughter.

Okay, so that's off the subject, though I'm not sure what the subject of a memory book is. I'll stick with this room. In the closet I'd probably find her clothes, but I'm not going to check. The bulletin board is bare. In elementary and junior high, Emily Jane put up movie star posters. We painted thumbtacks with fingernail polish and pushed them into the corner of each picture. In high school, she had photos of friends and programs from concerts. Usually, she underlined her name if she'd sung a solo or was in a trio or sang with Dirk. At last, I've written his name. It feels good, honest. This evening—particularly in Cammy's house—his name has hovered, waiting to be recognized.

When Cammy called last month to tell me that Emily Jane had died, I first thought, *how eerie, because this very minute Todd's talking about Dirk Hawkins.* He was remembering a wrecked motorcycle he and Dirk bid on a full year before they took their driving test. "Even the handle bars were bent," Todd said as the phone rang. From the way it rang, I figured it had to be bad news and said so. My husband says—and he drawls out the syllables of my name to show his irritation—"Chris-tine, it's impossible to tell who's calling or the message by a phone's ring. A ring is automatic."

But I can tell. I can sense lots of things. Off the subject again, aren't I? Emily Jane used to laugh, "Chris, I love your thought process. You take an idea and turn it into a springboard. I never know where you're going."

"Except," I'd argue, "my ideas are guided by a logic."

Emily Jane would punch my arm....

So, I was talking about Cammy's phone call. When she told me of Emily Jane's death and that she wasn't having a funeral, her voice stayed absolutely level, almost a monotone. Then she said, "I'll call Emily's college friend, Savannah, and Ann, the woman she taught with in California. I'll work out a weekend so the three of you can spend several days in my house. A tribute of sorts."

Stupidly I said, "You want me to stay overnight?" Of course the other two would need to stay at Cammy's, but I live only four blocks away on Bonner Street. When I don't sleep beside Todd, he insists that he doesn't sleep well; that he rolls over to curve himself around my bottom and wakes at the sudden emptiness.

"Likely three nights," Cammy answered.

"We'll have a type of encounter group?"

"Don't know. I simply think Emily would approve."

Then I noticed the ragged seam in her voice, as if Emily Jane's aunt—Emily Jane's one relative—had tried to sew a binding over her grief. Suddenly I understood that my friend was gone, really gone, so I barely managed "okay" before I sobbed.

Todd's not big on sensitivity, but he left the table—we still have that Formica one we bought when we married—and held me tight. Even when hurting over Emily Jane, part of me responded to Todd— his solid chest, strong arms, the very essence of him. And part of me wanted, at that instant, to go into the bedroom and make slow, gentle love, to be cradled and to block out my pain.

From the day we entered kindergarten together, she, the happy white girl, and I, one of three black students in the class, had been best friends. I named her Emily Jane to differentiate her from the other Emily in our class. Emily Jane sounded prettier than Emily One or Emily Two, our teacher's choice. Many afternoons she walked home from school with me to our rambling old house on Center Street, alive with my brothers and sisters.

"They tumble around like puppies," Emily Jane told Cammy.

That described my family then and now, because the four Todd and I produced also created an atmosphere of loving confusion. Once, when Emily Jane and I talked about artists, writers, composers, and how tragedy seemed a common thread in their lives, she sighed, "I'll never be a great singer or a great anything, because I've been happy, and happy doesn't cut it."

Well, if Emily Jane had been happy, I had been ecstatic. What a good, non-tragic life I've led. Oops, I've wandered again. Where was I? Right, with Todd in the kitchen, and while we didn't end up in the bedroom, he did assure me that it was all right to stay at Cammy's. He pulled a chair away from the table. Its metal legs scraped against the linoleum, drawing attention to the fading pattern. Heather had begged us to replace it with tile. As I sank into the chair, the cushion puffed air. "The chairs always sound like they're farting," my son Greg had once said, and I tried to tune out his joke as I buried my face in my hands. For once, I wished my thoughts didn't dart everywhere, but they would line up in proper order behind the name, Emily Jane.

"Sorry you didn't see her before she died," Todd said, and I cried louder. "But maybe it's better. Maybe you'll remember her as you last saw her. I'll sure think of her singing with Dirk on a stage."

I couldn't answer. Sure, that picture was etched in my mind along with plenty of others, but I owned no final, conclusive picture. Emily Jane had arrived in Centerville this summer, the day after I left for Chicago for the birth of Jason, my grandson. When I got home and learned that Emily Jane was in town, I hurried to Cammy's house.

The front door was open; the screen hooked. I called, "Hello" through its mesh, and from the front parlor, I heard a moan. In the July heat, I shivered. Goose bumps dotted my arms. While I waited, unsure and afraid, Cammy stepped into view, a silhouette behind the screen.

"Emily's extremely sick," she whispered, her thin lips mashed against those tiny squares of screen. In that summer heat, where no leaves stirred and Cammy's flowers wilted, I, too, wilted. I braced myself against the rough green board that trimmed the front door. She continued, saying, "I'll call when Emily's having a better day. Of all people, you're the one she wants to see before..." her voice trailed away.

The call never came.

SAVANNAH

Conscious of Cammy's room and of the night, I pause and let the setting affect me before I make an entry in the journal I've been given.

Friday night—

I've always liked the night, especially a night heavy with summer. Right now, such richness presses so closely that it holds the eddy of cigarette smoke in this room, Cammy's room. The smoke curls toward the open window, but unable to escape through the screen, it loops toward me and Cammy's ladder-backed chair.

I glance around the neat, severe room. Yet, in the careful lines of the tucked white chenille bedspread or in the primrose decorating the back of the hand-mirror lying on the dresser, I detect a hidden passion, a barely-submerged sensuousness that lurks as well, within Cammy.

Inhaling, I tap my cigarette against the rim of a teacup commandeered from downstairs for an ash tray. Ann is expected any minute, or I'd smoke on the front porch. As a Californian, she'll be offended by cigarettes, and on a night when nothing moves, when blackness shapes wind-free pockets around every object, the smoke would hug the porch.

Cammy won't mind if I light another one after I finish this one. She'll forgive whatever I do, because from our first meeting, we established a link I can't explain. The link has merely strengthened since that October night after my roommate, Emily, suggested I come home with her for the weekend. As eighteen-year-old college freshmen, we were homesick. Too far for me to ride the bus to Mama in Hampton, Missouri, I'd resigned myself to counting days until Thanksgiving break, but Emily lived in Centerville, only an hour's bus ride from the campus.

"It's high school homecoming weekend. I know all the guys on the football team, know the queen candidates. Oh, Savannah, let's go." She probably hoped Dirk would be around. The dorm was oppressive, so I dipped into money I didn't have to buy a ticket. After class on Friday afternoon, we caught the bus.

When it let us off in Centerville, we ran down the main street toward her wooden, two-story house. Our luggage banged our legs, and Emily yelled, "I can already hear the band."

We planned to drop what we carried and hurry to the football field, but when Cammy greeted us, I suddenly didn't care about going with Emily. Not knowing the friends she'd bump into at the game, I saw myself with a self-conscious grin, standing behind her as she tossed introductions over her shoulder. I could never enter that high school world, just as she could never enter mine, if ever we took the bus to Hampton.

With minimal protests, Emily left me in the parlor. In the warm fall night, I sat near a window propped open with a broken broom handle. Lace curtains hung limply on each side of the pane. Due to the angle and lamp light, the glass trapped Cammy's reflection. It mimicked her thin body as it bent, to sit in a companion chair on my right and captured her regal features, reminiscent of New England, of an Edith Wharton character. What a contrast to me, who spoke of the South. Full-hipped and so full-breasted that I longed for winter and men's crewneck sweaters to conceal my bosom. As well, I had a full face with thick lips. At age twelve, I started hoarding pennies to buy lipsticks, hoping some advertised new color or combination of colors would reduce their shape.

Oh, yes, we were complete opposites in age, in body types, in experiences, in race, but an intuitive something linked us. Later, I likened it to when one spots a stranger across a room—man, woman, it doesn't matter—and instinctively senses that that individual is shy, has suffered a trauma, is involved in a messy affair.... Well, I spotted secrets in Cammy; she in me. Each treading with a certain caution, afraid that what we feared would catch us, that what we worked to forget, avoid, or ignore would snare us. So, that evening, against the background of yells, garbled words over the public address system, and the sporadic bass drum beat that filtered through the air, we spoke easily, confessionally. Long before Emily crept into her room, I'd confided to Cammy my growing certainty that my unknown father was white, and I'd revealed my conflicted desire to learn more about him.

ANN

Since it's too hot to sleep, I'll record my initial impressions of how the house looked to me when I arrived hours ago.

Friday, after midnight

The angular lines of the house are as Em detailed them. Set on plains, backed by nothing or by a wind break, it would be a stark farmhouse. Gentled by a lawn, by what in this midnight time seems rows of zinnias and marigolds, secure behind maples or locusts, and cradled by neighboring houses, it's Em's childhood home in a small Midwestern town.

That's what I initially thought as I parallel-parked my rental car before 731 Polk Street. So, maybe that's where I should begin this journal that Cammy handed me, she, like an apparition with long, white hair that flowed down her back to blend with a crisp, white nightgown.

When I approached the house, I glimpsed a figure in the hallway behind the front screen. I felt it appraising me, felt its suspicion, felt it was Cammy. I didn't alter my pace, didn't acknowledge her presence. Instead, I listened to the satisfactory click of my shoe against the concrete sidewalk, a confident sound. No hesitation, no fear, and that bolstered me as I mounted three wooden porch steps and moved beneath the dim exterior light fixture with its layered circles of insects. Because a white arm shoved open the screen, I needn't put my luggage down to knock on the door.

But when I entered the hallway, my composure slipped. Something of Em waited here. If I could blink more rapidly, turn more quickly, or somehow part the curtain of today for a scrap out of yesterday, I'd see a young Em run down the inside staircase, curls bouncing a half-second after each jarring step. Or, I'd see a teenage Em standing in this spot, face against the window watching for Dirk, or—

"I'm Cammy, Emily's aunt," the woman said as the screen door closed behind me. "Thank you for making this trip."

Shifting my luggage, I shook Cammy's hand, bony and firm, as I'd imagined. "I'm privileged to have been asked."

Her eyes were large in a thin, oval face; her posture erect. As she regarded me steadily, I sensed anew that she classed me as an enemy, or at the least, an alien. She knew the other two women well—Chris, Em's friend from childhood, and Savannah, the college roommate. However, I came from near San Francisco and had shared moments and secrets with Em that lay beyond her scope.

This led to significant thought number two: *Cammy's asking Chris, Savannah, and me to commit memories to paper so that she can read them and weave together missing pieces of Em's life.*

That thought didn't surface, though, until after she'd escorted me up stairs, muffled by a fading runner. Under the yellowed light the runner looked purple with a golden garland, an intricate floral design. I focused on the rug, not on the nightgowned woman before me, because this rug had known the pressure of Em's feet. How many times had she gone up and down? Thousands? Did she choose the middle? Or sometimes did she skip steps or tread only on the right side or on the left?

When Cammy stopped, I glanced ahead to the room at the hall's end. Em's room. It overlooked the street. I had hoped I could sleep in there, but likely Chris rated that one. Across from it on the right, the door also shut, must be Cammy's room. The older woman wouldn't put me in that one, either. Obviously, I'd stay in the rarely-if-ever-used back guest bedroom.

Cammy pointed to the bathroom beside the guest room door. "Once in a while, the toilet runs. As I told the others, jiggle the handle."

I nodded. How many years since I've been a guest in a private home, shared a communal bath? I wished I could give Em my impressions, hear her laughter when I confided silly questions that flitted through my mind. *Are the others night or morning bathers? Both? Tub or shower women?*

"It's late," Cammy gestured toward "my" room, and from somewhere in the folds of her gown produced a composition book, the kind I'd not seen in ages with its "100 Sheets 9 ¾ x 7 ½ label."

As she descended the stairs, I realized that she'd given her room to Savannah. Behind "my" door waited a chipped walnut dressing table with a smeared mirror, circa 1920, and a pine dresser that rocked when I laid my hand on its ledge. No caster on the right front corner. A double bed with brass headboard missing a porcelain corner knob was topped with a mottled pink chenille spread. I tossed my carry-on onto it, kicked off my heels and sat in the final cast-off, a lumpy rocker.

"God, Em," I whispered as tears stung my eyes, which were irritated from the airplane's recycled air and from straining to read unfamiliar road signs as I left Des Moines. I did nothing to prevent tears that coursed down my cheeks and trailed across my jaw line.

When Em had known she was terminal, when she decided to die in Centerville with Cammy, had she bid goodbye to each room? Was her vision jaded by more than three decades on the West Coast? Or did she examine every bit of mismatched furniture and find a story in each one? Or did the rooms simply represent sentences in her life, ones not worthy of comment?

I dug a Kleenex from my blazer pocket, then hung my jacket in a closet perfumed by moth balls. I removed my clothes, welcoming air upon my body. But in the humid stillness, it was debilitating to unpack, so I lay on the bed in bra and panties. Sheets and mattress had snared heat, and I longed for air conditioning. With the composition/memory book, I fanned my face. Its attendant *whish whish* broke the quiet, and I strained to hear a passing car, a cricket, but darkness, like a sponge, absorbed any noise. In my East Bay apartment, had I ever encountered pure silence? As I sat upright, a bedspring twanged. Ah, a noise.

Wide awake, I placed both feet on the floor and studied the book. That's when I thought I might as well write something with all these hungry pages to fill. The spring twanged a second time as I settled on the edge of the bed, uncapped my pen, and began page one. But now I face the problem, what to say about Em? Days and years with her don't proceed in linear fashion. Seated on this sagging mattress, I conjured but snippets of our friendship, fragments out of sequence.

Somewhere, sometime, when I taught art at four elementary schools and she taught music at the same, our paths crossed. We were traveling teachers, hired to provide "enrichment."

For months, I'd guess, we'd occasionally pass in some hallway, either entering or exiting classrooms. We'd smile, nod, exchange inconsequential greetings. So, what emerges as my first solid image of her?

One day I arrived a few minutes early, and as I neared an opened classroom door, I heard a pitch pipe and next the throaty voice of the music teacher leading fifth graders in "Barbara Allan." The voice wasn't excellent, but it had a something—a folk singer's quality, an earthiness that evoked joy and pathos. Then I saw Em, or at least her profile. Black hair tumbled over her shoulders and her white blouse. In one hand she held the music book; with the other, she directed. But the head tossed back remains the sharpest image. As she belted out, "Oh, Mother, come and make my bed," I wished for my destroyed sketch pad to line out the Barbara Allan she suggested.

She turned slightly, caught my stare and grinned. Oh, Em had this marvelous grin that exposed uneven teeth. "You can spot those of us who were po'," she later laughed. "We're the ones with the scraggly teeth."

Mine couldn't be called "scraggly" thanks to braces wired on by a dentist who winked at my mother. "While Ann won't have perfect occlusion, I guarantee that she'll be marketable." I'd cringed at that. I didn't aspire to marketability, but to filling rooms with paintings and not children's belongings, which was the obvious consequence of being marketable. Well, I got my wish, or my punishment when Robin, my daughter died....

So I stood in the hallway watching Em sing, watching her become the song. That's it. That was her effect. She became the music. When the last note faded and she said, "Boys and girls, that was lovely," I stayed.

The regular classroom teacher appeared from the back of the room, and Em stuffed papers, pitch pipe, and book into a blue cloth bag before joining me.

"You have a haunting voice," I said and flinched at such an inane remark.

Apparently excusing banality, she wrinkled her nose and gave a half-shrug. "For someone with a limited range, I'm not bad on ballads in a classroom."

"I'm Ann Thompson." Now, I sounded too formal.

"Well, I'm either Emily Jane or Emily, or—"

"Em?" I said, and that it would be.

CHRIS

Saturday morning

Good, Hazel Hasler's rooster is crowing. Morning's long overdue. Night lasted forever. I couldn't sleep. At first, as I tossed around, I decided I was restless because Todd wasn't beside me, so I tried the mental imaging, courtesy of my sister Margaret, that I've used when Todd and I have been apart—such as the time I went to the Ozarks with my sister Valerie, or when I flew to Chicago to be with Julie before, during, and after Jason's birth, or when I visited Emily Jane in California. Of course, that was it. Emily Jane. This room has too much of her.

I kicked off the sheet and hoped its crisp noise would drown our high, thin, little girl voices as we played paper dolls, right over there on the fading rug that Cammy braided. The snip of scissors blades clattered against our words as we cut out clothes or "body suits" that we'd drawn. Our anatomy was pretty bad. We weren't far off on breasts, although I've never seen any as pointy or perky as we drew. We didn't know about pubic hair, and a penis—based on my brothers'—resembled a worm. After we attached these bodysuits to our paper dolls, we tried in some general fashion to simulate lovemaking between our one male paper doll and a huge harem of females.

In the predawn blackness, I clamped my eyes tight to make my world even darker, to hide from the light of Emily Jane's smile when she, at seventeen, sat at that dressing table pushed against the wallpapered wall. She arched her back and breathed, "Oh, Chris." Her smile was so radiant that some of it lives in this room and not solely in my mind. "He does love me. Dirk does love me." She fumbled at her sweater's neckline and withdrew a chain from which dangled Dirk's class ring, the back section of the band hidden under grimy adhesive tape.

"And Cammy says?" I asked.

Emily Jane kissed the ring, pressed it against her left breast in the area of her heart, then slipped it under her sweater. "Nothing. She doesn't know, and I'm not telling her."

The silence between us said that this was hard because she wanted to confide in Cammy. But the silence also said, "This is one more secret between us, one more proof of our exclusive friendship."

This secret, her going steady with Dirk, wasn't of the same magnitude as our earlier, deepest secret, but it was almost as meaningful since I was the only one she told about Dirk, and I was the only one who knew about her actual relationship to Cammy.

That I had learned on a gray spring day when flowers and trees weren't yet convinced to bud. Rain streaked on the window right beside this bed, where Emily Jane sprawled. Maybe she was twelve. She wore a plaid flannel shirt, her favorite, that rubbed her skin and reminded her of a heat poultice on her chest without the odor of Vicks Vapor Rub. I guess she wore jeans. Since I was chilly, I crouched by the floor register. I'd gotten so tired of heavy skirts, of dressing for winter, that now, when the calendar said "spring," I insisted on wearing cotton. A faint trickle of heat rose from the register and warmed portions of my body, which I rotated over or onto the square vent.

How the subject of family came up, I've forgotten. Possibly, once again, Emily Jane had envied the fact that I had parents, brothers and sisters.

"I have just Cammy." Her voice was muffled because she lay on her stomach, face flat upon the spread. "She's not my aunt, you know," and because she sounded dreamy, far away, I thought *Emily Jane's writing a line for a song.* During the past year she'd been picking out melodies on the piano and drawing notes in music books with staffs and lines and spaces.

She raised her head turtle-style. "But you've already figured that out, haven't you, that Cammy is really my mother?"

Oh, boy, I could fill pages of this book trying to describe my shock, and then I might not capture how the blood raced to my head, how my breathing slowed, how my body froze over the register. Emily Jane rolled over. "I'll grant you the story sounds sad and dramatic. Mother and Father driving too fast. Car spins, crashes against a bridge railing, tumbles over the side into the river, killing them. Mom's younger sister, Cammy, takes infant Emily and devotes her life to raising the orphan."

"You don't think your parents are dead?"

"Sure, Dad and his wife are dead. I've seen their death certificates. Cammy keeps them in that battered hat box in her closet along with photos of her sister and sister's husband. Get this. Cammy's complete name is Camellia Emily. That's very significant."

So that the mild heat could climb up my legs, I stood on the vent. "I don't understand," I said.

"Well, recently, Cammy's said a couple things when I was talking about Dirk that led me to believe that she loved my dad. She said he wasn't good enough for my mother. A cover-up, see. And she avoids speaking his name. It was Jared. I may never learn the details, but I'm positive—you know those feelings that tingle in the pit of your stomach when something is true—that Cammy and my dad had an affair. I think it happened after her sister Amy, my alleged mother, had married Jared." She cupped her hand toward her flannel-covered bosom, a motion that would fit nicely with one of her songs. "I'm the love child."

She continued inventing the scene between Cammy and Amy, when Cammy told her sister, "I'm pregnant." Then she acted out Jared's reaction. "See, I think that Jared and Amy had a huge fight about his affair while they were in the car. I bet she slugged him. That's why he lost control of the car. That's why they died."

"Wow." I forgot my chill and the crumpled folds of my limp, pink skirt. She and I were lost in the enormity of this fabricated history until I asked, "Were you born yet, when they, you know, fell over the side into the river?"

Emily Jane shook her shiny, black hair. "Don't know how pregnant Cammy was, but I feel I was born sometime after their deaths."

Once more I squatted on the register to warm my bottom. I wished I'd picked cotton panties that day instead of nylon. "Makes sense," I finally agreed. "Would help explain why Cammy's always been so close to you."

"And why she never married. Oh, Chris." She nailed me with her expressive eyes. "We have to play along, have to keep her secret until she's ready to come clean."

My head hurts as does my heart, and with the sky lighter, I think I'll pull on my saggy, baggy shorts and tiptoe from the room. I need a few minutes with Todd, a few minutes with today.

SAVANNAH

Saturday, 6 A.M.

Last night, wishing to go no further with my story, I reined in the direction that my hand was bent on pursuing. "After all," I reminded myself, "this is supposed to be about Emily."

Anyway, I stubbed out another cigarette, climbed into bed, and awaited sleep, which hid in the corners of the room. Thoughts somersaulted and answers to my questions whirled until I realized I couldn't separate Emily from me, nor separate Cammy from us. Even when we operated in supposedly independent spheres, the three of us were connected. What each *had been* influenced, what each *was* when we got together; and that, naturally, influenced how we acted apart. Thus, if I write in this journal about years or events in which Emily wasn't physically present, still because she shadowed them, they are about her. And I assume that my life cast shadows over her. After graduation, when we didn't see each other for extended periods and communication was through letters or during the rare, quick visits when we met at Cammy's house, I believed our four years at Monroe College shaped her days as well as mine.

I heard something downstairs. If lucky, I could steal a few minutes alone with Cammy.

Through the slit in the nearly-closed sliding doors of the parlor, I saw her seated at a desk sorting papers. Pressing my mouth to the opening, I spoke her name. The doors protested as she pulled them apart. Automatically, I checked behind me up the stairs, for surely such noise would wake the others. When nothing stirred, I stepped into the parlor and closed the doors.

She'd rearranged the room. The chair I'd occupied on that October night was gone, and its replacement was not beside the window but beside the desk.

"I moved things around to accommodate the hospital bed." She waved fingers toward the southern corner. I looked; although, of course, the bed where Emily died last month had gone to some other patient.

"Am I interrupting?"

"No." Again she waved her fingers in invitation toward the chair. "Just organizing letters that over the years I've thrown into cubbyholes."

Seated in the wing chair, I saw Emily's large, looping and wondrously open handwriting across the envelopes. Her hand would move rapidly as she wrote, and she'd laugh that with a couple of words consuming several lines, she wished the professor would grade her term papers on quantity, not quality.

Cammy fingered the topmost envelope. "Comforting to see her handwriting." Then she pushed back her chair, walked to the window, stretched her arms above her head, and leaving the echo of popping joints in her wake, turned to me. "And, Savannah, how are you?"

"Extremely glad to see you." At that, she smiled.

Infant sunlight invaded the room and tinted the lace curtains a saffron shade. *Surely they're not the same curtains from thirty years ago*, I thought, and a wave of sadness hit. How young Emily and I had been when we'd ridden the bus from Monroe College to Centerville. My oldest stepson's child is eighteen, the age Emily and I were with our dreams, our—

For one horrible second, I verged on tears. From elementary school, when I first knew that in some indefinable way I was different, through high school, I'd trained myself not to cry. To stop tears, I had some pet techniques. Onto my mental screen I could toss a nonsensical picture of a goony bird that made me smile, a picture of kids stoning a dying cat that replaced sadness with rage, a picture of Mama's shoes where she'd painted cardboard circles black to insert behind the holes, and that shamed me. Or I could hold my eyes wide open and not blink to prevent tears.

But the near-tears moment ended with footsteps in the hall. At the not-quite-secured double doors, Cammy said, "Christine is undoubtedly going home to check on her husband." She spoke next of starting breakfast. "But don't offer to help. I do better fixing food if I'm alone."

After she left, I studied the desk. Emily's letters were in a stack. Those from me were scattered to the right. I selected one I'd mailed from Monroe.

"You'd asked," I'd written, "how or when my suspicions began. I can't pinpoint any particular time, but ever since I was little, I was conscious of something. For example, our neighbors often had relatives and friends. No one ever came to visit Mama and me.

"Our cottage was set apart from other houses by a vacant lot. Near us, to the west, were railroad tracks, and we felt vibrations from freight trains that pounded the rails. On the other side of the tracks lay a white section, one Mama said contained nothing but 'poor white trash.' Our lonely cottage enhanced my feeling of being segregated in a segregated Missouri town."

As scenes overlapped, they blotted out sentences scrawled in my tight penmanship in Parker blue ink.

Into view swung the cottage with its small living room, smaller kitchen, bedroom that Mama and I shared, and bathroom where rust stained the lavatory sides beneath dual leaking faucets.

On muggy Missouri nights, when Mama had finished working—either cleaning houses over on the north side or ironing clothes (usually men's white shirts) in our living room for a doctor's wife—she and I would sit side by side on the top step of our stoop. Sometimes she helped me catch fireflies in a Mason jar. "Jar flies," she said when the insects lit up the glass. I think she forced my attention on them to divert me from the obvious, that I was the one child not playing with other children outside after dark.

On our poor street of simple houses, we couldn't shut out the lives of others, or the shouts and laughter of kids having fun. Kids weren't mean to me. Basically, they ignored me, as if adhering to their mothers' rules: "Don't go playing with that Savannah Hanson." Occasionally, when kids had asked me to join them, Mama said, "No."

When I asked, "Why not?" she'd answer, "You're better than they are. They're trash." Despite pleas or arguments, Mama remained adamant.

Yet, obviously, we weren't superior. Our cabin was one of the worst on the block. Some other people had cars. True, many didn't run and car parts littered sidewalks, but Mama didn't even drive. In nice weather, she walked to work; in snow or rain, she accepted rides from her employers.

I'd watch from the living room window, sitting on my knees on the coarse tweed sofa, waiting for that "fancy car," as Mama called it. The driver steered carefully to avoid potholes in our street. Mama exited from the passenger's side. Usually, I'd see other black faces in the back window, making me aware that the fancy car would deliver others to homes, where they had families. If Mama lugged a big basket of ironing, I'd jump from the sofa and open the door.

How could we be so superior when we owned no transportation, when we rented this ugly, cramped house, and when Mama had a worse job than Mrs. Lillian, who lived catty corner, and worked in the school cafeteria? And Mrs. Randall, on the other side of the vacant lot, was a waitress at the Over Easy Restaurant. And how could we be so superior if no one ever called us, if the mail carrier left no personal mail, if Mama had no friends, and if we had no family?

She told me that she'd run away from mean parents.

"Didn't you have any sisters or brothers?" I asked, as I sat with my primer on my lap. I remember the smooth movement of the iron as it leveled wrinkles from a shirt sleeve.

Mama leaned slightly over the ironing board, which consumed most of the space between the sofa and the bedroom door. "No."

"Did your parents try to find you?"

"Hiss," the iron said to the fabric.

"Not to my knowledge."

"Didn't they love you?"

The tip of the iron clinked against a button. Mama rested the iron on its end and repositioned the shirt. "Doubt it."

"Why did they have you?"

She tested the iron with spit on the end of her finger. "Things happen," she said, and I sighed. Her answers were never satisfactory. Her gaze never met mine when she delivered her cryptic one-liners.

When she spoke of my father, she simply said, "He went away."

One time—it must have been when I was eight or nine—we walked home from the grocery store on an autumn afternoon. A man trotted across the park with a child on his shoulders. I'd never had that experience, never would, and anger goaded me. "Why did my father leave? Where is he today?"

The friction of the brown paper sack rubbing against her frayed cardigan seemed to be her answer until she said, "Have no idea."

"Don't you care?"

Mama didn't break her stride, didn't even peek at me from the corner of her eye. "Not anymore."

I wanted to hurt her, to force her to give me something solid—a bit of a story, a description, one fragile root from yesterday's soil, so when we'd outdistanced the park and no one was around, I said loudly, "Guess nobody much liked you. Your parents never cared enough to find you. You must have had an aunt or some relative, and they haven't found you. And my father—he took off."

She kept walking, acting as if I'd not spoken. Ashamed, I lagged behind. I didn't doubt Mama loved me. She'd save my life, would throw herself, if necessary, in front of the truck heading toward us.

I dropped further behind, taking in once more, the nearly-transparent circles on her sweater's elbows, the dejected fabric of her figured skirt, the snags in her stockings, which she rotated so the worse runs wriggled up the inside of her calves. But, these clothes were clean as were mine, not grass- or-jam stained.

To her back I directed one final comment. "Mama, why are we all alone?"

She turned and surprised me with a smile. "Child, how can you say that? We're not alone. We have each other."

Later, that same autumn, I wondered if indeed we might have more than each other.

It happened in the middle of a night when the wind increased, rattling windows and teasing loose shingles on the roof. I scooted over to cuddle against Mama, to wedge my face into the folds of her flannel nightgown, softened by her warmth. But her side was empty. With my eyes shut, I curled up in her place and listened for the *shush shush* of her peeing. When she'd pad back to bed, she'd chuckle. "Thanks for keeping my side warm." I'd inch toward my cooler half, and when she arranged herself, getting the blankets just so, she'd scoop me close against her.

Oddly, though, I heard voices. I crept to the bedroom door, stealthily twisted the knob and peered out. Although the table lamp was on, Mama faced the front door blocking my view, so I couldn't tell who else was there. Obviously a person Mama chose not to invite in. Only phrases escaped from their low-pitched conversation. The stranger sounded like a woman. "…should know."

"Appreciate…Cora Lee."

Mumble. Mumble. When Mama stepped forward, they hugged. The arms that encircled Mama's back were white. I bit my bottom lip to keep from crying out. The woman, whose face I never saw, left, but Mama stayed by that front door. Cold, I retreated to bed. Her footsteps, deadened against the homemade rag rugs, beat louder on the bare floor. In the kitchen the water faucet shuddered; the teakettle clanged against the burner. Full of questions, I fought sleep.

Whenever Mama crawled in beside me, if she did, I was asleep, and when I awoke, she was dressed for work and organizing my school clothes on our bedroom chair, her habit on weekday mornings.

"Who came here in the night?"

She laid my bleached-white anklets on top of my bleached-white panties. "Some dream you had."

"I saw her," and Mama swung around, her eyes wide. "At least her arms, Mama. She hugged you and she had white arms."

"Maybe the rest of her was another color." Mama laughed. "Come on. Get up. Tell me more of your dream over breakfast."

As we ate our oatmeal, I detailed my account, but when Mama smiled and said, "What an imagination," I didn't mention the name, Cora Lee.

The double doors to the parlor parted and Cammy asked, "Coffee?"

While my mind made its re-entry from the past, I sat quietly, and then she noticed the letter in my hand.

"Take your letters," she said. "They're yours."

"Thanks. I'll put them upstairs. Join you for coffee in a second."

As I stacked them on the bedroom dresser, it dawned on me. Mama and Cammy were similar. Not given to talking, they carried an aura. Both had detached themselves from society. Both were alone, because where were condolence notes to Cammy? Why hadn't the phone rung? Had anyone sent cards or flowers when Emily died?

ANN

Saturday, A.M.

I awoke to the smell of frying bacon. My stomach growled in hunger. Ignoring the reality of calories and cholesterol, I dreamed of that greasy pork taste, letting my lips moisten around the texture of fat marbling crunchy strips of meat. My stomach growled more loudly.

All right, I'd get up and take a run, then come back and shower. Surely by that time, the other two bathroomies would be done. I pulled on my running shorts, tank top, knotted my shoelaces, and began my stretching routine. Em, never a runner, but "a damned fast walker" as she liked to say, hated limbering up. Impatient, she wanted to be outdoors. But I enjoy the feeling of my resistant body gradually succumbing to suppleness.

As I tell Em, as I *told* Em, such is a metaphor for life: resistance being planed down to an acceptance. But how can I accept one more needless death? An instant weariness settled, making my warm-up an effort. Like a tonic, I required a friendly word, some kind contact. I'd call my husband.

When I stepped into the hallway, indistinguishable syllables floated up the stairwell, a weaving of female voices—alto and second soprano. Oh, Em had introduced me to music.

I descended to the entryway where the phone—my God, one with a rotary dial—was centered on a small round table beside a magazine rack that contained the Centerville phone book. Was it even a fourth the size of ours?

My forefinger hooked into the "9XYZ" circle. No, wrong area code. Seth wasn't in our apartment, but in his Santa Barbara apartment, near the other nursing home he owned. This was the second weekend of the month. He came to me on the first and third.

In California, it was 6:00 A.M. Although I'd wake him, he'd understand. With every laborious turn of the rotator, I felt as if time, too, bent itself to this curve of slowness. The voices from the kitchen were paced as if the day allowed for leisurely conversation, as if work, committee meetings, appointments, and schedules didn't demand attention.

Seth's phone rang. In an anticipatory world, I heard his sleepy "Hello." In the world of Cammy's house, in the world where Em was dead and I stood holding a black receiver tethered to a wallboard, I heard no response. I counted the rings. Why didn't his answering machine click on with his amiable, "Hello, you've reached Seth Thompson's number. Leave yours, and I'll call you back"? Eager to leave last night, had he forgotten to press the "on" button? Had such eagerness been fueled by plans to meet Morgan, to spend the night with him?

Em was the only person to whom I'd admitted my suspicions that Seth might be bisexual. "You and he are my best friends," I'd said by way of an inadequate introduction to the topic.

"And best friends," she'd replied, "are more important than anything else."

From such a foundation of friendship, I could say that sex with Seth was also friendly, nothing like the wild sex with David, my former husband. Unlike David, however, Seth had the uncanny ability to read my mind at times, to contribute insights, to enrich my world, to joke and talk easily—just like Em.

She had asked, "Does it matter if Seth does or does not have a man in Santa Barbara? Does it matter that his life is compartmentalized? We all lead compartmentalized lives with some merely more subtle than others. Don't you have the best of his life, actually all of it, when he's here?"

I sank onto the bottom stair step and rested my forehead against the balustrade. Perhaps my movement, the resultant creak as I resettled my weight, sent signals through the house, prompting the sharp tattoo of heels from the kitchen. Through the stairway posts, I saw Cammy march down the hall. From this angle I made out sections of her—a shoulder in a tan blouse, a leg in generous brown pants, a sturdy SAS shoe. But the voice was whole. "Scrambled eggs?"

I bent backward a couple inches for eye contact with blue-faded eyes, a contrast to Em's sparkling, large ones. "Actually, I thought I'd go for a run."

"And not come meet the other two?" She had me. How could I appear so ungracious?

Before Cammy introduced us, I knew the one in baggy shorts must be Christine. She would have been a cute teenager, for traces of cuteness lined her smile, her features.

"Sorry we didn't meet when I came to California to visit Emily Jane (Em, I mentally corrected), but you were away on a trip," she said. True, Seth and I had driven north to Victoria, B.C.

The other one, Savannah, had never been cute. Exotic looking, she sported a magnificent chest. What had Em said about her? College roommate, but what else?

Without asking, Cammy poured a cup of coffee and set it at the vacant place, my spot. Well, so much for my usual green tea. Dutifully, I sat as she spooned scrambled eggs and four strips of bacon onto my plate with its blue plaid design.

Cammy sat across from me with a militaristic posture that dampened my supply of small talk. As if waiting for orders, the others watched her. My fork, scraping the plate, seemed extraordinarily loud.

"Naturally, you're wondering why I invited you," she said, "what we're going to do, and if there'll be a—a service." Her voice faltered, and the hand suspending a mug, trembled. She licked her lips, placed the cup on the table, and put both hands in her lap out of sight. "Emily specified no service."

At that, Christine sniffed back tears and fumbled in her shorts pocket for a frazzled tissue to blow her nose.

"Since each of you knew Emily at various times, I thought that if we were together for a weekend and explored some memories, we might create a person with an entire lifetime that we could remember."

Ah, my instincts were right, but in the morning light the concept lost any sinister quality and became intelligible. No one spoke. A fly buzzed from the window over the sink, a window with yellow tie-back curtains that collected the sunshine.

"Today I'd like to take you to a couple places in town that I associate with her."

Christine stuck the dissolving tissue against her lips and nose.

Savannah laid her hand on Cammy's upper arm. "Sounds lovely," she said, and now I detected the slightly slurred syllables that hinted of the South.

"Nothing's fixed, no schedule, but we could walk there this morning after," and she looked at me, "Ann has her run."

It was too late in the morning, and I'd eaten too much for a decent run. By the time I fought my way down several blocks in that strangling Midwestern humidity, beads of sweat dotted my bare midriff and the back of my neck. My sports bra clung as if a size too small. My feet were leaden. My body resisted this, but my brain said, "run." As at other junctures in my life, I needed to flee, needed to push myself, needed to do something.

A woman spraying a hose over a scorched flowerbed regarded me as I jogged past. It accentuated the fact that I was the lone crazy individual gasping for breath along a dappled sidewalk.

When I run in the East Bay hills and wind sweeps off the strait, I drink in such freshness that the cottony webs of despair evaporate. Even in the fog, Em and I would take our run/walk. Far behind, she'd often not reappear until we huffed our way up the final hill to our apartment complex, where we'd agree that problems had diminished.

After my daughter died, I ran and ran. I delighted in taut muscles, in slenderness. My legs were someone else's. My shape was new. I was new, not Robin's mother, nor David's wife.

And when David had an affair, when his mistress announced she was pregnant and he agreed to marry her, I ran into a second life, returning to college for a teaching credential. There I met Seth, another returnee, working on his MBA. He refused to run with me, but would patiently read on a park bench as I threw myself against a shoreline breeze, or he'd study in the front seat of his Volvo while I conquered hills.

Now I leaned against the trunk of some foreign, non-California tree, before a Norman Rockwell-type house with spacious porch and swing. Wooden shutters decorated windows on both levels. The house, too, appeared foreign. Homes should be of stucco, painted in Mediterranean pastels, like my cream-colored childhood home on the Peninsula, south of San Francisco.

Once more, I forced myself to run over an upended sidewalk with the WPA 1940 insignia. Surely Em followed this route on her way to city center. Nope, downtown, I corrected myself. I tried to implant Em on this street, tried to see her walking fast. Instead, I saw her the first time she'd power-walked as I ran, which was shortly after we became friends, while she still lived across town in that tiny duplex where the bed folded into the wall.

When renters in the apartment adjacent to ours parked a U-Haul near their door and began loading furniture, I called her about the vacancy. Over the weekend, Seth and I helped her move next door. Her belongings, her California possessions, are still next door as Em had paid rent in advance. I'd need to speak about that with Cammy, I guessed. I'd not unlocked the door with my
and had let her plants die because I couldn't face that silence. We'd believed that she'd return, that she was only visiting in Iowa. We didn't believe that she was deathly ill. Well, in two weeks rent would be due. In two weeks, the apartment would have to be cleared.

Again, I paused. With hands on my knees, I sucked in huge draughts of air, scented with the fragrance of some obnoxious funereal-smelling flower. "You're tired," my brain said. "Go back." Before conceding defeat, I half-heartedly ran in place.

I paid no attention to the lawns on my right, nor the occasional car on my left. When I first took up running, I trained myself to stare straight ahead, to concentrate on a single direction and disregard the pitfalls of peripheral vision. I trained myself not to feel. But feelings and the periphery intrigued Em. I'd establish a good stride, be running strong, and she'd yell out in her husky folk singer voice, "You're missing the wisteria. Ann, on your left, that dead tree—" Her poignancy would cause me to lose my stride. Studying the object or the panorama, I sometimes regretted shredding my sketch pad. During that second, I'd flirt with re-embracing art, my original love. Yet, unfortunately, art meant moving inside. Only when I merged with the subject could I paint. Going inside, becoming one with a subject, courted pain. That's why I'd discarded pad, pencils, paints, and easel. What I taught children—essentially craft projects—was safe.

Thinking of Em in these jagged moments also courted pain. What would I do without her? Thus emotion, not exertion, stalled my breathing and my gait. I wasn't proud of the dispirited *shuff shuff* sound of my feet, but I'd not worry. At Cammy's I'd shower, try Seth once more, and be the guest Cammy wanted.

The house lay a block ahead. With the goal so near I increased speed, brushed a trickle of sweat from my forehead, and as my arm descended, spotted a man standing, backed against a pickup parked across the street from 731 Polk.

He studied the house, and as I neared, I knew he studied me. Although I continued straight ahead, from the corner of my eye I noticed the tall, lean cowboy physique. Probably my age, he wore jeans with such ease that they weren't apparel, but accents for a posture—half angry/half confident. Despite the sun, the heat, and the god-awful humidity, I managed my fancy pace. Knees up. Shoulders back. To someone at a distance, my body would look damned good.

While I refused to acknowledge him, I felt his appraisal as I cleared Cammy's steps, hooked the screen door behind me, and entered quietly. Wrapped in an old-fashioned coolness, I stood in the hallway, letting my heartbeat stabilize.

By the time I turned around, the man had climbed into his truck and sat behind the steering wheel. I couldn't distinguish his features inside the shaded cab, but I had the overall impression of sexuality.

How long had it been since a man in my age bracket had emitted such magnetism?

The truck engine kicked over, and the pickup rolled down the street. Feeling suddenly empowered—an "in" term we bandied about in the teacher's lounge—I dialed Seth's number and experienced amazing relief when he immediately answered and asked, "You okay?"

"I truly don't know. I seem to be in sort of an altered state."

How warm his soothing laughter. How great to listen to his explanation of a six o'clock drive to the doughnut shop. "If you get there before seven, you can buy the ones hot from the fryer." I'd not remind him about calories and fat, would forget about his increasing waist line, would glory in happiness that he'd not spent the night with Morgan.

Seth supplied the pep talk I craved and repeated plans of flying from Southern California on Friday, so we could spend extra days together.

Not until I reached the midway point on the staircase did actuality strike. Maybe Morgan was in Seth's apartment. No reason, beyond my vague assumption, that he'd go to Morgan's townhouse. Maybe that's why Seth went for doughnuts at such a ridiculous hour, to share them with a lover. I was shaken. I took a deep breath, but some four steps later, however, questions about my husband vanished before the realization that the sexy cowboy must be, had to be, the infamous Dirk Hawkins.

CHRIS

Later on Saturday morning

The last time I wrote in this journal I wished for a few minutes with today, my normal today. Well, I got my wish all right, with all levels on which my today operates. First, I eased downstairs and along the hallway, aware that Cammy was in the parlor, in that room where Emily Jane died.

The kitchen was so still that the pendulum of the clock (Cammy bought it at the auction when the elementary school was demolished) hit against the morning with brazen strokes.

On the back stoop I noticed the peeling paint and wondered if Cammy would repaint before fall, or if she'd let it go until spring. After snow falls, she doesn't use this back entry much and puts clothes in the dryer with great reluctance. She prefers to steady the wicker basket piled with wet laundry on her hip, go down these three steps scooped in the middle and head for the clothesline. The clothespins that she never removes form precise rows like uniformed stick men in ranks. Precise, alert, as Cammy's always been.

I love how early morning smells. In the alley I breathed in the hollyhock scent. Some people might argue that hollyhocks, like dandelions, for instance, have no aroma. But, yes, they do. Faint and dry. I retain the memory of their smell through the winter months just as I retain the sight of their blooms. I fingered a silky, white, open bell-shaped one. Emily Jane and I must have made hundreds of hollyhock dolls.

Very near this stalk, we once lined up an assortment of upside-down blossoms on a warped two-by-four board. We were so involved in a pretend world that we didn't hear Lester Nielson, neighborhood and class pest. Sneaking up behind us with a big stick, in one quick, vicious swing, he crushed the dolls and our kingdom.

Emily Jane leaped up and threw herself on Lester. She clawed and bit. Stunned, I stayed on the ground. Lester must have been stunned too, because he didn't fight back. About the time that blood reddened the fingernail tracks she'd etched on his cheeks, he hit her with the stick. I jumped up and grabbed it, and right then and there, Emily Jane and I took him.

Lester let out a howl after Emily Jane wrenched the stick from me and beat him on the calves. When she and I backed off, Lester had blood streaming down his face. Long scratches—pink on his white arms—extended from below his T-shirt sleeves to his wrists. Our wild breathing filled the alleyway. Emily Jane and I were mighty. Lester knew this and wisely ran off.

In high school, when he was pretty good looking and no longer a pest, he asked Emily Jane for a date, even though everyone knew that she was nuts about Dirk Hawkins. "Ever since you attacked me, I've admired you. You fought with pure spirit."

I, also, admired the way she'd gone after him. Never had I seen that fierce protectiveness, and I didn't see it that often in the future, but it was there. She would protect what was important: people she loved, her world, and vital secrets.

By the hollyhock stalks, I removed my sandals, for I suddenly longed to feel the stubbly grass, the weeds and gravel as I had when she and I traveled the alleys. That meant I proceeded carefully, because my feet are tender. But that also meant I paid attention to the backyards and how the morning woke them.

Okay, enough about today as lovely. When I unlatched our rear gate and crossed beside my garden ripe with tomatoes and corn, I was still in a memory and wonder mood about what makes every day Today. Todd would be fixing breakfast. I'd surprise him by slipping up behind him and pressing myself against his back.

He fooled me. At the table, he dipped a corner of his toast into a pool of egg yolk on his plate. Methodically, he lowered the toast. He was not in a memory/wonder mood. Usually, Todd eats fast, consuming food as if he's an empty tank and the gas station hose is under high pressure. When upset, his actions are slow.

"What's wrong?" I put my hands on the back of one of our chairs, aware of the curling duct tape I'd stuck across a tear, aware that he chewed a bite about twenty times before he said, "That kid." Todd needn't add more. Even if he had, the buzzing in my temples would have drummed out his words. That kid. Evan. My nephew. Not even my child, for heaven's sakes, but Grant's son. Grant, my youngest brother, is a decade younger than me—the unpredictable one in my family. The one I like the best, he left Centerville the day he graduated from high school.

As I walked to the coffee pot to fill my special cup, an actual China cup without a chip or a crack that I'd found at the thrift store for a dollar, I thought, and not for the first time, *Grant and Dirk Hawkins have a lot in common.*

I set the Mr. Coffee carafe back on the warmer and sipped from my cup, "Good."

At that, Todd smiled. "I take it you haven't had any coffee yet?"

"Nah, everyone's asleep over there."

"How goes it?" and I could feel him trying to break through the immediate gloom to understand my loss and these few unreal days. And I could feel, as well, his unspoken truth that Evan was of *my* family, that he'd had nothing to do with my involvement, that from day one, he'd not wanted any part of this kid.

"We've four of our own," he'd stressed. "We have our hands full. We don't need Grant's problem."

I couldn't dispute that, but when Grant carried in that baby wrapped in a dirty blanket with a puppy dog pattern, something unprecedented happened. Instantly, I felt a bond with Evan, one I'd not known with any of mine. And I knew before Grant spoke that he'd splice together a version of another love affair gone wrong, but this time, darn the luck, there'd been this little accident, a child. And while he promised to live in Centerville, work at a steady job, and be both father and mother (the situation with birth mommy was very fuzzy) to his son, I accepted the fact that Evan would be my fifth child, despite the fact that he ostensibly lived with his dad in an apartment.

As I brought my cup to the table, I returned Todd's smile. "It's hard at Cammy's. That's why I sneaked home this morning."

With his left hand, Todd squeezed my forearm. "Missed you last night."

I nodded, hopeful that we could re-establish our usual closeness before we dove into the business of Evan. Not to be, for Todd cocked his head in the direction of the hallway. "Came a few minutes ago looking for you."

"And?"

"In the bedroom." Todd moved to the sink with his plate. As a stream of water poured over the dish, he sloshed the remains of breakfast into the garbage. "As usual, he's in some kind of trouble."

I headed down the hallway and rapped on the closed door, a cheap hollow core door that failed to keep out sound. Doors in our house are useful only for restricting sight. While you can't see someone bathing, you sure can hear water splashing in the shower or hear someone's hips go "scrunch" against the bottom of the tub. Snoring, crying, and the attempts to walk noiselessly after curfew zip right through the thin wood. In Cammy's house, built circa 1900, sound doesn't travel. Behind the door, in Emily Jane's room, she and I could be assured of privacy, spilling out confidences that no eavesdropper could ever overhear. But such insulation never gave us any warning signs of Cammy's approach, so sometimes Emily Jane and I jumped when we opened her door and discovered Cammy.

"Yah?" Evan answered.

He'd stationed himself against the wall about a foot from the window, so he could check the driveway and keep the door in view. From a young age, he'd learned never to lose sight of entrance and exit possibilities. Now, at sixteen, he was merely less overt about the space he picked.

"What's new?" Needlessly, I shut the door.

Evan clamped his lips into a "don't know" expression and fiddled with the window blind cord. My stomach tightened, and I felt that breathlessness I generally have when I'm sure something's wrong with one of my kids.

"You might as well tell me." I claimed the lumpy twin bed, my son Scott's reject, that Todd had moved into Julie's former room for the nights when Evan stayed with us.

His Adam's apple slid up and down while he rehearsed what to say. "It's August," I reminded myself, "and summer school's over, so it can't be trouble with teachers." Yet, he'd never mentioned grades. Could he have dropped out as he'd periodically done during the school year? Would he tell me, as he hadn't in the past, that he'd received Fs or "Incompletes?" Had he quit the roofing job he'd had for less than a week? Been fired?

"Got picked up last night," he finally mumbled.

Instead of offering more facts, which were never his strong suit, he tugged a paper from his jeans pocket. A ticket, quartered into half the size of a trading card, was so badly creased that I spread it on the green bedspread beside the hole my son Greg burned when playing throw-lighted-matches-into-the-air.

"It's for driving without a license?" I rubbed fingers over the furrows to decipher handwriting buried in the grooves.

"Yah."

"But you don't have a car."

"Drove Buck's."

"Who?"

"Guy at the roofing company."

"He loaned you his car?"

Evan opened and shut the blinds. "Not exactly. I kind of borrowed it, and another guy and I took it out south of town. Had it back in under an hour."

"You stole the car."

"Nah. Anyway, I didn't hurt anything, and we were going to fill the gas tank. It'd been on empty."

"Plus no license."

"If Dad would only let me get my license. You don't know how it is to be the only guy my age not driving."

I did feel sorry for him—sorry that Grant wouldn't let him drive. ("Shit," Grant had told me, "he'd crack up a car and there'd be all hell to pay.") And I felt resentment. Sure, Grant was right. Evan would push a car to its limits, would be one of the teenagers attracted to the hilly country roads south of town, who at one hundred miles per hour might shatter a fence post with the force of collision. My resentment, though, stemmed from the fact that once more Evan was in trouble. Once more I was the one who'd help him.

"Does your dad know?"

"Nah, he took off yesterday in his truck on a run to Arizona. Mophead's with him."

We laughed. When Evan laughs, his face shines. An inner light pulses through the skin. I love that, for usually he's too serious.

"She's still around, huh?"

He hunched his shoulder, his nothing-I-can-do-about-it posture.

"Grant know you call her 'Mophead?'"

"Nah. Probably wouldn't think it funny, but her hair's all wild, like a mop."

A shaft of sunlight crossed the upper window pane as morning advanced. I must get back to Cammy's, so again inspected the limp unfolded ticket.

"There's no court date on it," Evan said. "A notice comes in the mail."

"Okay, next week we'll decide what to do. For now, go on to your job."

Evan shuffled his feet. His sneakers squeaked rubbery noises on the pine floor boards. "You do still have your job?"

"Not exactly."

I exhaled loudly and collapsed against the headboard, welcoming the scarred wood strong against my shoulder blades. Evan stood just outside my line of vision. Good. I'd seek comfort in the familiar wall and part of the ceiling in front of me. "You're going to tell me that this Buck is your boss? That you've been fired?"

"Since you figured it out, I don't need to tell you."

Suddenly, I was tired, lightheaded. I'd slept poorly last night. An energy-draining day lay ahead, and here was Evan. "If there's more, I don't want to know."

"Chris, I'm sorry." When his voice trembled, I felt tears, like an automatic reflex, flood my eyes. I couldn't cry. Couldn't.

"So, what will you do today?" I asked

"Ride around on my bike. Watch some TV."

"Evan—"

"I know. Stay out of trouble."

"You could hang out here, but I'm at Cammy's today, tonight, and tomorrow."

He weighed his options: Our house and manage to avoid Todd and Heather? Home from college for the summer and employed at the 24-hour drugstore, she'd constantly beat on the bathroom door after he started his shower. "Come on, Evan. I need to get in there. Evan, don't use too much hot water. We've only a thirty-gallon tank." Or to Grant's apartment? On Centerville's Main Street over the hardware store, the two-room apartment where Evan slept on the couch would never be his home. "I am," he'd once said in a moment of unusual analysis, "a person without a home."

"Since Dad and Mophead are gone, I'll go to the apartment."

Rising from the bed, I handed over the ticket, which he stuffed into his pocket. I longed to hug him, but his stance said, "Touch me, and I'll turn into a statue," so the best I could do was say, "We'll get through this. It'll work out."

His "Yah" was hollow, without conviction.

I stalled returning to the kitchen and Todd's reaction. Before his lips could frame the question, I could hear him ask, "He took the car?" A vein would throb in his right temple. "Drove without a license?" As if trying to prevent the intensity of his emotion from exploding over the room, his jaw would jut out.

Thank goodness, the kitchen was empty. His breakfast dishes soaked in the sink, and on the table a note on a junk mail envelope against my K-Mart Special sugar bowl said, "Off to the shop. Love you."

I held the envelope in my hand as I re-crossed the backyard. A talisman of sorts, an omen that things would turn out with Evan. But how? Would the judge levy a fine, a big one? Jail him? Send him away to a rehab camp? What if the judge ruled that Grant and his revolving door policy with women weren't suitable? Might the judge have a social worker inspect that apartment? Would she/he recommend a foster home? Would Todd and I be asked to take him, be legally responsible instead of existing in this current limbo land, where Grant allegedly was in charge of Evan, and I filled in the major areas?

"Oh, Emily Jane," I whispered. "Wish we could talk or I could write you."

Under my bed beside my other secret box, I stored a Whitman's Candy box in which I saved her letters. Way back when, in a letter from California, she'd dubbed me "Baby Maker," after I'd written of my third pregnancy. And when Evan entered my life and I wrote about his fights and his school suspensions, she answered, "You'll do fine. You're a pro. You can't have been making and rearing babies and not have learned an incredible amount about them."

She'd kept reassuring me. When I called upset about Evan's fury, worrying that his feeling of abandonment, like an ugly sore might never heal, she'd said, "He has you, Chris, and he's one lucky kid. Daily I deal with students who have but a single adult in their life. More times than not that adult's unreliable. One girl lives with an alcoholic great uncle—"

As I progressed along the alley, sounds invaded—a lawn mower, the spin cycle of a washing machine. What if I thought about them rather than Evan? What if I imagined Leland Mitchell guiding his mower over a yard that he mows weekly so that it resembles a pink scalp that shows through close-cropped hair? I struggled to invent pictures of Ruth Benson shaking a box of powdered detergent and squinting at the washing machine agitator. In her whiny manner, she'd insist that powdered soap was cheaper and more effective than liquid detergent. But pictures and voices wavered, overpowered by Emily Jane's rich voice. "It's going to be okay, Chris. I just know it will."

She'd emphasized this in her apartment, the evening after we'd toured San Francisco and brought crab and French bread back for dinner. We ate and drank wine. Under its influence, I admitted my deepest fear, one I'd never confessed in coherent fashion, for Todd and I merely alluded to it with partial sentences and half-truths. "If only Evan doesn't do anything horrible," I'd say to Todd, afraid that if I spit out the actual words, I might set into motion some kind of self-fulfilling prophecy.

"What if Evan kills someone?" I blurted out to Emily Jane.

With an impatient hand, she shoved black curls from her forehead and centered her wine glass on the coffee table. "Why torture yourself with that question?"

"I try not to, but he's had so much against him. What if—"

Slender silver bracelets jangled on her arm as she pounded the coffee table. "He has you. That weighs heavy in the equation. And remind yourself that countless others have had bad lives and never murdered anyone."

"Like Dirk?"

Emily Jane's smiles are memorable, but she had different smiles for different people and events. The smile for Dirk, however, surpassed all of them. And though, as my daughter Julie would put it, "They're no longer an item," the smile for Dirk was undiminished. "He's broken more than a few hearts, but he's left an indelible impression. Evan will, too." That's when she enfolded my left hand with both of hers. "It's going to be okay, Chris. I just know it is."

Oh, she knew a lot and kept a lot in confidence, had since we were young. Quite simply, I trusted her. She'd never lied, disappointed, or shamed me. She accepted my immature addiction, my "cutting out paper dolls" fetish that dated from when she and I played paper dolls, and I experienced the most intense pleasure in the act of cutting.

NOTES WHEN SUMMER ENDS

Nothing matched it. When I bought a book of paper dolls at the dime store, my heart raced, and all the way home I tasted the excitement of that first cut, of aiming the blade points toward tabs and dress ruffles, of staying right on the line, of leaving scalloped ribbons of paper, of listening to the clear snip of scissors.

By late elementary grades, Emily Jane and I had outgrown paper doll sessions. Yet, I'd not outgrown the desire to cut. In a magazine, I might see a flower or a design, and the need to cut it out would surface. I even stole a magazine from Adele Harper's house because I was compelled to cut out some farm animals marked by thick, juicy borders.

Mom subscribed to *McCall's,* and each month before she read it, I tore out the Betsy McCall page. In the midst of the commotion at our house, I don't think Mom ever realized a magazine page was missing. I hid these in my bedroom drawer, stockpiling them for times when the urge was strong.

On the Saturday afternoon before high school graduation, Emily Jane dropped by and discovered me guiding scissor blades around Betsy's fingers. She stared at my hand, and I dropped the scissors.

"It's some kind of compulsion," I whispered in an effort to explain the unexplainable. "Usually I do it when I feel pent up. Like I need to discharge some electricity or something."

With a shrug she smiled her you're-my-friend smile. "Seems pretty harmless to me."

After Todd and I married, she came by our rental on the edge of town one morning. I was cutting out a tree stamped by firm black lines in a brochure. She said nothing. I replaced the scissors and brochure in a manila envelope—that was before I had a box—and hid the package in its nest beneath the dish towels.

Today, the box beneath my bed has an emergency ration: scissors, a paper doll book, and sheets of gift wrap with paper doll designs. When this weekend's over, I'm sure I'll lock the bedroom door and dip into my stash. Since Emily Jane's death, I've resisted, but....

I entered Cammy's kitchen, where she stood at the stove, hand twirling a fork in an egg mixture that spread across the bottom of a dented cast iron skillet.

"Scrambled eggs are nearly done," she said. "Would you go tell Savannah we're ready? She's on the porch, smoking a cigarette."

As I moved down the hallway, I kept my gaze on the screen at the end to avoid seeing the front parlor.

Savannah rested against the railing. She dangled her cigarette on the far side, over Cammy's marigolds. I listed that detail in my reasons-to-dislike-Savannah column.

"You're Christine," she announced, which I didn't credit as noticeably intelligent since the only other possibility was Ann. "I met you—good lord—years ago, one of the times when I came back from college with Emily."

Okay, because she greeted me easily, I could give her a mark in the reasons-to-like-Savannah column.

"When I was pregnant and Emily Jane threw a baby shower for me." To stake out my territory, my priority in our relationship, I stressed the older name.

Savannah snubbed out the cigarette and flicked it in a perfect arc that ended in touchdown beyond Cammy's flowers. "And I hid out for most of the shower with Cammy in the kitchen. I think I helped serve the cake."

She needn't explain that she'd avoided inserting herself in a situation that wasn't hers, and I liked her for implying that but not justifying it.

"Must have been something in that cake, because I went on to have three more babies." It was a feeble statement, but she did me the courtesy of laughing. As we re-entered the house, I hesitated on the threshold. "What about Ann? She eating breakfast with us?"

"Guess she's sleeping in. I've never met her. Have you?"

"No," and because she didn't comment further, I gave her another tally point in the good column.

SAVANNAH

Saturday, 1:30 P.M.

Behind the bedroom door, I light a cigarette. Heavenly. While we lingered over lunch at Rosie's Diner, I exercised willpower and denied the fact that a cigarette completes a meal. I paid attention to Cammy's vignettes about Emily. The ones she recalled concerned minor everyday occurrences—Emily's skinning her knees while roller skating, playing "dress up" in sheer curtains, and presenting a concert from the stairs' landing at age three when she'd memorized verses of four songs. Michelangelo supposedly said, "God is in the details." Apparently so.

I glanced at Christine and Ann. Fine, they listened intently, giving Cammy the audience she deserved.

That's why she's invited us, I thought, *so she can assuage this need to talk about Emily. And that's why we must make entries in these books.* So, Cammy, when you read this, you'll know that despite understanding your intentions, I'll write what I feel led to write. And I'll start by admitting that at lunch I felt close to Ann and Christine because they hung on your words and because I could sense them gluing your reminiscences to theirs, expanding their concept of Emily.

When Cammy faltered in her memory parade, she drained her coffee mug and rose. "Tonight, after supper, we'll talk more, but I have an errand to run now."

As she extracted bills from a change purse tucked in her pants pocket, Ann asked her, "Then, this afternoon?"

"Whatever you'd like to do. Supper's at six."

Cammy laid money atop the check and set the salt and pepper shakers onto that. As we protested her paying for us, she walked away, out the door.

"Well?" Ann raised an eyebrow at Christine, as if the local resident had been elevated to person in charge.

"There's a garage sale over on Webster Street."

Ann laughed. "Why not?" and looked at me, but I shook my head. I'd defer for a cigarette.

I could tell Cammy wasn't home, that the house was empty, when I stepped inside. Funny how a house is altered by people. Without me at my house, are the rooms flat? Does my husband feel the difference? Or does Benjamin relax into his easy chair, unlace his shoes, ball his socks into them, and scratch his toes, relieved that I'm not around to point out that flakes of skin from his feet have scattered over the carpet?

Cammy, I don't know if Emily would approve of Benjamin, because he's fifteen years older than I. She might believe he's too staid. I wish, though, she'd have had a chance to hear his soft speech, see his smile, feel his gentleness. Emily, however, didn't like Nigel, whom I dated twice in college ("too stuffy," she said) nor Ron my boss when I worked briefly as his assistant at the insurance company, and she met him at his best, when he and I attended a convention in San Francisco. "Bor-ing," Emily wrote later, and that one word was the complete text of her letter.

A creaking, rhythmic noise comes from outside. From the bedroom window, I see into the neighboring yard where a child, about six, I'd guess, pumps herself higher and higher in a swing. Her chubby fists cling to rusting chains, and her legs thrust back and forth in a dedicated manner as if she must gain altitude and break free from this atmosphere.

When young I loved to swing, would occasionally go to the school playground on summer evenings. Alone, I'd propel myself upward, imagining that with each exertion I gained on the stars, where I might locate a landscape solely mine.

In a letter to Emily, I once confided about my search for a place where I felt complete. "But everyone is searching," she replied. "I think the best most of us can hope for is a temporary setting that, at least for a while, speaks to us."

"For you is that Centerville?" I asked in the next letter.

"In one sense, but there are other places where my spirit has said, 'This is it.'"

If I remembered those spots, I'd record them in this journal for you, Cammy, but of most importance is the truth that this house, you, Christine, and yes, Dirk, gave her the most basic sense of belonging.

Where did I first find that "temporary setting that, at least for a while speaks to us?" Diamond Grove, Missouri. My fourth grade class, having completed a unit on native plants, took a field trip to the George Washington Carver National Monument. I'd not wanted to go. Field trips meant a buddy beside you on the bus and beside you in line. No one ever chose me as a buddy, so the teacher assigned another unpopular kid as my partner. In second grade, the girls quickly paired off, so the teacher had no choice but to team me with Ezekial Wilburs, who drooled.

But this particular trip began auspiciously, for the day before, Crystal had joined our class. Skinny, with a whipped-dog-please-be-nice-to-me attitude, she was ignored, so I was prepared to share the bench seat with her at the back of the bus.

In the visitor center, though, I experienced that fledgling brush against a sense of belonging. We learned there about Carver. Born a slave, he'd been stolen with his mother from the Moses Carver farm by bushwhackers. Moses offered his one horse and three hundred dollars in ransom for the slaves, but the bushwhackers returned only the half-dead baby. The childless white Carver couple became George's foster parents. With Mama not telling me my personal history, I yearned for that. Probably so did Carver, who'd also been denied his personal past.

Although we could follow the nature trail without a ranger, Crystal elected not to run ahead, but remained close at my heels. I didn't care. Transported by these surroundings, it was my turn to ignore someone, to ignore the other kids who chased and yelled. Responding to the past, I dawdled by the site of George's birthplace cabin. So small. About fourteen feet by fourteen feet, as I remember, and yet, the adjacent white couple's cabin site measured but two feet larger.

By the cabins', I remember the "hanging tree." Stark, without leaves or branches, it affected me. Legend goes that bushwhackers hung Moses from this tree, whipped him, and applied live coals to his feet, torturing him for gold he didn't have.

The path wound toward a spring from which George carried buckets of fresh water for the household. I stopped by the pond even longer than I had at the cabins sites or at the shorn tree, because the statue, "The Boy Carver," seemed alive, as if his ears picked up the melody of croaking frogs, or traced darting minnows. Poised to jump over a fallen log, at any second he would race toward the walnut grove.

Perhaps I should credit the statue of a young person by himself and yet not alone, or the April day, or the untapped part of me for my response. During these moments, Crystal remained but a blur. Not until she tried to stop a sneeze did I consider her and realize that on some level she intuited my need for silence, that she understood something unprecedented was happening to me.

As we circled the pond, she walked a bit closer. Springtime sunlight danced across her arm and while I knew a kinship with her, I also knew this place wasn't as important to her as it was to me.

She bent down and selected a stone. When we again sat on the backbench seat in the bus, she handed it to me, warm from her touch. I treasured it for years. It rested on the corner of my desk that faced the wall opposite the bed that Mama and I occupied until I left for college.

The irregularly shaped smooth rock symbolized my first real friendship, for Crystal and I, although never in each other's homes, were best friends at school. She moved from town in junior high and after that, when she sporadically sent letters, I tied them with a shank of ribbon and stacked them beneath the stone. The stone, as well, symbolized my ill-defined awareness that my difference from others might stem from something related to my unknown family, and finally the stone represented a place where I embraced an attachment, where I felt at home.

ANN

Saturday, after lunch

I'll guess it's three o'clock Central Daylight Time. This guest room's minus a clock, and I forgot my watch. Undoubtedly it's at home by my desk lamp, so I point the hands on its face at one P.M. That's *my* time, and I yawn, aware of jet lag.

I walked back from the garage sale by myself and found the front screen door unhooked, never the case where I live.

"Cammy," I called into the gloomy hall, but walls and rug swallowed the name. At the top of the stairs, I noticed Savannah's shut door, but since Christine's was open, I neared it. She'd left me abruptly at the garage sale, after we'd zigzagged across a lawn overflowing with leftovers. Seeking some plateau, some common denominator for conversation, we struggled with disjointed topics.

We joked about a purple artificial flower arrangement with a polka-dotted bow and doubted any fool would shell out five dollars for a manual typewriter. Christine examined a mug with a gold TEXAS on the side, then quickly replaced it as a pickup idled by the curb. Over the top of a novel, whose end flap I skimmed, I saw it and the driver were the same as those parked by Cammy's this morning. Dirk Hawkins.

"Mind if I take off for a minute?" Christine asked, and with an apologetic smile she hurried toward the shiny black cab.

The man, this Dirk, leaned across the seat and the passenger side door swung wide. Impossible to determine if they exchanged words or not, as Christine climbed into the cab, they pulled away.

Not interested in the book, nor anything at this yard sale, I ambled along studying heartland architecture, how sunlight streaked lawns and diffused itself through water whirling from sprinklers. "Store these details and sounds," I told myself. "Imprint nuances." They could function like a subtext when/if I cleaned out Em's apartment. I attempted to see with her eyes. How did this street appear when Centerville was her entire universe? How did it change when she returned from college and on every subsequent homecoming?

Thus in that reflective state in Cammy's house, I approached Em's former bedroom and felt grateful that Christine's clothes and accessories didn't mar it. I could scan items once important to Em.

David, husband number one, accused me of coldness when I quit crying over Robin before he did. Perhaps he had a point, or perhaps because I soon ceased crying over my daughter's death and over Em, it was because I handled emotions in another form. Don't enter yesterday, live for the day. Stay in the now, is my mantra.

Starting to my right, I touched everything in the room. As if blind and investigating through my fingertips, I circled, stroking the closet doorknob twice, which probably had known her hand more often than the wallpaper or the curtain.

I was by the overstuffed chair when I heard the phone ring. Seth? I dashed down the stairs and managed to grab the receiver on the fourth ring. The man on the other end wasted no breath on amenities. "Benjamin Holt for Savannah."

When I rapped on Savannah's door and she answered, I saw the just-abandoned journal and pen. As I said, "phone for you," I wondered what she wrote, wondered as she passed me in the hallway, if she too, when alone in the house had been drawn to Em's room. Although her voice traveled upward, distance clouded her words. Her tone, however, sang of happiness, reminding me that Em would tell her first graders when they sang with great enthusiasm, "That's a happy song I'm hearing."

In "my" room, I could tempt no breeze through the raised window, so with the door ajar, I picked up this journal. The open door issued an invitation, apparently, for Savannah stepped beneath the transom. "Thanks for calling me. My husband."

"Everything all right?"

While the phone voice held music, so did her smile—a gradual widening of the lips, a gradual crescendo. "Fine." A few measures of silence elapsed and then, surprisingly candid, she said, "Emily worried that I'd have a marriage without feeling. Not true."

I thought of Seth, of feeling that existed mainly in language.

"We're a team," she decided. "No, more than a team, and have been so from the beginning. Benjamin was my last boss. He and his wife owned a print shop, and after she died, he advertised for help. I was between jobs, ready for a change. Well, he hired me. Benjamin, another fellow—a part-time printer—and I did it all."

"Do you still own the shop?"

"Benjamin retired, turned it over to his son, but he can't stay away. Every day he drops in. It's fine with me, but not with the son. Benjamin called just now about a shop for sale. He read me the specs from an ad in one of his printing magazines; wondered if it's worth pursuing."

"And?"

Beneath her sandals, the hall boards reacted as she redistributed her weight, a reminder that we were strangers in a strange house, brought together by strange circumstances. "It would mean a move to Birmingham, but that's a minor inconvenience. We'd have a goal, and if it's what he wants, I'm all for it."

Savannah folded her arms across her spectacular chest. "Might be good to move, to have a new house. Emily would definitely approve. She's scolded me for not insisting on a new place. After Benjamin and I married, I moved in with him and his sons, into the house he and first wife Sandy bought."

"And you're still there?"

"Yes, and it's worked well. Although Benjamin loved Sandy, he loves me in a new way, a way perhaps reserved for second wives, when one's been given a second chance."

I refused to think of David, of his new love, of his new chance.

The porch screen door banged and Savannah called over her shoulder, "Cammy?"

"Me," Christine answered.

"Where do you suppose Cammy went?" Before I could make a guess, Savannah—apparently locked into the subject of marriage—asked, "Wonder why she never married?"

My heart lurched as I said, "Em?" Yet a portion of my brain exalted. Savannah didn't know. I must be the only one under this roof who did know.

"No, Cammy."

Christine paused beside Savannah. Her face was damp with perspiration, and her eyes were swollen. When she said "I've been with Dirk," her throat sounded full and raw. *The name, Dirk,* I thought, *is one familiar to us all, a name that unites us.*

"We drove out to the pond where as teenagers we'd go park. Just talked about her."

"She always loved him." *Damn, how trite that sounded.*

Chris swiped the back of her hand across her eyes. "And he her."

"Is he married?" Savannah's question lessened any sentimentality that we two generated and demonstrated she'd not forsaken the marriage theme.

"We didn't get into that. Somehow, it didn't seem important." Chris looked tired, despondent, so I suggested we find something to drink. I hoped for wine, but settled on iced tea stored in the refrigerator in a vintage 1950 Kool-Aid pitcher.

At the kitchen table, Chris sucked on an ice cube, maybe to busy her mouth so she'd be exempt from launching any discussion.

Savannah surveyed the room, her gaze roaming over the glistening gas range with a saucepan atop a burner, the sink with dishrag folded in three parts and draped over the mixer faucet, the identical crisp linen dish towels properly aligned from a metal rod.

So I spoke. "I've never met Dirk. Em showed me pictures and talked about their singing together in high school, about how she loved him, about his marrying, about meeting him occasionally over the years."

"They kept in touch," Savannah agreed. "I don't think regularly, but she wrote me when he contacted her. The last time was a weekend in Denver."

I started. "Really? Are you sure? She never told me." It had to have been a weekend I'd gone with Seth. Why such a secret? Why never mention it? Why, when I knew so much about her, had been with her—

Chris spit the ice cube into her hand. "Seven years ago at our last class reunion, she and Dirk sang their old duets and sneaked away that night."

"That's news to me," Savannah said. "I knew that she'd come to Centerville for a reunion but not that Dirk—"

"They could never have married." Chris deposited an ice sliver onto a paper napkin. "They were too intense. They'd have used each other up. They just needed to get together sometimes and release the passion that had accumulated."

We wandered then through the territory of high school romances and how they had influenced us. Chris had married her high school boyfriend, was happy, and had never been tempted by anyone but Todd. Savannah evidently had no memorable high school boyfriend, so she emphasized her later relationships, and I had several boyfriends, but the best one, David, came after college. I didn't reveal why he and I divorced. Instead, I stressed Seth's companionship.

"So because of Emily's intense love for Dirk she couldn't marry?" Savannah asked.

Chris nodded. "Right. Dirk's had at least two wives, but Emily Jane—well—she stayed true to him."

I should have let it alone. Maybe my dislike of lies prompted me to set the record straight, maybe I wanted to assert my significance in Em's life, maybe I reacted from hurt over Em's silence concerning the Denver weekend, or maybe I felt confessional, certain that at some point I would include the revelation in this journal, but for whatever reason I said, "She did marry."

Savannah's brown eyes widened and Chris, as if participating in the childhood game of "Statues," didn't move. Next door the little girl yelled, "coming" to some invisible command, and the refrigerator motor purred steadily before my heart's rapid banging obliterated sounds.

"You're telling us that Emily had a husband." Incredulity tinged every southern-coated syllable.

Why did I do this? Oh, Em, are you angry? I'm not much of a best friend, am I?

"She would have told me," Chris asserted flatly, "or" she added with a quick concession to Savannah, "us."

I sipped my tea. Mother would have termed it "scared water." Anemic in color and flavor, it furnished no help. "I think she was so embarrassed by it that she never told anyone. If I'd not been involved, I would never have known. His name was Richard, and he was a processed food salesman. Well, his name remains Richard, and he continues to sell food to institutions."

Neither smiled.

"My husband owns two nursing homes, one in the Bay Area; the other in Santa Barbara. He's one of Richard's customers."

I could sense Chris thinking *So?* And Savannah thinking *Come on, get to the Emily part.* "After Em had lived in the apartment beside us for many years, I introduced her to Richard."

Numerous scenes, numerous minutia backed this statement. I saw Em on a summer morning step over the low fence that separated our adjoining patios and clear the jade plants in their redwood barrels. She was barefooted, dressed in black shorts and a shapeless white blouse. Her hair, in its normal untamed manner, fell about her face. She collapsed into the lawn chair beside mine, then glanced at the sliding glass door to the rear. "Seth around?"

"Nope. Santa Barbara weekend."

She wiggled deeper into the cushion, so that the base of her skull lodged on the top of the chair. "Bad view from here," she decided. "I'm in a direct line with the cellulite on my thighs. I never dreamed it would creep around to the front."

Almost finished with a mystery, I regretfully marked the page with a memo sheet from Seth's Bay Side Nursing Home. "Try a fitness center."

"Yeah, right. It's a place where young people go and so do hunky men."

Hunky men set her off. As if she were printing lists on columns drawn on a chalkboard below titles "Positive Traits" and "Negative Traits," she recapped the pluses and the minuses of every man since Dirk with whom she'd had a relationship.

Feeling immensely wise, I said, "Your problem is that you compare all men with an adolescent male."

"I sure used to, but no more. Dirk was pure pleasure. In college, a girl who roomed down the hall from Savannah and me got engaged in her senior year to this wimpy fellow. For two years she'd carried on a torrid affair with a football star. We couldn't figure it, but one night she said, 'I've had my passion, and I'll never forget it. But I need to marry a guy who'll bring in lots of money, be an excellent father, and not cheat on me.' 'Pretty clinical and cold blooded,' I later said to Savannah, but she thought it made perfect sense. Well, finally, I can agree with that engaged girl. This white-hot love with Dirk is seared into my system, but I'd like a good man in my life like Seth."

Simultaneously, we smiled, but my smile felt a trifle controlled. Without question, Seth was a good man, but on that morning I would have traded a bit of such goodness for a wild romp in bed. However, I'd not bore Em with that announcement. She'd nodded sympathetically at varying anecdotes about my sexy marriage to David that ended with Robin's death, at my decrying the shell people he and I became. Brittle and dried, we no longer craved sex or each other.

"Well," I stretched, as if by physical activity I could shake off the past, "it's all a trade-off, isn't it?"

I went inside for coffee, leaving her on the patio with the morning sun pushing through the oak tree leaves to print a mosaic across her hair. From the cabinet I grabbed mugs, a Christmas gift from Wilcox Food Supply, Richard's company, and suddenly thought of him. Divorced, no children that I knew of, and a decent fellow—might work.

Weeks passed before we could arrange a dinner, but on a fall evening, Em skirted my plants on the patio barricade, slid back our screen and entered our living room.

"Hi, beautiful." Seth greeted her as he straightened napkins and silverware I'd tossed on the table, after I'd hurried home following a lengthy faculty meeting that had lasted until 5:30.

Em *was* beautiful. She resembled autumn, the deep browns and yellows of leaves. That still life—Em radiant and mysterious—haunts me. That image influenced Richard, as well, for when he arrived seconds later, he brightened and stepped closer, as if to be encompassed by the force field she emitted.

Force field, that was it, because Em wasn't pretty. Nose: "ideal for a peasant" she said. Lips: "downright impoverished." Hips: "designed for breeding, but I'm not testing them." But she lived vibrantly. And at times, such as that night, such aliveness obscured disparate parts and provided another definition of beauty.

It was an enchanted evening and when Richard asked to walk her home, she left with him. After Seth and I loaded the dishwasher, he held a drinking glass to the wall that divided our kitchen from her bedroom, "to hear if there are any suspicious noises." Under the night's spell, we laughed without reason. Seth hugged me, and when I kissed him, he didn't tilt his head away or pat my arm like a brother. He returned the kiss. We made love in the bedroom and fantasizing that he was David, I came. When I shocked Seth with my tears, he ineffectually murmured, "There, there," but he held me.

The Em-Richard romance skated smoothly ahead throughout October; then accelerated in early November, due, I'm convinced, to Christine's letter.

I found out about the letter on a Wednesday evening. Although Seth generally flew to Santa Barbara and his facility on alternate

Fridays, he'd gone that morning when his new director of nurses phoned, distraught over an unexpected state inspection. Thus, alone that night, I'd dialed Mother, who lives on the Peninsula. As she raved about my sister's kids, I fed her obligatory comments. Not envious that Carla has two sons, I sensed Mother's unspoken messages beneath delight in her grandsons. *You and Seth would have pleased me if you'd had children. It would have been healthy for you to have had another baby. You'll be alone in your old age.*

She told me that she'd bumped into David, "Yesterday in Safeway. He had his daughter with him."

I knew that David and his wife had a child—or was it children—but I'd sealed off that knowledge. A daughter. I wasn't going to ask if he'd inquired about me. Obviously, Mother didn't intend to tell me. "He's looking very handsome," she said. My patio door opened with Em's touch. In a tepid greeting, she waved an envelope. Although she, too, looked tepid, I was thrilled to see her, as I longed to conclude this conversation. Invariably Mother mentioned David, whom she'd adored or Robin, her one granddaughter. Sometimes her voice carried a subliminal accusation that I'd been complicit in Robin's death. If I'd not gone with the watercolor group that day, if I'd not hired the neighbor's teenage daughter as a sitter, possibly Robin wouldn't have ridden her bicycle alone around the block. Possibly the car wouldn't have struck her. Or possibly I would have summoned help more quickly or efficiently than the terrified sitter so that Robin wouldn't have lingered in a coma for six weeks until we vetoed life support systems.

"Talk to you soon, Mother," I said and signaled for Em to sit down.

"Nope," Em answered. "I'll pour us some wine first."

"Were you at Crawford Elementary today? Bad day?"

"It was manageable," she muttered while she bumped bottles in my cupboard to unearth our crisis ration, a jug of wine brewed by another teacher. Such powerful wine it was, that Seth, Em, and I agreed its sole purpose was to knock out the drinker.

Not bothering with wine glasses, Em tipped the jug so that liquid gurgled into tumblers.

We saluted each other, and she sprawled into Seth's recliner, her choice when he was away. "God," she said after a hardy drink, "this is awful stuff."

"Anesthetic's not designed for taste."

She set her glass on Seth's *Provider Magazine* in order to extract decorative notepaper from its matching envelope. Notepaper. Christine. Based on lamb, bunny, and kitty stationery, I'd formed definite impressions of Chris. Em creased the sheet in half before reading aloud, "Guess who walked into Todd's shop today? Just the way I wrote that, you know who. Todd said Dirk looked terrific. Straight out, Emily Jane, I need to tell you that Dirk's remarried. Todd didn't get her exact name. Something like Gwen or Lynn or maybe Wyn, but who would name a baby 'Wyn,' like hoping she'd be a winner?"

I filtered home brew through my teeth, grateful for the sharp taste and residue, the almost instant disintegration of reality. Silly to wallow in memories of David and Robin, to allow Mother's comments to disturb me, and Em should do the same. she shouldn't mourn Dirk's remarriage.

"You thought Dirk was going to come back for you?" That sounded harsher than I intended, and I flinched when Em paled. Then she straightened her posture, her spine no longer flat against the rust-colored fabric.

"No." The letter scratched against the envelope as she re-inserted it.

We finished our drinks, compared school notes, naturally, and she asked about Seth's director of nursing problem. She mentioned Richard's condo in Fremont, and as if diagramming sentences, analyzed anew my marriage, the fact that Seth split his time between two nursing homes, and the necessary "space," it gave me.

"And, Seth as well," I said. "He'd been a bachelor for too long to relinquish privacy and autonomy." His spartan Santa Barbara apartment proved this. There, he could space photos of mountains and waterfalls in perfect order on living and bedroom walls. He admired rooms that reflected no personality. On the few occasions I'd gone with him, I'd chafed to leave. By choice, I seldom went.

Em took her glass to the sink and rinsed it. "I think next weekend, a long weekend, I'll stay with Richard in his condo."

She did spend more evenings and weekends with him. The four of us met for dinner and a movie, but with Thanksgiving and Christmas fast approaching, my spare time dwindled with the increased art projects in various classes.

For me, November and December were especially difficult. The car had struck Robin on the day after Thanksgiving, a day when our watercolor group figured that "normal" people would shop, leaving Ohlone State Park vacant to ready itself for winter. Before I ripped it to shreds, I had a credible sketch of November light gracing the shell mounds at the park.

Throughout that "holiday" season, David, I, my parents, Carla, and David's family staked out the hospital. Now that period blurs with but minimal specifics as keepsakes: an ice cream roll with a Santa design in the middle served at the cafeteria on Christmas Day; rain, constant it seemed, dimming the window pane in Robin's room; the bulging ankles of a nurse, which caused me to wonder if she suffered from gout and interested me enough that I intended to read about gout in my home medical volume. Strange, I suppose, that I can't recall Robin. Thin, of course. Wan, definitely. Head bandaged, yes. Tubes and I.V.'s ruled her body, but I can't see *her*. The gaunt faces of our families superimpose themselves upon each other because we all looked the same—altered.

Robin died for me the day after Thanksgiving. Granted, she continued breathing until January, but from my first glimpse after she was wheeled from surgery, I knew that Robin, my Robin (the child I could cruelly remind myself that I'd not wanted), was gone.

During that interminable six-week period, while the family argued medical opinions and balked at discussing organ donations with hospital staff, I grieved. I believe that put me weeks ahead of the others, for I didn't endure days of torture where hope raced with despair.

Therefore, I struggle to avoid this season. Seth and I travel, or if demands at either nursing home, where staffing's perennially short around Christmas tie him down, I take off. I've eaten Christmas dinner alone in Waikiki, have attended plays in London with a theatre group, and have driven up the coast to Ft. Bragg. One Christmas when San Francisco's fog canceled Em's flight to Iowa, she and I drove south for a weekend on Catalina Island.

Since for me the day after Thanksgiving marks Robin's death, that's when I visit her grave. It's better, because none of the family goes then, so there's slim chance I'll run into David. I could meet him anywhere and act friendly and gracious—except for the cemetery.

I'd wanted Robin cremated after the organ donations, and had sought comfort in disposing of ashes as I chose, scattering fragments in settings she'd loved: by the park sand pile, near a pasture where a sway-back horse nickered at her delighted, "Here, boy," by the backyard stones memorializing two turtles and her cocker spaniel Jupiter.

But in foxhole fashion, David and his parents dug in, piling high the space around them with emotionally shoveled dirt. So I capitulated. If it meant so much to them, I could handle it. Had I foreseen that thirty-six months later, David and I would divorce, I would have held firm, for the grave's permanently on the Peninsula in the province of David and his replacement wife.

Over the years since then, I've reread the tombstone dates, studied the smiling kindergarten photo that David inserted behind a Plexiglas oval, and touched those incised letters, "Robin Grayson." Before her birth, David and I had agreed on no middle name, just as we agreed to change our predetermined name to Robin when we spotted the bright bird on our front lawn the morning that I went into labor.

Just once, Seth went to the graveyard with me. The children's section disturbed him, particularly in late November when rain or fog usually weighs upon us. Especially though, he hated the glittery plastic windmills that spun on graves, the teddy bears, dolls, trucks, and tiny tinsel-decorated fake Christmas trees.

NOTES WHEN SUMMER ENDS

What did I bring? Some natural object of special import—a green pebble I discovered while running, a dried cat tail from the marsh at our marina, a robin's feather that wafted onto my patio on a spring breeze.

For the last couple years, Em has gone with me. Not knowing Robin, she brought items she imagined would appeal to my daughter.

On this particular November day—the November day that relates to Richard—Em showed me symmetrical red leaves that had drifted onto the playground as she left campus, ones she pulled from her jacket pocket after I'd parked at the cemetery and we'd walked down a slope. "Have you firmed up Christmas vacation plans?" she asked.

I stared straight ahead in an effort to ignore a woman about my age when Robin died, stringing handmade stars in a sapling beside a fresh grave. "Depends on Seth. If he can get away, we'll try Death Valley. If not, I'm thinking about Hearst Castle."

"Well, your dilemma is solved. Come with Richard and me to Reno. We're getting married. Now, for a moment, say nothing."

As we stood at the grave, I smiled at her. "You do surprise me."

In answer, she released the leaves that spiraled downward. How long had it taken before this plot looked as if it had always belonged in this fenced property? At the bottom of the headstone, I laid an acorn, a dark brown marvel that I'd narrowly escaped crushing on the sidewalk beside our complex.

"I wanted to tell you here," she said. "I want no one else—well, Seth, naturally—to know. After we're married, I'll call Cammy at some point, and after vacation, when school resumes, I'll announce it."

I glanced from Robin's eternal smile into Em's exuberant eyes. *Thank you, Em,* I thought, *for such a gift.*

So while customers packed stores buying presents, Em and I shopped exclusively for The Dress. Not white. Not floor-length. Not sparkly. Not cute. We picked a peach-colored dress that highlighted her eyes and dark hair.

Curled up on her love seat, I listened while she called Reno wedding chapels, and debated with herself about where and when to host a reception for faculty and friends in January. I gave my input to her and Richard about pooling furniture, and begged them not to move into his condo, but live next door in Em's condo.

The morning of the wedding, scheduled for 4:00 P.M. on Christmas Eve, Seth and I drove to Reno. Light snow dusted the car near Truckee, and it mellowed us. Seth and I, Californians, are spellbound by snow. Bounced between divorced parents, neither of whom had welcomed him as a child, Seth relived a series of unpleasant Christmases. As the wipers on their low, metronomic speed scraped flakes from the windshield, he said, "Maybe if ever I'd had a white Christmas, I'd have some better memories."

"From now on, Christmas will come with great memories. We'll remember Em's wedding." I laced my fingers through his on the hand closest to me.

The wedding was tasteful. I'd worried that it might be tacky or a packaged ceremony, but Em had selected a Bach prelude for the pianist. The official who read the service added personal remarks, and a photographer unobtrusively snapped pictures. Em was gorgeous in her dress; Richard proud in a new blue suit.

At an early dinner, Seth and I toasted them. I kissed Richard's cheek, hugged Em, and said we'd expect them in five days, when they'd move Richard's possessions into her apartment. But, five days later, Em showed up alone. Haggard and drawn, she needed a shampoo.

"My God, let me pour some of that rot gut wine."

"Got anything stronger?" she asked and then sighed. "It's over, Ann, and you can't tell anyone about my stupidity. Promise?"

I took in the dark circles under her eyes; the left hand minus a ring. "What happened?" Images chased each other—Richard beating her, confessing he wasn't divorced, demanding money for debts, insisting on sex with a dog or some other aberrant sexual practice. Yet, Em had slept with Richard, had spent plenty of nights at his apartment, and he at hers, so sex shouldn't be the issue.

"Wouldn't it be easy if I could tell you one horrible thing? But it's everything. Suddenly I realized that this was it, that Richard's snorting and farting while he slept would only worsen as we aged, that his stale morning breath and his strenuous gargling sessions in the bathroom would be the smells and sounds to greet me for the rest of our married life.

"If I deeply loved him, little things wouldn't annoy me, at least initially, but by the end of the second day I was tense and angry at the way he flossed. He doesn't even do it in the bathroom, but in front of me. And he plasters his hair over the patch where he's balding, which irritates me.

"I reasoned with myself that this was part of adjusting, lectured myself about overreaction, but down deep, I knew. I convinced myself that separate households were the answer, like you and Seth have, so I suggested he not sell his condo, that we try a commute marriage. He said, 'That's idiotic. I've already accepted a deposit. It would be a ridiculous waste of money. Besides, what would people think?' I told him that we needn't concern ourselves with others and pointed out how well you and Seth have managed. 'Seth's nursing homes warrant two addresses,' he said, 'but I need and want just one home.'"

They'd parted amicably enough, agreeing that marriage was a mistake, one about which they'd keep quiet.

Then Em laughed. "Plus, the sex was mediocre at best. No way he'd ever improve. He's but a novice in Dirk's league."

With that line, I concluded my story. Savannah and Chris regarded me as do incredulous children, as do some of my students when mesmerized by an art project. Then the floor creaked, and the three of us turned. Cammy stood just inside the door to the hallway. Her chiseled expression and her unrelenting gaze told us that she, too, had listened and hung on to every word.

CHRIS

Saturday, late afternoon

Well, Cammy took us on part one of her trip this morning—to the high school and to Rosie's Diner for lunch. It was hard for me then, and it's hard for me now. I sit in Emily Jane's room with sweat blotching my clothes. I'd forgotten how hot and close the second floor can be in this old house with the bedroom door shut. I have to have it shut because I need privacy before we gather for the supper Cammy's fixing.

First of all, the down-memory-lane trip was hard, because we walked by the hardware store. No sign of Evan. Not only was I worried about him, but I was walking with Ann (Cammy and Savannah led off). As if I could see our town—pitiful little nothing town—through her eyes, I noticed the neglected hardware store apartment. A shade with a big gash covers one window. The other window that fronts Main Street is bare. Not a hint of a curtain. I doubt any female stays with Grant long enough to dress the windows or put plants, even a miserable geranium, on the ledge.

Secondly, when we turned down Taylor toward the high school, we passed in front of Todd's shop. He was busy in the office talking to Mr. Wiser, a lawyer, who continues to complain about his Chevy overheating. Todd, listening intently to Mr. Wiser and marking on his clipboard, didn't see our procession. I sent Cammy a silent thank you for not pointing out my husband or his business.

If Ann, Savannah, or any outsider with education witnessed the interchange behind the plate glass window, they would assume the trim man in the suit works out with weights, is important and professional; the balding, greasy man in coveralls with a slight paunch that gives the elasticized waistband a workout hasn't gone to college and switches television channels whenever a male ballet dancer leaps across the screen. Such assumptions would be correct.

Next, entering the high school building was rough. I've put four kids through C.H.S. With each of their involvements, it became more their school and less mine. However, on this August morning without back-packed kids in clusters on the lawn and in the hallway, with Cammy's thumb on the door latch that Todd, my kids, Emily Jane, and I touched, I exhaled a couple Lamaze–like "who-whoose" into the air before I stepped into a dead hall.

Cammy made a sharp right into the auditorium. Even to me it appeared cramped, and to Ann and Savannah it surely seemed antiquated.

"This is where Emily sang," Cammy said.

Most likely, Savannah and Ann saw a vacant stage with a stale velvet curtain. But for me, ghosts ruled. Dirk and Emily Jane, in their black choir robes, left the chorus perched on tiers to take center stage for their duet.

A huge knot lodged in my throat, so I slipped back into the hallway. How? How could this be over, completely totally over?

Backed against a locker, I practiced deep breathing and decided to stay here. Let Cammy say whatever she desired. The performances she detailed for her audience would not match what I remembered anyway. But my time alone was interrupted by the school custodian, Earl McKenzie, who'd been in our graduating class.

"Hey, Chris," he called out as he walked toward me, "taking a nostalgia trip?"

"Sort of," and I explained why I/we were there.

"Sure surprised and sorry to hear about Emily Jane. Found it funny, though, that there was just that death notice in the newspaper. No article, no funeral. Not even much of an obit. Me and the wife talked it over. What to do? Send a card? Take food by?" He shrugged. "We did nothing."

"Me neither."

"So why the mystery? Did she have AIDS or something?"

"No, cancer. But why the mystery? Cammy's not said. Maybe she'll answer that this weekend. What can I say? Cammy's one unusual woman. Always has been."

Earl raised his hand in warning at footsteps coming from the direction of the auditorium. I had to admire Earl. After he nodded at Cammy, he just plunged in, "Condolences about Emily Jane."

"Thank you." Her words were clipped; her voice strong, but what must she feel like? What's it like to lose your only relative, for to my knowledge, Emily Jane's her only family. For what did I actually know about her? Nothing of her history, nor anything about her finances. She'd not held a job. What did she do for money? Cammy had always been the aunt-mother. Involved with Emily Jane, I'd had no curiosity about Cammy. She'd been a backdrop, like that curtain in the auditorium.

"So, no services?" Earl persisted.

"None."

"Any kind of, well, a memorial gift or anything?"

"Emily wanted nothing."

"And we're respecting that," Savannah said. As if protecting Cammy, as if closing ranks, she stepped forward beside the older woman.

"Sure, sure, if that's what she wanted." Earl scratched his chest, debating, and finally came up with, "She really could sing." We nodded, and he ambled down the hallway toward the custodian's room that once had loomed as a forbidden area, where maintenance men in khakis probably cussed and told dirty jokes.

"Now, for Rosie's Diner. Whenever Emily and I ate out, and it was rare, we'd go to Rosie's. Whenever Emily came home, we'd treat ourselves to grilled cheese sandwiches."

Could I choke down anything over the lump that refused to completely dissolve?

If I could only curl up in some safe place where this group or Heather, Todd, or Evan couldn't find me, I'd bawl my eyes out. Instead, I joined Ann behind Cammy and Savannah, en route to Rosie's.

NOTES WHEN SUMMER ENDS

As if a tour guide, Cammy pointed out sights. "An invasion of Bermuda grass is taking over that lawn... That's where Judge Atkins lived, a pompous man." Well, journal, I wondered if she often walked this way, ever visited others. How little I knew of her. But, how little I know of anyone really. In high school, I'd swear I knew Emily Jane as completely as I knew myself. But over the years she'd had experiences that shaped and re-shaped her. If we'd had that last conversation, what would we have said? Even when I spent four days with her in California, she didn't reveal much about her current life. With me she remembered our past, and since she'd kept up with my family life, had come home for Julie's and for Scott's weddings, she listened to my problems. In letters and in phone calls, she'd given helpful advice about Evan. But, what did she *think*?

Cammy hung a left at the corner. I guess to take us along the shaded street that parallels Main, a street with the house where I'd grown up. Paint peeled from the porch and torn shingles dangled over the storm gutters. The people who bought it after Dad died and after we put Mom in the Care Center, are absentee landlords.

Cammy slowed. "This was Christine's home where Emily spent many wonderful hours." I smiled and knew a second of superiority about my memories, ones that neither Ann nor Savannah could touch. Next, though, sharp pain flooded throughout my body, because everything that used to be was gone. Gone, impossible to touch. Yet that was nutty. What was there to touch? Memories are fluid. Time erases and inflates them. Never could I ask Emily Jane, "Did we paint the south wall of the dining room with finger paint, or did I imagine that we did it?"

When I'm upset, movement helps, so I started walking. Behind me, I heard the others tag along, and at my elbow Ann said, "You were privileged to have shared her childhood."

"Yes," I whispered, surprised at this friendliness, and yet, I quickly asked myself *Why are you surprised? Wouldn't Emily Jane pick good friends? Aren't I doing her a disservice to assume that Savannah and Ann aren't worthy?*

"Sometimes," Ann continued, "when we had philosophical conversations, we discussed friendships, how at various junctures in your life, you require different people. Invariably, though, Em returned to her premise that basic friends stay, and often there's only one. For her, it was you."

Before me, trees swam and the concrete sidewalk wavered. "Thanks."

We cut back to Main to the farthest business, a run-down dining car. The original Rosie was dead, and her granddaughter now managed the café. Business had declined, mainly because of restaurants opening along the highway to the north where Centerville's expanding. Thus, I didn't expect many booths to be occupied. I also didn't expect to find Candi, my daughter-in-law, in the back booth. Deep in conversation with a man in a suit, she didn't notice me. As I scooted across the leatherette bench seat, I saw the back of the man's head. Expensive haircut. He didn't get that at Larry's Barber Shop where Todd goes, or at Quick Shears, the eight-dollar shop by the highway that Evan likes. So, while Cammy poured out memories of grilled cheese sandwiches, I wondered about Candi and Mr. Faceless.

Candi and Scott have been married for almost three years. Our relationship? Civil sums it up. The two had dated in high school where Scott, unlike his dad, was a major football star, voted most valuable player in his junior and senior year. He'd been popular, and understandably so, because Scott's one of those easy people with a sunny smile. Charming, but sincerely charming.

Candi, the only child of a dentist, has a mother too stuck-up for Centerville. Claudia's friends live out of town. She travels extensively, maintains a gorgeous house because she hires help, and resents the fact that Candi loves Scott.

They sent Candi to a private college. Scott, on an athletic scholarship, attended State. At the end of freshman year, Candi transferred to State. Soon, she and Scott lived together, and after graduation they married. Scott got a coaching job in the next town. It still strikes me as odd that my son coaches at Elmwood, our traditional rival, and that he married such a cold fish. At least that's Todd's name for her, as she's a bit deficient in the warmth department. Yes, civil, that's our relationship.

Todd and I have rarely been to their home. She has fragile living room chairs, upholstered in white brocade. "Froo froo chairs," Todd said. "Non-kid chairs," I answered. I mean, honestly, what kids—even outstanding kids—don't leave finger smudges or drag something greasy across cushions?

Obviously in the booth at Rosie's, my mind operated on several levels. Scott's marriage, fancy chairs, and did that mean they'd never have children, Candi at the diner with this fellow, and Cammy listing special occasions when she and Emily Jane had dined here. "When Emily lost the regional Songfest Contest, our consolation? Order a grilled cheese. When she managed to pass algebra," Cammy smiled, "how did we celebrate? Grilled cheese sandwiches and jumbo fries."

Oh, my, the Emily Jane level is a sorrowful one. But perhaps it's not a level. Maybe everything relates to Emily Jane because I could write her about Scott, whom she'd known since birth. Unnecessary to explain background or feelings, or—

I felt horribly lonely. No, I felt like I wasn't there, like my head had separated from my body. As if from a distance I watched Cammy, and to ground myself, I silently said, *I'm sitting across from Cammy and catty cornered from Savannah, with whom I've spoken what? A couple hundred words? A woman I'll likely never see after this weekend. And Ann, her hands curved on the closed menu as if ready to play the piano, I'll not see again. Just by happenstance we are in Rosie's Diner.* Why, if I'd been born in Elmwood, for instance, I would have missed by a few miles knowing Emily Jane. If Savannah had another roommate, if Ann had taught another hour at the schools, if Cammy (whether aunt or mother) had decided not to raise Emily Jane—Life is so dependent on chance, on timing, isn't it? And if we hadn't come into this restaurant at this moment, I wouldn't have spotted Candi with darkly-handsome business-suited man, a complete opposite to stocky Scott, who looks best in sweats.

I peered around Cammy's ear. Good grief, Candi was glowing. It reminded me of standing beside Emily Jane before her bedroom mirror. "See, Chris, I have the Glow, the sex glow." Then she blushed about making out with Dirk. In the mirror I faced my own virginal reflection.

My stare must have shot across the diner because Candi glanced up, right at me, and I felt a pang of fear for Scott.

The waitress neared and as each of us dutifully ordered grilled cheese sandwiches, Candi gathered up her purse and left the booth with Mr. Handsome. "Hi, Chris." Great, when she paused at the table, she was nervous. She didn't introduce me to Quality Haircut, and I didn't introduce any of my group.

"I'll call you," she said, "later today?"

"I won't be home."

"Well, we'll talk soon, real soon." She swallowed. "Until then, don't tell anyone that we—that we met today, okay?"

The waitress moved off. Cammy and the other women listened now to this dialogue, while Mr. Studly Handsome worked on a sophisticated smile, sort of sucking the inside of his cheeks to make his features more pronounced.

I hated to agree with her, to appear like an accomplice, but I couldn't break the mood necessary for Cammy. So I said, "Look forward to talking to you." Then in a moment of strength, for which I'm proud, I smiled at Cammy. "What about the time that Emily Jane said, 'Instead of a birthday cake, let's eat grilled cheese sandwiches?'"

I'm sure I didn't imagine that the three of us bent our heads more closely together and leaned toward Cammy. As she began the account the diner door closed behind Candi and her Studly friend.

SAVANNAH

4 P.M. Saturday

I've pulled down the yellowing window shade in an effort to prevent some of the heat from invading Cammy's room. With the sun pounding against the aging blind, the room takes on a sepia color. Once more, I've studied Cammy's possessions and have smoked a cigarette, stalling techniques to avoid this journal. Sometimes I have so much to say that I'm overwhelmed, realizing that there's no way I can cram everything into this book. At other moments, I feel that nothing I say can interest anyone. Who truly cares about my ideas, my dreams? What difference does my life make? This afternoon I acutely feel the latter, but I'll write something, will give my version of what happened after Ann's recital about Emily's marriage, of what happened after she and Christine left the kitchen.

Cammy remained by the cabinet, so I picked up our iced tea glasses. "Ann could be lying," I suggested, as I rinsed them at the sink.

"No, I'm sure she's telling the truth."

I set the glasses upside down on the drain board, turned off the faucet, and wiped wet fingers across my rump before glancing at her. She appeared calm, with the outline of a smile around her lips. "As I said, one reason that I invited the three of you here this weekend was to learn about Emily. I'm succeeding. For example, she never told me much about Dirk because she knew I didn't approve of him. In return, I failed to tell her about her parents, always intending to do so—" Cammy cleared her throat. "Getting the full picture fascinates me. Come," and she crossed behind me to a solid white door in the kitchen wall, which when opened released a musty basement odor.

At the foot of a flight of wooden steps, a fluorescent light illumined a library table covered with books, note cards, and manuscript pages.

In one corner, a floor lamp overlooked an easy chair with an afghan. To its left, a pile of books, some with scraps of paper protruding as place holders, nearly consumed an end table. A thickly woven area rug lay before the chair, and I pictured wintered nights; Cammy reading in that chair, her orthopedic shoes removed, her long slender feet burrowing into the rug tufts.

Books filled cases along three walls. "Most of them are biographies," she said.

"A way to gain a full picture."

"To try for a full picture," she corrected. "A biographer can't possibly know or include everything. Can a biographer overcome prejudice, particularly if it's a subconscious one, if the writer isn't even aware of a bias? If there are multiple biographies of a subject, I read them all, but no matter how many or how few there are, I often attempt my own interpretation."

She motioned toward the library table where her handwriting lined the manuscript pages.

Along the fourth wall, a bank of file cabinets divided the space from the furnace, the washer and the dryer. She eased open a drawer crammed with file folders, marched her fingers across the labeled tabs and selected a file. "This might interest you."

I pulled back the library table's straight chair as I read the printed capital letters, "Mary McLeod Bethune." Just as I'd been intrigued by George Washington Carver, so had I been fascinated by Bethune. In school, I'd written several term papers on her.

Cammy turned on her floor lamp, produced reading glasses from her pants pocket, and picked up the biography atop the pile.

Skimming through the pages, I read again of Mary's birth in 1875, the fifteenth of seventeen children. Obsessed with the desire to learn to read, she walked five miles daily to the black elementary school during the brief months it was in session.

I quit scanning and carefully read paragraphs neatly written in Cammy's tight script, markedly unlike Emily's generous scrawl. Cammy's sparse sentences conveyed a power, so that although acquainted with the framework of Bethune's life, I read each word. I appreciated Mary's scholarship to attend high school, and easily created a mental film strip of the girl in hand-me-down clothes boarding a train in her native South Carolina to ride to Scotia Seminary, clear in North Carolina.

For the first time, Mary ate with a fork, slept in an actual bed, shared a room with just one other girl, and began adopting a philosophy that "If you do not extend love, you will not receive it."

At last, she taught school in the South and married. "But, Albertus lacked his wife's energy and dedication to teaching," Cammy wrote, "so she took her son Albert to Palatka, Florida, where she launched her own school."

From previous research, this part was vivid, how with a dollar and fifty cents, she rented a ramshackle building and furnished it with discards and items from the dump.

Traveling a route I'd traveled before I re-experienced her fight to improve the school that grew into a college, and her battle with discrimination, and then I found my favorite quote, which Cammy had underlined with a red pencil. "When Mary asked for a contribution and was refused, she would say, 'Thank you for your time. No matter how deep my hurt, I always smiled. I refused to be discouraged, for neither God nor man can use a discouraged person.'"

At this point, Cammy's book snapped shut, so I read no further about Mary's work with President Franklin Roosevelt, the United Nations, the archives for black women's history....

"Thanks, she was one of my idols," I said.

We sat lost in our own thoughts until Cammy said, "You wrote once that your father was dead; that you intended to find his grave."

"Never did. After I married Benjamin, I gave up that idea. Benjamin and his three sons became all the family that I need." I shifted in my chair. "I've never told you My Story, have I? My letters have given portions out of sequence." So, in Cammy's basement, I spelled out the affinity I'd felt at the Carver Monument in grade school, then dealt with junior high years when other girls had mere bumps on their chests, while I developed such big breasts that I had to lean forward in order to see my knees.

From where had I inherited such size? One evening I pressed Mama for family background. "I won't talk about family. They kicked me out."

"But why?"

"They were uneducated, which means you have to get an education, must graduate from college and—"

"But what about my father?"

"He abandoned me. Surely, Savannah, you can understand how painful it is to talk about that, about being discarded."

"But I must have paternal grandparents? Aunts? Uncles?"

Mama answered that she'd lost track of his family, which told me that somewhere there must be relatives.

Throughout high school, I kept to myself, declining dates. Boys asked me out because of my breasts. Avoiding eye contact, I carried books before my chest and wondered from what gene pool I'd inherited their size. On my thin, tall Mama, blouses hung virtually undisturbed, with barely a mound on each side of the front buttons.

She scolded me about stooped shoulders as I crouched over the kitchen table doing my homework or "lessons" as Mama called it.

"If I throw my shoulders back, my tits stick out," I yelled one night.

"There is never any excuse for vulgarity."

"There is, there is. When I'm forced to carry around 40C's, when they bounce and flap during P.E., when kids stare at them, when they keep growing, when boys brush against me to feel them, when I can't imagine ever getting pregnant because they'll balloon into size 90F's, when I can't figure why I'm cursed with them, then, yes, it's time to be vulgar, to call them what they are, tits. I'm a cow with huge udders, and isn't that what farmers call them—tits?"

"Teat is the preferred pronunciation for nipple," Mama said distinctly, and then we laughed. She bent forward and kissed my forehead. "Sweetheart, I'm sorry you're unhappy. Thousands of women would love to have your problem. There'll come a time, I'm convinced, that you'll be happy with your bosom."

Mama was right. The time came in my senior year. In geometry class, my desk lined up with Franklin Waverly's. Intent on math, he ignored my chest. When he walked me home from school, he identified birds and insects. He seemed unfazed by our cottage and its location. Mama approved of him. "He's polite and studious."

Through the winter, Franklin and I dated, and when he could borrow his dad's car, we went to movies, bowled or roller skated. His kisses were tender. In the spring, if he had the car, we sometimes parked on country roads. His kisses became longer, more ardent.

One May night, when the moon shone full, we sat in the car, his arm loosely around my shoulders. He spoke of the moon, of the flat Mare Serenitatis, Mare Crisium, and Mare Nubium. From that, he moved into popular misconceptions.

"As in Man In," I laughed. We catalogued others, and then talked in general about other fantastic ideas, about fantasies.

"What's your fantasy?" he finally asked.

"To learn about my father."

"If I could, I'd make it come true for you."

Touched by his honest desire, I asked, "And yours?"

He gulped. "Don't get mad, Savannah, please, but my fantasy is to see your breasts. Just see them," his voice broke, "in the moonlight."

As I unbuttoned my blouse, he removed his arm from my shoulder. Neatly, deliberately, I folded my blouse across my lap. I unsnapped my bra, and as I laid it on my blouse, his breathing grew louder. "They're beautiful; the most beautiful things I've ever seen, and the moonlight—it bathes them."

I glanced down. With the moon lightening my skin, casting shadows through the dusty windshield, I saw my breasts as lovely for the first time and was grateful to Franklin.

With hands clasped between his thighs, he studied my chest for some ten minutes. Sounds of his rapid, hoarse breathing competed with an owl's hoot, a night bird's shriek. When I shivered, he watched entranced as my nipples tightened.

"Franklin, I'm chilly."

"Oh, sure, sure. Thank you. Thank you very much."

On subsequent nights, he asked to stroke them with fingers warm and butterfly gentle. Hands that cupped my breasts were loving. If kisses could be called "adoring," that's what I felt as his lips tattooed each breast. Tenderly, he sucked my nipples. Because Franklin cherished them, so did I. He never proposed sex, never explored any other areas of my body. For me, it was a hallowed experience that lasted until August when he left for college on the East Coast.

Franklin was the lone male who worshipped my breasts. Benjamin, a major league fan of legs (Sandy, wife number one, had fabulous legs), in the beginning days of our marriage, would massage my bare shoulders where bra straps had dug a trench and sympathetically ask, "Hon, ever consider breast reduction?"

Money, pain, and time dampened any serious consideration of surgery. Sometimes, though, when the moon cast a white-yellow through our bedroom window, I left our bed. In a shaft of light, I'd let my nightgown drift to the floor. As light caressed my bare breasts, I'd remember how I'd fulfilled a fantasy for Franklin, and how he'd never actualized mine—to learn about my father.

Next, for Cammy in her basement, I identified another piece of the father puzzle that took place during my freshman college year. For the Thanksgiving holiday, I rode the bus home, my first trip back to Hampton from Monroe. On a scholarship with a tight budget, I'd counted the weeks until I could see Mama again. An uncharacteristically warm November allowed Mama and me to wear only cardigan sweaters for wraps when we walked to the grocery store for our turkey. On Carter Street, we met a large white woman heading in the opposite direction. Something about her seemed familiar, and as we neared, instead of glancing away as whites and blacks usually did, Mama and the woman nodded.

An attractive woman with a heavy bosom, she frankly appraised me, and after we passed, I turned. Over her shoulder, she continued her scrutiny.

"Who?" I asked

Mama didn't answer.

White arms around Mama. "Her name's Cora Lee," I said. "She came to our front door one night, didn't she?"

Mama got very busy pushing up the stretched-out sleeves that sidled down over her wrists. "That," she finally said in her subject's-closed tone, "is something you must have dreamed."

On Thanksgiving morning, the weather changed. The sky darkened, and the wind chased itself around our cottage, making the oven heat welcome. When Mama lit candles on the kitchen table, their glow cheered the grayness that dyed the window pane. We recited our thankful-for list. As usual, Mama said, "I'm thankful for Savannah," and as expected said, "I'm thankful that she's receiving an education." Then she added, "And I'm immensely thankful that she is home. I have missed her."

That made me newly sensitive to Mama's existence, to those evenings when coming from work she'd open the front door onto silent rooms. After a quiet supper, she'd read her library book with the tick-tock of the living room clock, her one noisy companion.

"I'm thankful that I am still able to clean houses."

That raised questions. Was Mama's health poor? In her mid-forties, she could apply for other jobs. Why, with her drive, her intelligence, and her confidence, had she chosen the role of housecleaner?

"All right, Savannah, your turn."

I gave my stock responses, ones I'd enumerated for years; then tacked on, "I'm thankful for Emily my roommate and for her Aunt Cammy."

If Mama wondered about Cammy, if she felt hurt at their inclusion, or if she had questions, I don't know, for her stoic expression stayed intact.

After our feast and dishwashing, Mama lay down on our bed. In the living room, I switched on the lamp and arranged my file cards on the chair arm before opening my Western Civ text, a used book. If I didn't underline—a luxury non-scholarship students enjoyed—I could resell the text to the bookstore in May. Thus, I took copious notes. As my pencil lead bit into the cardboard, the phone rang, its bell so shrill and startling that I scattered the cards.

Mrs. Simonton identified herself as one of Mama's employers and apologized about intruding on Thanksgiving Day. "Mama's resting," I told her.

"Seems the parents of our daughter's fiancé, from New York, will arrive on Saturday. The problem? We've never met them, and I need the house spotless. Could Emmaline, your mother, possibly clean tomorrow?"

I promised to tell Mama when she awoke, and as I started back to the arm chair, I bumped the little phone table with its uneven legs. Several slips of paper slid from beneath the phone, and as I put them back, I noticed Mama's handwriting: "Cora Lee Hanson."

Stunned, I didn't bother to read the phone number printed beside the last name. Hanson. Hanson. My name. Mama's last name.

As I replayed that incident for Cammy, I once more experienced the visceral reaction of that Thanksgiving afternoon, that certainty of a relationship with Cora Lee and maybe a relationship with others in the white part of town.

Upstairs, someone tread on kitchen boards that sang a high-low melody, bringing Cammy and me into a basement setting and late afternoon.

"We'll talk more tonight," she said, and refusing offers of assistance, left me at the library table encompassed by lives packed into the shorthand of words. I stood up to return the Bethune manuscript to the file cabinet. As Benjamin had taught me in the print shop, I jogged the pages, rapping the bottom ends against the table top. Then I noticed the first pages of the handwritten sheets that lay there. I read but a few lines. Cammy was writing Emily's story.

CHRIS

Just before supper

One afternoon, Heather stomped into the house after school. "What a freak show kind of day," she announced. Today qualifies, at least so far. I mean, it was freaky waking up in Emily Jane's room, freaky hearing Evan's problems, freaky trailing around to the high school and eating lunch at Rosie's Diner. The big freaky was seeing Candi and car salesman (that's what I decided he was) and being with Dirk. (Hold on, journal, I'll explain that in a minute). But *major* freaky was Ann's story about Emily Jane's marriage.

It's hard to believe. Emily Jane and I shared everything. Wouldn't she have called or written me? So what if she were embarrassed about a really short marriage? Didn't she think I'd understand? But, then, what Dirk said amazed me too. (Yes, I'll get to that soon). First, I need to record the supreme freaky event: Cammy's entering the kitchen so quietly that she took us off guard. She didn't say, "Impossible that Emily Jane married," or "I'm hurt Emily Jane didn't confide in me." Nope, she asked Ann, "Do you have a picture of this Richard?" A picture!

Savannah scooted her chair over so Cammy could join us at the table, but aloof, Cammy stood by the cabinets. One hand knotted into a fist rested on the counter, and I noticed how the veins protruded, like the skin had fallen away. I must confess, I glanced down at my hands to check my veins. Surely, bulging veins is a sign of age.

"Don't think so," Ann answered. "I didn't take any pictures when Richard and Em dated, and she tore up the wedding poses."

"Whatever happened to him?" Savannah asked.

When Ann shrugged, it called attention to her shoulders. Graceful shoulders. Another body part moment, I guess, but I suddenly realized how varied we are physically. Ann with her neat, athletic body;

Cammy, tall and stately; Savannah, bosomy, and warm-chocolate; me, some twenty pounds overweight, sort of falling apart below the neck but not doing badly in the face wrinkle department.

"Richard sells food products to my husband and to other facilities. I just don't see him anymore. Seth, my husband, said Richard had remarried, but gave no details. Men—"

She needn't complete that sentence. We know that men don't tell the neat stuff. Even Dirk—now I can get to him—left lots unanswered.

"Seems almost like old times," he said after he'd picked me up at the garage sale, and we'd ridden along Polk Street for several blocks.

"Almost is the key word," I pointed out.

He flashed me that winning Dirk Hawkins grin, and I laughed. As Todd says, "There's something about Dirk that makes you laugh. The guy could be feeding you a mega-lie, and you'd feel good."

"What are you doing in Centerville?" I asked.

"Stopped off on my way to Houston. Coming from Minneapolis." He didn't explain why he'd been in Minnesota before he asked about Todd and the family. "Still helping to raise Grant's son?"

"Still is another key word," I said, and we laughed together, a deep satisfying laugh that Emily Jane would have loved to share. "I'm a grandma as of a month ago," I told him as he swung off Polk to slow before the high school.

"Looks good on you, Chris," he answered, but he wasn't looking at me, but at the double-decker building. He'd rolled down his window and rested his left arm on the door frame. Sunlight washed over his arm and struck his T-shirt sleeve and pocket. Recalling packs of cigarettes he once carried there, I asked, "You quit smoking?"

Dirk turned toward me, and in that movement I took in his thinning hair, the frown lines like grooves in his forehead, the creases locked onto his cheeks and around his lips. Sunglasses with opaque lenses shielded his eyes, but I figured (and when later he removed the glasses, I was right) that his eyes were more sunken, more melancholy than when I'd last seen him some seven years ago, and definitely more troubled than in high school.

"No choice on the smoking. I had to stop. Bad for my voice."

"You've kept on singing?"

"And playing." He nodded his head toward the space behind the seat, where a guitar case rested.

From the passenger side window, I noticed the Hillyer's house across from the school. What had my neighbor told me about them? Right. That Don Hillyer was injured in a car accident last spring; the emergency room nurse (that would be Grace Tomkins) had nearly fainted when she undressed Don down to his bikini panties and a bra with an extender in the back.

How had Don handled this rumor/situation with the True Brethren Fellowship that he pastored at a rural church? I was ready to tell this to Dirk, but he speeded up and headed south toward the lagoon.

"Are you in town alone? For long?" I asked.

Wind roaring through our rolled down windows defeated my questions. I wasn't sure he heard because he answered, "Damn, the bumps have been smoothed out."

I nodded. After a fatal car wreck, the city council allocated money to fix the "roller coaster" hills that led in one direction out of Centerville.

His foot, in a scuffed cowboy boot, slid off the gas pedal. "Yep, I'm alone. Have a room at the motel."

Originally there'd been a dirt parking area beside the lagoon. "In the olden days," as Greg my youngest, referred to them, we'd sat or lain in cars. After a girl in Julie's class filed rape charges on some out-of-town guy who brought her here, the council voted on funds to bulldoze the parking spot. Now, trees towered over the space where Todd, Dirk, Emily Jane and I once killed the car's motor and the lights. Now you parallel park along the gravel road and cross a culvert to reach the lagoon. No one has assumed responsibility for cleaning it, due to a land sale and dispute over who actually owns this pond.

Dirk shut off the engine and exited the truck with the agility and controlled easy moves that he'd had since kindergarten. That kind of confident swagger that athletes have no matter how old they get. As he rounded the hood of the truck, I thought, *From this distance he could be mistaken for the Dirk of thirty-five years ago.* Long lean legs in jeans, a great tight butt and flat belly.

"You have grandkids?" I asked as he guided me from the truck and down the side of a ditch. (Emily Jane teased me about my vertigo, which bothered me even on a three-foot decline.)

"Could be. Chances are there are some I don't know about." He pulled me up the opposite incline, and I followed him on a trail by trees with thick overlapping branches. When in the world had I last been here? I guess when Heather was a toddler and Todd had joked, "What about going to the lagoon to be by ourselves?" Kids often interrupted us or plain exhaustion deterred us from lovemaking, so I paid my sister Margaret to baby sit, and told her we were off to a movie in Des Moines.

On a fall night, a weeknight when we'd likely not compete with high schoolers, we parked at the lagoon. The moon was wonderfully bright, and it shed some wondrous spell over us. Never did I love Todd more fully. No, I didn't conceive number four in the car. That night was strictly for love, for us.

In the August heat, Dirk and I clung to the trees' shade. I'm not heat-tolerant. Funny, I know, for a Midwesterner, but Mom blamed it on my getting overheated as a child. Helping her pick strawberries, I keeled over.

Twigs splintered beneath his cowboy boots as Dirk threaded his way around trunks and stumps. "It's here, Chris," he called out, sounding jubilant. He hurried ahead, and with his hands swept leaves from a park bench. Again, he grinned. "Obviously, it's not been used much recently."

"I've never seen this before." I ran my fingers over the top back slat. "It wasn't here in high school."

"Was put in after we graduated. Sometimes Emily Jane and I met at this bench when she came home from college and could borrow Cammy's car."

Apparently, I looked puzzled because he smiled. Crinkles accented his eyes and vertical lines marked his cheeks. On Dirk, lines are fine, rugged. "Yah, no one knew that she slipped out of town. Probably you've forgotten that I took off the summer after high school graduation, worked as a field hand. When Emily Jane was a freshman in college, I came back to Centerville. Worked for the John Deere dealership." He gestured. "Have a seat. I'll grab us some cold ones."

As I waited, I rubbed my palms along the bench. So Emily Jane once sat or lay here. She'd never mentioned this bench or their meetings, and like a needle jab, betrayal pricked. I told, or wrote, her everything. She is—was—my best friend.

Dirk carried a cooler. With practiced hands, he popped beer caps and handed me an open bottle. It did taste fantastic. As she converted to California, Emily Jane drank wine. No thanks. Give me a beer any day.

Sometimes Todd and I sit on our back step, watch the stars, and divide a six-pack. This summer we dragged a throw-away mattress out of the garage. (Wish someone would tell me how to dispose of it. The garbage people won't haul it off, and the mattress is too bumpy and stained for our thrift store). In the backyard, we sprawled on it, and the coolness of grass rose up like an air-conditioned mattress pad.

Utterly romantic, except for the act of drinking. First, I lay on my side, dug my elbow into the mattress, bent my arm and propped my hand beneath my jaw bone, as Todd did. But when I raised the bottle to my lips, beer dribbled down my chin. That meant I had to sit up to drink. I'd sit, drink, lie down. Sit, drink, lie down. Finally, Todd got annoyed.

"You worked at John Deere," I said, picking up on Dirk's last sentence.

"A mistake, but I didn't know what else to do. Lived at home. Another bad decision." He drank. "Anyway, I pulled down a good salary, so I sent some money to Emily Jane. When she could, she'd buy a round trip bus ticket for one night. If it wasn't freezing, we came here. Sometimes, though, we hit Hoagie's Road House and we'd sing. Hoagie paid us in food and beers."

My hurt deepened. "I didn't know."

As if sitting bothered him, Dirk stood up and paced. "Unless someone saw us at Hoagie's and said something, no one knew that we met. It was our best time. We had this secret, this rendezvous. Our singing was never better."

I rested the chilled brown bottle against my cheek and incongruously thought of Mom placing a bottle of hot water against my stomach once when I had cramps and another sister had dibs on the hot water bottle, and at the same time, thought of how Dirk and Emily Jane must have shone at Hoagie's under the spot that funneled light onto the stage—actually a crude elevated table-like extension at one end of a square building.

The ancient roadhouse reeked of booze, vomit, and often sewer gas. The toilet was awful. Emily Jane and I always went into the cubicle together and closed our eyes when we squatted above the seat. No way would we allow any skin to come within inches of that dirty, broken half moon. However, with our eyes closed, we couldn't read the walls penciled with phone numbers and sexual promises and a lipstick printed verse, "Don't change pricks in the middle of a screw/stay with Stanley's/whatever you do."

Hoagie's, across the county line, must have been in business when our parents were young. Why officers never shut it down beats me. Maybe graft? Gossip swirled around it about prostitutes, brawls, and disappearing customers.

Todd, Dirk, Emily Jane and I rarely drove that rutted back road to Hoagie's as teenagers. For us, it was a titillating and frightening dark rectangle with rough-cut tables and chairs that suited the men who frequented it. Yet, Hoagie encouraged "musicians" to perform—sort of an early open-mic arrangement.

In our senior year, Dirk and Emily Jane worked up courage to sing one night. Even the blotto drunk guys listened. A year or two after this, Dirk and Emily Jane would have sounded sensational. At least I'm sure Emily Jane did because of the voice training at Monroe.

"Sorry, was daydreaming," I apologized.

Dirk knocked the toe of his boot against a stubborn weed, trying to uproot it. "Yah, we were awesome." His voice was tight. "You know, after she graduated from college and moved to California, we sang only once more at the last class reunion."

"You did see her, though, after she moved."

He drained the bottle. "Denver, L.A., Vegas... ."

In the background under all that vegetation the lagoon shimmered, its constant green scum looking like a field. Could fish live in it? Did that covering destroy their oxygen? Did they need oxygen? I should have paid more attention in science class. Dirk popped another cap.

"Why do you think you didn't marry her?"

"That would have worked?" He scoffed. "Hell, Chris, could you imagine Emily Jane in a mobile home? Sticking it out with me? But we sure had something, didn't we?"

I finished my beer and shook my head when he indicated a second one. "Another sounds terrific, but this has already been quite a day, and it doesn't appear like it's going to slow down. Better stay clear headed."

"Once I did suggest marriage. Called her in the middle of the night from a bar. She laughed, told me I was lonely, and I was. Tammy had taken off. Emily Jane said, 'You're drunk.' She was wrong. 'No,' I argued, 'but I needed some beers to get up the nerve to tell you that you're it. The only one I'll ever really love.' She cried and—"

He heaved the bottle toward the water. The remaining beer formed a curve as it sprayed from the neck. I followed the trajectory as he said, "Christ, why did she have to go and die."

When he brushed the back of his hand across his eyes, I cried, too. Dirk took a step in my direction. *He's going to sit beside me*, I thought, *take my hand*. Instead, he pivoted and headed toward the lagoon. We each cried alone. At last, I was the one who went to him.

On the marshy shore, he put his arm around me. "When did she get sick?" he asked. "I didn't see her for a year, and she said nothing in our phone calls."

My mouth, firm against his chest, meant my words were muffled. They sank into his shirt. "Must've been last August that she wrote about a biopsy. I called her. She said she'd have a lumpectomy. Made it sound like nothing, like a scratch. In October I was in line behind Cammy at the grocery store. She, like I, thought everything was over after the radiation treatments. In the spring Emily Jane wrote that things weren't good and she was coming home, but I never saw her. Was in Chicago for my grandson's birth when she died."

His breathing was unsteady, and his hand tightened on my shoulder. "Why no funeral?"

"Not sure. Cammy just said that's what Emily Jane wanted," and I explained about Cammy inviting three friends.

"Maybe you'll learn more this weekend," he said, at which my inner voice chimed in with, "You already have learned much more."

A frog hopped on a dead branch that stuck above the surface. The frog observed us and, deciding we were boring, opted for the lagoon, creating ripples in the green net.

"I should get back," I said. Our strides matched, mainly because we proceeded at a snail's pace to the truck parked in the sun. The black interior had sucked in the heat. As we drove to town, I didn't care if the wind whipped my hair or not.

"Who were you with at the garage sale?" he asked, and as I spoke of Ann, I wished I felt no jealousy, wished the desire to be Emily Jane's best friend wasn't so childishly necessary.

He dropped me in front of Cammy's, and I walked in to Savannah and Ann and her unbelievable tale about Emily Jane's five-day marriage. And that forced me to face the recurring questions: do I know only what Emily Jane wanted me to know, or do I know only what I cared to know?

A band gripped my temples. An anxiety attack? I'd never had one, but my daughter Julie's neighbor described the symptoms to me in Chicago, how you can't breathe. That's what I felt, breathless. I opened the bedroom door, but the hallway was also packed with dead air. The neighbor had said, "Breathe into a paper bag." I'd go home for a few minutes, breathe into an Anderson's Market sack, and "get a grip" (a Julie expression). I hurried downstairs and through the kitchen. That's when I noticed that the basement door was ajar. Cammy's voice rose from the bottom of a flight of stairs, from a place Cammy's always called hers alone.

So, I changed course and retreated toward the front of the house. That way she wouldn't see or hear me and suspect that, yet again, I was sneaking home. Out the front door and down the sidewalk; then I veered left into a no-breeze afternoon. Hot, it was incredibly hot and humid. Our small house, shut up all day, would be miserable. I'd raise some windows, turn on the fan, and when Todd got home, I bet he'd think, *What a wife, coming over just to make me comfortable.* I breathed more easily with that thought. It cheered and calmed me, but then a shiny red car drew up to the curb, and the tinted window on the driver's side smoothly descended to expose Candi's forced smile.

"Christine, do you have a minute?"

I wanted to say, "No," wanted to reach my house and wander through each room, where gradually I'd be restored, sort of like climbing into a relaxing bath tub and by degrees feeling every kink and ache disappear. But for the second time today, I sat in the passenger seat of a vehicle. This climate-controlled luxury car, though, was years ahead of Dirk's truck. The blasting air conditioner dried the sweat on my forehead and along the path where it had trickled between my breasts.

"Nice car," I said because, unlike our van, it mowed down the rough patches on Polk Street. (Todd's convinced that Mervin Harrison's road crew repaved the street while in a communal alcoholic haze.) And unlike our van, the interior was spotless. She studied the road but indicated she'd heard by a twitch of her head. "A birthday present from my parents."

I also studied the road as I recalled my gift, a set of wine glasses. Really, they looked classy, I assured myself. A tool salesman gave them to Todd at Christmas. Thinking they'd make a nice gift for someone, I stored them in a cupboard. Unfortunately, the box got a bit battered, and when I soaked off the sticker (left a damp rag on it for half an hour) that said "Arnold's Tools," the sticker's glue removed part of the cardboard, so I suppose the gift might have appeared used or recycled.

Candi steered around the corner. Ah, we weren't going to my house. "Was surprised to see you in the diner," she said, and before I could blurt out, "Not as surprised as I was to see you," she asked about the women at the table. Clear to the new park—it's out along the highway—with its molded plastic play equipment and wood chips piled around young tree roots, I offered thumbnail sketches of the others. Probably that was the most I'd ever said to her. When had we ever been alone?

"It must be awful to lose a best friend." She stopped the car in the biggest wedge of shade at the park.

Not expecting such sympathy, I felt the too-familiar prick of tears and turned to watch two toddlers try and climb the slide itself rather than go up the steps. They grasped each side and planted feet on the slick surface only to slip, drop to their knees and revisit the slide's lip.

"I never had a best woman friend. My friend was and is Scott." She unlatched her door and walked toward the nearest bench.

Again, I crossed a grassy strip, and again I sat on the unforgiving slats of a bench. Why can't a bench be solid, so that lines won't imprint themselves on the back of your thighs? Your hips?

As she sat, Candi's chain bracelet clanked against the wood. *Pricey*, I thought. She didn't buy that at Gilbert's Variety, where I got my dolphin earrings. Did Scott buy it?

"You're curious about the man in the diner."

As I nodded, my inner sound track asked, "How did she become so composed at her age? At my age I'm not that put together."

"He's Buck Nolan. His dad recently retired, so he's sole owner of Nolan Roofing Company."

I made one of those "oof" noises that people do when the wind is knocked out of them. Buck Nolan.

"Yes, Evan's former boss, the man whose car he stole."

"Borrowed," I contradicted.

She tapped exquisitely manicured fingernails—ones coated with a deceptive innocent pink sheen—on a bench slat. Sunlight glinted on the expensive bracelet, one Buck Nolan could afford. "That leads to my confession and my proposition. You've undoubtedly deduced that Buck and I are involved."

As I glared at her and "The Glow" that infused her features, pictures revolved in my mind: Scott greeting me every morning with his sweet smile; Evan against the bedroom wall, the ticket clutched in his hand.

"My proposition is that if you swear to say nothing about this, if you never *ever* tell Scott, if you in no way let this information affect how you act toward me, then I promise that Buck will go to the police, swear he made a mistake, that Evan didn't "take" his car. Charges will be dropped, and Evan can have his job back."

My gulp was extraordinarily loud. The aroma of frying hamburgers on a nearby grill smelled heavenly and idiotically I thought, *I'm hungry. Cheese sandwiches aren't all that satisfying.*

"Why?" I asked.

"The affair? Can't answer that. I love Scott. I have since high school. I love my life, my part-time job."

"You're working?"

Irritation tugged at her lips, and her voice was testy. "I thought you knew. A dentist friend of Dad's is establishing a practice in Elmwood. I help out three afternoons a week."

Silently I informed her, "No, I don't know of your job or of your life. We aren't exactly buddies." And then one part of my mind asked the other part, "What if you keep this secret? Would that forge a bond with Candi, provide an opportunity for a more equal relationship?"

Candi fiddled with the bracelet, and I imagined studly Buck snapping it around her wrist as they lay in bed.

"Maybe," she said, catching my fixation with the bracelet, "I was simply curious. I've never slept with any man but Scott. Maybe it was the last chance for a fling before we start a family. When we married we decided on a five-year plan, five years for us to get finances in order, to travel, to— Then we'd have a child. We've been married three. Scott adores coaching, is happy in Elmwood, and he's ready for a baby. My life as Me is almost over."

Arguments pushed against lips that I wisely kept sealed.

"And could be," she smiled, "that the bad boy image attracted me. Buck's not the committed type."

Like Dirk, like Grant, I thought. But images of Scott persisted—ruffling my hair as he left the house; tossing a football to Greg; bringing Heather a milkshake when a boyfriend stood her up. "You can't hurt Scott," I whispered.

"Never." Candi's gaze was wide, direct. "That's why you can't give him even a clue. I've been careful. Today I shouldn't have had lunch with Buck, but I figured Rosie's was safe, and that I could use the excuse of getting a roofing estimate if I did bump into anyone I knew. But running into a mother-in-law unnerved me. I'll not be out in public with Buck again."

"You'll stop seeing him?"

"Not yet."

As if to reinforce her case, she dredged up details of how she'd met Buck, but I tuned out. Frankly, I'd heard too many stories for one day. So I focused on the family eating their hamburgers and on the toddlers who now squeezed sand through their fists, as I surveyed "my options" (Heather's current cliché). However, pictures of Evan paraded before me—his refusal to be separated from "blanky," which I'd sewn for him; his sobbing in my arms when a gang of middle school boys jumped him; his handing me a clumsily wrapped plaster-of-paris heart he'd crafted for Mother's Day. I'd agree with Candi. To keep him out of trouble, to keep him employed, I would promise much.

As we strolled back to her car, I thought, *If anyone sees us, they'll think 'Look at that mother and daughter, so intent, so involved. Isn't it lovely how daughter is confiding and explaining so precisely.'*

The air conditioner's blast helped. "How can you be positive Scott won't learn of your (I couldn't say 'affair') involvement?"

"I told you. I've been discreet. But if someone suspected and dared tell Scott, I'd simply deny it. He'd believe me. The one person he'd believe over me is you."

Pain shot from my chest to my temples. The band was back. I longed to sob and massage my forehead. In favor of Evan, I'd sold out Scott.

Candi's damned bracelet thudded against the steering wheel.

"At least give him back that stupid bracelet," I said. "How do you intend to explain that?"

Keeping her left hand on the wheel, she unclasped the latch with her right and dropped the bracelet into the pocket of her pants, which sported some designer label, I'm sure.

We said a sort of goodbye before our house, which all at once appeared shabby. Since shabby has described it for years, more truthfully I should say "shabbier" and "smaller."

No one had watered for a while, so islands of brown dotted the front lawn. I attached the sprinkler head to a hose striped intermittently with duct tape, and for the thousandth time wished that we had extra in the bank account for an automatic system. Better I should wish for an intact hose. I set the sprinkler in the worst island, placed a bucket beneath the faucet that dripped and turned the handle.

"Shit." The whirl of the sprinkler sprayed my pant legs. Too weary to reposition the hose, I dashed for the door before the next revolution pelted me. As I ran my thighs jiggled—another reason to embrace the bleakness that was suspended, cape-like, inches from my back. Well, I couldn't cover myself in unhappiness, nor could I wander room to room gaining comfort because Heather—home from work early—occupied the living room floor. In front of the fan, hands clasped behind her head, she lifted her upper torso in the modern version of sit-ups.

By the time I'd changed from the soaked pants into a pair with only a tiny stain on the right leg—a stain I could conceal by holding my hand over it, if I didn't forget and move—Heather was upright. "Mom," she announced, "you must replace this shag carpet. It's too '60s."

I sank into Todd's lounge chair, grateful for the tattered corduroy fabric and his smell that enveloped me. "It's not on today's list or even tomorrow's."

With a grin, she mopped her damp forehead. "Okay, but on tomorrow's list put 'Get Grandma's laundry.' Yeah, Aunt Margaret called. Has a fever. Can't pick up Grandma's clothes at the Care Center."

"It's not my week," I protested.

"Hell-o, Mom." Heather squatted beside the chair to stare up at me. "See, Aunt Margaret's sick. No can go. Needs substitute. You."

"It's the last full day at Cammy's. I don't know her plans. What about Esther?" Surely my brother's wife could fill in.

Using the lounge chair arms as support, Heather pulled herself from the floor. "Esther and Lincoln are on vacation. Remember? And, no, don't even think of asking me. I work from eight to six." She ambled away into the kitchen. So, somehow, on Sunday I'd have to include a stop at the Care Center. Sometimes Mom recognized me and talked fairly rationally. Usually she regarded me with vacant eyes. The next-to-last time that it was my week to pick up her laundry, I'd persuaded Grant to accompany me. She didn't recognize me, but her face lit up when he said, "Hey there, Mom." The bad boy, her best-loved child.

On one visit I knelt beside the wheelchair. "Mom, Emily Jane died." She ceased trying to braid the pom-poms that decorated ties on her pink bathrobe and repeated, "Emily Jane. Your friend?"

While I nodded, pleased with Mom's lucidity, my mind battled to combat our environment—stale air, pitifully sparse family photos on her half of the dresser, her bald roommate who constantly screams, "Operator, operator."

"She loved our home and family," Mom said in the most rational sentence she'd uttered in months, and I cried. She spread her arms wide, as she once had, and I sort of flopped down, bruising my knees on the tile floor, and I burrowed my face into the fleece robe that hid her stick legs.

I forced myself from Todd's chair to check the kitchen clock: 5:15. In less than an hour, Cammy would serve supper. I must get back and must call Evan.

As Heather removed a microwaved entrée, I sent a mute command, "Take it into the living room and eat in front of the TV so I can use the phone."

She chose the table. So much for mental powers. I debated. Call Evan from Cammy's? But what if he weren't home then or now?

As the clock registered declining minutes, Heather bit into her personal-sized pizza. Perhaps I should go ahead and dial Grant's/Evan's number. On the third ring, Evan answered. "Good news," I said, then wondered how to proceed with Heather beside me, spiraling mozzarella strings with her tongue.

"Heard great things this afternoon about you and your job. I just wanted you to know that you must be doing well. I'll fill you in later when I have more time."

"Can't talk, can you?"

"Right."

"But you're trying to tell me that I still have a job at Nolan's? That something happened about the charges?"

"Absolutely."

The sharp intake of his breath betrayed his coolness. "I'll stay in tonight. Call me, okay?"

"It's a deal."

I replaced the receiver, aware that Heather had digested every syllable along with her pizza slice.

"Someone likes Evan?" she challenged as she slithered the back of her arm across her mouth in a Todd-gesture to remove tomato sauce.

"Yep, couldn't give him the complete compliment as I'm late. Turn off the sprinkler in an hour?"

I stepped out the back door into the alley and plodded toward Cammy's. For the very first time in our married life, I would keep an important family secret from Todd. Together we'd faced everything— Scott's tonsillectomy, my false fear that sixteen-year-old Julie was pregnant, Greg's shooting out the neighbor's garage windows, Heather's cheating on a test and failing history. He'd waited up with me to scold Heather when she broke curfew; had agreed that Scott couldn't play in Friday's game after he and the football team winched a goat onto the principal's roof, and with my prompting grounded Greg after he lurched into the house with bloodshot eyes and slurred speech. When my brothers and sisters voted to place Mom in the Care Center and to sell the house, he'd been there with me.

For the first time in my fifty-three years, I had no one—not Todd, and definitely not Emily Jane to whom I could admit what I'd done to save Evan.

SAVANNAH

Saturday night

On this second night in Centerville, I'm alone upstairs. Downstairs, I imagine Cammy is pulling a nightgown over her head as she prepares for sleep on the parlor sofa. I'm glad for this solitude. After supper and after both Ann and Christine left the house, I trailed Cammy into the kitchen. With a crisp white dish towel, I dried plates, glasses, and cups that she rinsed free of soap suds.

"What about the photos I put on the table?" With her dishrag, she conscientiously scrubbed fork tines.

"Good idea. I liked the one you put by my plate—Emily in her choir robe, beaming at her award."

"Third in the state for the junior high girls' trio." She organized silverware in the dish drainer's corner holder.

"But the picture by Ann's plate disturbed her."

Cammy nodded. "Think she's out now running it off." She upended her plastic dish pan, and as the water gurgled down the drain, she wrung moisture from the dish rag and untied her apron. "Care to go back downstairs?"

We descended into a constant haven. Since light never infiltrated from any window, it could be whatever hour she decreed it to be, whatever season she adopted. Near the library table, I said, "You're doing a version of Emily's life. Will you read our journals and include sections from them?"

As she settled into her chair, she smiled. "That was my intention, to use the journals and what I gleaned from conversations. But I'm reconsidering. Would I be guilty of invading a privacy? Of lifting material and twisting it? Won't I—regardless of what the journals say—force my view of Emily onto the pages I write?" She paused and kneaded knuckles on one hand. "A bit of arthritis."

As I sat down, I carefully avoided looking at the handwritten manuscript.

"Go ahead," she nodded in my direction, "read what I've written."

"No, that's your story."

"And what about your story—not of Emily, but of the search for your father?"

"That is My Story, isn't it?" So I continued with my storyline of what happened after I'd found Cora Lee's name and phone number, which confirmed that we had some type of connection.

On that Thanksgiving Day afternoon, I started for the bedroom. I'd shake Mama awake and demand that she answer every question. But, at the closed door, I thought, *Do I truly want my suspicions verified? Can I handle ugly truths? What if my probing injures Mama? She's all I have.* Therefore, I did nothing. Read my assignment, dutifully delivered Mrs. Simonton's request and pretended I'd never seen Cora Lee's last name.

I boarded the bus for Monroe on Sunday. From my window seat at the rear of the bus, I watched Mama grow smaller and frailer as the driver accelerated. I couldn't hurt her, couldn't bully the past from her.

And I did manage to suppress concern about my background beneath an avalanche of demanding assignments. Since I'd never been a top student, worked part-time at the campus library, and since Emily entertained me with ideas, I had limited opportunity to reflect or agonize. Although Emily infrequently dated, she urged me to date, then invariably disapproved of my "bloodless" choices. However, in the spring, she did approve of Malcolm Everly, who also worked at the library, when he suggested we meet for coffee at a downtown café. "Now that guy has life," she said, "has the spark you need." And she repeated her theory that I was too cautious. Malcolm was one of half a dozen African-American male students who shared a boardinghouse on the fringes of the campus. So, on a Sunday afternoon, I wandered through a largely-deserted city center to a scruffy café to have coffee with him. Some older white women near the door glared as I joined Malcolm at a table in the rear. Smart and attractive, he did exude "life," but those qualities paled beside the sense of comfort that I enjoyed in his presence. Like me, he was on a scholarship so owned no car. When we did meet, we walked. And when our evening library shifts entailed locking up, we took our time—talking, for Malcolm had high principles. His goal, to be a preacher, interested me, for I'd never attended church. Yet, his career choice equally dismayed me because he wouldn't be rich or have job security. Plus, when he spoke about his personal savior and his wide brown eyes glistened, I couldn't imagine being the wife of such a preacher. The "spark" that Emily observed, was for Jesus.

On a night when we shut library windows against sounds of cicadas and chirping crickets, when we locked out the wispy fragrance of tea roses blooming against the brick wall, I asked, "Does Jesus personally save you? For instance, if you're driving a wreck of a car down the highway and a tire blows, would he reach down and guide you to safety?"

As he eased the fastener on the top pane with the long wooden window pole, he answered, "It's possible. Miracles occur every day. All that's required, Savannah, is faith the size of a mustard seed."

Automatically, I tugged books forward so their spines would be aligned with the shelf's edge. "Getting back to the blow-out, if Jesus can protect you, why doesn't he do it constantly? He sounds capricious to me."

Worry knotted his forehead. "Not capricious. Oh no, see, when he doesn't intervene in the case of death it's because it's the person's time to go, or when he doesn't intervene in a problem, it's because the person must learn a lesson. If that person confesses that Jesus is his or her personal savior, then the person benefits from the lesson, or if it's time to be called home to heaven, then the individual is carried there in Christ's bosom."

In slow motion, we advanced to the next window. "Then a person has no control over a situation. You don't know if Jesus is going to assist you or not."

"Oh, Savannah, you don't get it. Of course you have no control. When Christ is your personal savior, he's in charge and you trust him; you relax."

So went our discussions. Sometimes after we turned the key in the main door, we rested on the concrete steps admiring the campus, pretty in the soft bath of street lights, I'd make statements like, "Well, if there is a heaven, I hope it's serene and green like this."

"Not *if*, Savannah. There *is* a heaven. Jesus our personal savior guaranteed us of that." He quoted biblical passages and loaned me his Bible where he'd keyed vital verses. Family names, at least from slavery days on, fit in a diagram, like a tree with branches, in the front of the book.

When I returned his Bible, without having read beyond the "begats", I told him, "I'm envious."

"Of?"

"Your faith, your memories, your family."

"Some memories aren't good," he conceded, and I felt sure he referred to discrimination. At Monroe, as at his home, we other blacks were apart.

I was in a rather different situation on campus, because Emily had surprised housing officials by requesting a black roommate. "Made perfect sense to me," she explained. "Chris, my best friend since kindergarten, is black. Why break up the pattern now?" So she and I shared a room in the oldest, least expensive girls' dorm, where a few other nationalities were also housed.

Under the shelter of night, however, Malcolm would speak more freely to me. "But memories and life are challenges. They're my cross. They test my faith. And my family—oh, I bless them. They're everything."

He bragged about his mother's sweet potato pie, his sister's newborn who weighed twelve pounds, his brother's ability to play the harmonica, and his dad's rising in first light on cold Sunday mornings to coax heat from the furnace at church.

"I have no father," I said.

"You do have a father. Your heavenly Father far surpasses any earthly parent."

My smile must have been sad, because he draped his arm around my shoulder. It was the first time he'd dared do more than pat my hand, and I liked his touch. Quite easily I could grow accustomed to it, could crave more than a touch.

Emily strode into the library one late afternoon. For some reason, forgotten now, she had a camera. "I've one exposure left. Here, Malcolm, pose beside her."

He and I obediently stepped closer behind a library cart packed with books to shelve and Emily depressed the shutter. The flash blinded us, and as we bumped against each other, she called out, "Oh, I've got one more," and aimed the camera again.

Therefore, that second picture shows us with hands extended as if groping for one another. That was the shot Mama later saw.

I'd traded a single chaste kiss with Malcolm, had vowed to write, and then had ridden the bus home, where Mama knew of a possible summer job at Hendricks' Variety Store. Although several applied, Mr. Hendricks hired me. "I'm impressed," he said, "that you're a business major."

Mornings I walked to work, and evenings when I returned to the cabin, I often found a letter from Malcolm or from Emily in the mailbox. In one of hers she enclosed the snapshots, which I left on the bedroom dresser. When Mama arrived from cleaning houses and entered our bedroom, she spotted them, lying in full view on the dresser.

She stomped into the kitchen where I scraped carrots over the sink. "Your boyfriend?" She spat the question and waved the photographs in the air.

"Sort of."

Mama's wail terrified me as did her collapse in a chair by the table. I dropped the paring knife and ran to her, throwing my arms around her in a protective circle, inhaling the bleach and Lysol residue embedded in her hair and skin. "What is it?"

She mumbled and repeated, "You can't get involved."

"Why not?"

She wouldn't look at me, so I brewed some tea. As the summer evening drained the kitchen of color, we drank in silence until she set the cup upon the table top with a definitive thump. "I forbid you to drop out of college."

"I'm not dropping out. Mama, Malcolm and I are hardly a couple. We work together in the library." And although I explained about the pictures, I couldn't pacify her.

She clutched my hands. "Promise you won't fall in love."

With an incredulous laugh, I attempted to point out that one couldn't prevent loving, but, Mama, clearly agitated, kept saying, "You have to graduate, you have to get a career."

In an effort to calm her, I said. "He's going to be a minister. He's in love with Jesus and God. He's told me to substitute a heavenly father for my missing biological one."

My words shocked her, although that hadn't been my intention. She squared her shoulders, tilted her head back slightly, set her jaw, and ran the tip of her tongue over pale lips as if preparatory to a declarative speech. "Your father."

I tensed. The stove, the cabinets, the faded (but starched) curtains were sharply defined as if they and we had been transported into a dimension beyond the third. Even Mama's sigh and the hands she pressed against her cheeks looked and sounded clearer than normal, more pronounced.

"Sorry, I can't go on, can't talk about it. Just trust me, Savannah. You mustn't get involved with Malcolm. You mustn't. You can't take any chances of having your educational opportunity destroyed."

So yet again, I abandoned the topic with Mama. However, I wondered about her rationale. Did she believe that what I didn't know couldn't hurt me? Hiding from reminders of her history, did my relationship with Malcolm nudge her into cordoned off territory? Then in moments of complete paranoia, I questioned if Malcolm and I might be related. In the photo, did Mama see my cousin? My half-brother?

At work, such speculations receded before mounting responsibilities. From stocking shelves, I was promoted to clerking. Two weeks later, I placed orders and dealt with suppliers. "You're a quick study." Mr. Hendricks's drawl contrasted to "quick." "Wish you weren't going back to college. I'd hire you permanent. Can use you at Christmas, though, and for sure next summer." His compliments pleased me as did the satisfaction I gained from working well and hard. However, Sundays and evenings proved long. I missed Emily, and I missed Malcolm.

He wrote me in August. "I'll not return to Monroe. Dad's sick and I need to work. My brother insists he'll quit school, that he and Ma can bring in enough to keep the family going. Impossible. Stanley needs a high school diploma, and I don't have to have a college degree to preach. Some of the pastors who inspired me were self-educated. God does provide."

Behind his bravery lay anguish. No one in Malcolm's family had ever attended college. He'd have been the first graduate, would pave the way for Stanley, for cousins, second cousins, nephews and nieces. And Malcolm idolized learning and books. His hands caressed covers. With reverence, he stamped due dates in the front of library books. "Look," he'd say in horror at a book's broken spine, doodles on a page margin, deep pen tracks defaming paragraphs.

Reading glasses cemented with tape rode upon the bridge of his nose, and once, as we walked beneath a forest of leafing branches, he said, "I pray it's God's will that I keep my sight. I do derive such pleasure from the written page."

Ignoring the "God's will" part, I opted to discuss reading. "It's not given me so much a sense of pleasure as a sense of power, of knowing more. I read for facts and information."

He halted beside a spindly trunk, defeated by the healthy stand of elms. "And not to find out how people think? Why they act as they do? Not to peer inside minds and gain wisdom?"

I laughed. "You and Emily would make a fantastic team. She loves analyzing and exploring emotions."

Well, fate had killed any chance that he and Emily would hold discussions, and fate had dealt a blow to the chance that Malcolm would be part of my future. I stuck his letter, written on both sides of a sheet of binder paper, into an envelope and addressed it to Emily.

During my junior and senior years at Monroe, I heard from Malcolm, about the swing shift at the furniture factory, about his preaching with Brother Samuel and about Brother Samuel's kind daughter. He never said he loved her, but praised her compassion, tolerance, and her acceptance at age ten of Jesus as her personal savior. Then the letters ceased, but by that time Malcolm's importance was overshadowed by Tyler Bradford.

The Bradfords, a locally influential black family, owned a limited chain of apparel stores, so as a guest speaker, Tyler addressed my upper division business management class. He delivered a concise, enthusiastic report packed with practical techniques on employer-employee relationships that inspired me and quickly readjusted negative attitudes initially displayed by some white students. After class, he lingered to answer questions from four or five of us and then walked with me down the hallway and out the main entrance.

I should remember what we said or wore—something, but every detail hides behind one impression: Tyler confidently striding to his parked car, turning toward me and requesting the dorm's phone number. He didn't write it down, just committed it to memory.

Since Emily had wandered through the local Bradford store, she knew the name and Tyler's importance. "Okay," she announced after he invited me to a movie in the next town, "we'll dress you right."

Nothing in my thrift-store-based wardrobe passed her test, so she borrowed a light pink lamb's wool sweater from another "endowed" girl in the dorm. Sonia grudgingly loaned her black sheath skirt.

"You look good," Emily said, and I felt good as I slid into the front seat of Tyler's Buick. As he closed my door, I glanced out the passenger side at Emily waving from our second floor window.

NOTES WHEN SUMMER ENDS

I'd never ridden in a Buick, and had never eaten a "light dinner" at a cozy restaurant after a movie. I'd never received a bouquet of flowers, which Tyler sent after our fourth date, by which time I'd exhausted decent clothes and girls willing/able to lend. So when Tyler said, "Dinner at my house on Friday with Mother," I moaned to Emily, "What will I wear?"

Temporarily, she was stumped. She'd been by the Bradford house on the outskirts of Monroe. Secluded behind massed maple trees, she said, "It's a baby mansion, and if he's taking you there to introduce you to Mommy, he's serious. Think sophistication. Black, something black."

I came up empty handed at the thrift store, and when I begged clothes from the other full-chested girl in our dorm, I learned she hated black and had nothing "that depressing" in her wardrobe. Who Emily contacted in the drama department, I've no idea, but when she got into the costume room she brought out a black dress with a fur collar from the 1940s. Carefully she removed stitches from the fur and with the iron depressed the pinprick holes that remained. But without the collar the dress was plain, and the collar's outline was a shade lighter than the fabric. "That just makes it easier to reattach the fur," she decided before experimenting with a white scarf.

I modeled the ensemble, stepping over potato chip sacks that littered the floor between our twin beds. Emily had stumbled upon a bargain on outdated chips at a discount store, so for snacks and on Sundays when the cafeteria closed, we stuffed ourselves on slightly-rancid Hiland's Best.

She viewed me from the floor, from a chair, and then from close range as she walked backward before me. "You remind me of a black Joan Crawford with big boobs."

"Great. Crawford was sophisticated."

The Crawford motif was an appropriate one for the evening as the Bradford estate matched a movie set in my estimation. I crossed a foyer with original paintings (not prints) on walls. I tread on carpeting so thick that it disguised the complaint in my right high heel. The texture, however, impressed me most. What a revelation that expensive furnishings felt different. The sturdy, floral cream couch conveyed an assurance. Overweight adults could sit or jump on it, and it would hold its own. "Do what you will to me. I'll not split a seam or let a coil bend." The end table said, "Abuse me. Bang a wet glass on my surface. Forget a coaster. Allow white rings to permeate my wood, and I will remain quality."

The fork in my hand came from a manufacturer who would sniff at forks we sold at Hendricks' Variety Store. The rim of the delicate crystal against my lips rated one adjective, refined.

But Mrs. Bradford regarded me with the iciest eyes I'd ever seen. When I failed to put my dinner roll on the proper small plate to my left, she formed a tight "o" with her lips. She needn't say she didn't like me, for her scrutiny of my clothes, her observation of my table manners gave one clear message: this young woman is from the wrong background. She's completely inappropriate.

I tried hard. I read etiquette books. Emily and I practiced small talk and gestures. I made sure my clothing was spotless, thanks to Mama's early training. I took Mrs. Bradford a potted plant that Emily "borrowed" from the botany department, but the woman's opinion failed to soften.

One evening Tyler, his mother, and I sat in the living room before the fireplace, listening to flames pop from the perfectly-trimmed logs mounded on the grate. When I lifted my brandy snifter, the glass captured the fire's orange rhythm, and I thought, *I love Tyler. I could live here, be an asset in the business, could be Mrs. Tyler Bradford, if only his mother would approve of me.* Even the phone's ringing in another room had a beauty, an elegance.

After Tyler left to answer it, Mrs. Bradford said, "That's probably Donald with a report about the Jamestown store." She gazed at the portraits of Tyler and his brother Donald on the mantel.

"Fine sons," I said.

"Outstanding sons. After their father died, they immediately helped with the stores. Donald's done a magnificent job these past few years in Jamestown. It's a tragedy that he will never have sons of his own. Such a stupid tragedy—contracting mumps as an adult. There are no more Bradfords. Tyler is my—our only hope to keep the family name, the family line, alive. That's why it's imperative that he marry well, a socially prominent woman. I have big plans for our future." She stared at me. "I control the money in this family. I control our destiny."

In my single bed that night I lay awake long after Emily quit studying and snapped off her light. I replayed scenes from the evening and Mrs. Bradford's frank statements. She wouldn't let Tyler marry me, and I doubted that he, groomed for eventual command of the stores, could throw all that away for me. If only I didn't love him so completely.

In the morning, a receptionist at Hampton General Hospital phoned. Mama had been injured in some kind of accident. As if shock impaired my eye-hand coordination, I misdialed the Bradford Store number. "I'll be right there," Tyler said, when I finally contacted him. "We'll drive down."

I studied the grime collected in the finger holes of the pay phone—a symbol of our dissimilar social stations and answered, "Not this trip."

"Savannah, I don't care about where you live." I smiled. How dumbfounded the neighbors would be if a Buick parked before our cottage, and impeccably dressed Tyler escorted me from the car and into the house.

"I believe you, but I need to see Mama alone. Just drive me to the bus depot?"

He didn't bat an eye at the paper sack I used for luggage since my cardboard suitcase had split. Instead he said, "Start preparing your mother to meet me soon. Start preparing her for the man who'll marry her daughter."

During the bus ride to Hampton, I alternated between panic over Mama and euphoria about Tyler's statement. Buffeted by this fear and happiness, for maybe he could stand up to his mother, I walked into Hampton General. Mama was in bed six of an eight-bed indigent ward. She slept, a thin, tired woman with her leg in traction. *Mama, you shouldn't be here,* I thought. *You deserve a private room, which as Mrs. Bradford I could afford.*

My stare and emotions apparently infiltrated her sleep, for she opened her eyes. "Honey, they shouldn't have called you from school."

"Tell me about this accident."

"I was cleaning for Mrs. Simonton, was vacuuming at the top of the stairs. The sweeper cord and I somehow got entangled, and I tumbled down the whole flight, breaking my leg, bruising myself. As soon as the leg heals, I'll be back to work."

Throughout the afternoon, I learned that the Simontons would pay a salary as she recuperated and that my presence disturbed her. "Please, go back to school." Unsure what to do, I headed home in the dusk and unlocked the cottage's door. As if a visitor, I surveyed the living room furniture and accessories, at their best in muted light. What poverty.

The phone rang, and as Tyler spoke, I decided there were more than two of me. Besides the "me" that Tyler and the Bradfords saw, there was the "me" that Mama knew, and there was the unknown "me" privy to the codes that waited to be deciphered, implanted by an unknown parent.

Tyler pushed to come or to wire money. When I refused, he moved ahead with, "I told Mother that we're getting married." He cleared his throat, and I waited.

"She doesn't approve, does she?"

"Savannah, she'll come around. She has to come around. I don't want a life without you." He gave an apologetic laugh. "Now tonight, Mother's invited an 'unattached' woman from Des Moines to join us for dinner. She's trying to fix me up, but you're it."

Later, as I set Mama's dented kettle on the stove, I heard a light rapping at the door. On the steps, Cora Lee simply asked, "How is she?"

"Broken leg. May be released next week."

"And then?"

"Don't know. I'll have to figure that out."

"She wants you in college," Cora Lee said, "I can come help out when she's home."

This is it, I thought, *my chance for information,* so I invited Cora Lee inside. Reluctantly, she complied, and as if aware that I had ulterior motives, perched cautiously on our sad couch, ready for a fast get away.

I didn't turn on the light by the easy chair where I sat. Opposite one another, enveloped by deepening twilight, we were nearly faceless.

When she said nothing, I asked. "How did you know that Mama was hurt?"

"Emmaline and I keep in touch."

Emmaline. She said my mother's name easily, intimately.

"You go back a long way?"

"Before you were born."

My heart raced, and I heard my shallow breathing, the panting as if I'd been running, which in one sense was true. "So," and because my answer waited right here, but feet away, I found it hard to shape the syllables. Not helping, Cora Lee remained immobile, a large bulk.

"You knew my father."

"Yes."

Surely she heard my breathing and the chair that protested as I pushed against its back and arms, foolishly seeking the stability of the Bradford furniture.

Without inflection, in a montone that seemed calculated, she asked, "What do you know about him?"

"Nothing. Mama won't tell me anything."

"Leave it at that then." Her dress rustled as she started to rise.

"Please, stay. Tell me."

"I won't go behind Emmaline's back."

Afraid that she'd take off, I spoke quickly. "I know that, but please, please understand how vital this is. I've been denied knowledge of my father for twenty-some years."

As she considered, her hands smoothed the dress material that shielded her knees. The rhythmic motion lulled me as well. "You ask

Emmaline," she said. "If she says it's okay, I'll tell you whatever you like."

"Fair enough, but answer one question tonight?" She didn't say "no" so I hurried on. "How do you know him?"

At that she stood up and discouragement flooded me. I put my hand across my eyes. Gently she patted the top of my head before crossing to the door. The knob rattled as she spun it, but at the threshold she paused. "Your father and I grew up on neighboring farms. He's my cousin." The door shut behind her.

ANN

3:00 a.m., Sunday

Even though it's another hot night, I periodically shiver. Even though the house is still—eerily still, actually—I sense that Savannah and Chris are also awake and probably adding comments to their journals. Will they, as I intend to do, recount the evening from their perspectives?

For clarity, in my own mind at least, I'll pick up from where I think I last quit writing, where Cammy had eavesdropped on the Richard-Em account before requesting Richard's picture. With an answer that disappointed her, I left the kitchen for a nap in "my" bed and awoke to the smell of frying onions.

Thick-headed, mouth dry, I was grateful for a vacant bathroom and a quick shower. Next, I was grateful that Chris and Savannah (she in the farthest corner of the porch) called out as I passed behind the screen door in the hallway.

"Cammy likes to fix a meal by herself." Savannah flicked ashes from a cigarette that dangled over the railing away from me. But to be sure that I didn't come in contact with second-hand smoke, I stayed out of range, sitting in a far-distant wicker settee.

Maybe my recitation of Em's marriage was positive, because they talked readily. Chris told of a time when Em (I refuse to call her Emily Jane) replaced her at a baby sitting job so Chris could go on a date with Todd. Savannah laughed about a movie they wanted to see. Pooling their change, they had enough for one ticket. Em paid, went into the theater, and held the exit door open so Savannah could sneak inside.

"She enrolled us in an auto mechanics course at adult ed," I said, "because she insisted, 'If we drive cars, we should know about them.

Shouldn't be dependent on men.' We lasted until break time of that first class."

Our humorous stories grew—Em at the wrong funeral, inexplicably losing a shoe during an airplane flight and limping into the terminal, and spending a summer as a mystery shopper in which she evaluated various fast food restaurants and gained ten pounds.

As we laughed, I was again reminded of music. Savannah's laugh, a smoky baritone; Chris's, a second soprano; mine, an alto. Our concert must have pleased Cammy, for when she stepped onto the porch with "Supper's ready," she smiled.

On a table best characterized as a study in minimalism, Cammy lit twin white candles set equidistant in glass holders. The four china dinner plates had a simple silver band. The equally stark silver needed polishing. Fold lines marred the tablecloth, which made me suspect that at the last minute she'd decided on dinner in the dining room and had pulled the cloth from a sideboard drawer, that she was indeed inventing this weekend as it/we progressed.

As we drew back our chairs, I think we simultaneously noticed that a snapshot of Em lay just north of each salad fork.

"I selected some pictures and randomly placed them, hoping they'd spark some questions, some reminiscences," she explained.

The one by my place setting, a studio pose, must have been taken when Em was about three, but I didn't see her. The smile, the intelligence in big eyes, that was Robin. Never having seen Em's baby pictures, I had no way of knowing how much she resembled my daughter when she was three. While the others ate orange Jell-o salad embedded with mandarin oranges, fresh tomatoes, breaded pork tenderloin, and fried onions mixed with green peppers, I remained locked in the Em-Robin similarity. Dimly, I heard remarks about the meal, and collected stray phrases from anecdotes spawned by each black and white snapshot.

Obviously my silence, lasting too long, lapped like an invisible wave across the table, for Chris asked, "Ann, you okay?"

I forced a smile. If I told them of Robin, they'd react as other people did. In the past, I'd occasionally been foolish enough to mention my child's death. Instinctively, listeners drew back before mouthing platitudes. Then they monitored future remarks, while surreptitiously observing me. If a woman offhandedly said, "I'd die before I did that," or "I laughed so hard I thought I'd die," immediate stricken apologies or an embarrassed pause ensued. In short, my situation proved discomfiting in most circumstances and isolated me in social settings. Better to keep Robin my secret.

Surprisingly, Cammy said, "Silence may be the most meaningful tribute to Emily."

I regarded her, eyes and facial structure unlike Em's. In that dissimilarity, in finding no hint of Robin, I found my voice. "Thanks, you're right. We can honor Em in many ways."

Although I tried to relax and engage in dialogue, I couldn't. The photo tugged at me. Once more, only phrases filtered through. "Halloween costume"… "flat tire she drove on"… "state music festival"… "rented piano." I forced down minute bites of food, but finally excused myself and in the bathroom sobbed into a hand towel. "Enough," I lectured myself. "You can get through this. You've done it before."

I reapplied makeup and returned to the dining room. "So, we had this pickup," Savannah was saying. "Emily'd borrowed it from somewhere, and we set off from Monroe. Near Clinton, where the auditions were scheduled, she discovered she'd forgotten the paper with the directions to this little studio. She asked at a gas station. The attendant had no idea, but a fellow leaning against the pay phone booth said he knew where it was. He was hitchhiking. If we'd give him a lift, he'd direct us to the address. He was shabby, and I shook my head. However, Emily was desperate.

"'Okay,' she told him. 'Hop in the back. Through the rear window you signal directions to my friend, and she'll tell me where to turn.' 'This is stupid,' I said, but she merely firmed her jaw and answered, 'Lock your door.'

"Since every second counted, Emily barely let the guy climb into the truck bed before she gunned the motor. She spewed gravel, and we lurched onto the highway, hitchhiker holding on to the side for dear life. We barreled down the road, saw the exit signs for Clinton, and Emily yelled to me, 'Watch where he's pointing.'

"The guy wasn't pointing at all. He had a death grip on the truck. I motioned to him, but his eyes were glazed. When we'd passed the last exit sign for Clinton, Emily bounced the truck onto the shoulder and jumped out."

Savannah stood, centered hands on hips in a not-bad imitation of an annoyed Em, and we laughed. "'You liar. You don't know where this address is,' she screamed at him. 'I do, too, but you're driving like a crazy woman. I can't let go of the truck.'

"'Okay, okay, give me the name of the exit.'

"Now," Savannah continued as she sat down, "I can't remember why he couldn't, but he did say, 'It's the exit by the billboard advertising something religious.' Emily glanced at her watch, threw the truck into gear, called out, 'Hold on, Savannah,' and effected a U-turn. She crossed two lanes of traffic—plenty of blasting horns—smashed some flowers in the central median and circled back toward Clinton.

"Hitchhiker was paralyzed. We exited by 'Repent Now,' and once in town and going the speed limit, he loosened his death grip and began pointing before various corners. At a stop sign, about half a block from the studio, he leaped over the side and ran off."

"And the audition?" Great. I sounded fine.

"I never heard her sing better."

Although we tossed around reminiscences for several hours, I failed to regain my equilibrium. Thus, when tales about Em started dwindling, I decided to call Seth. Just hearing his voice would restore me. Seated on the stairwell step, I dialed and on the third ring pleaded, "Oh, please, not the answering machine."

I didn't have to leave a message, for suddenly Seth answered. His "hello" was husky, as if he were overcome with emotion.

"Oh, Seth, I was worried you were out."

From the background came another voice, "Who is it?"

Morgan.

Seth must have mouthed "Ann," because Morgan said, "Tell her now's not a good time."

Was that the rustle of bed sheets? *Now's not a good time. Now's not a good time.*

Seth cleared his throat. "What is it, Ann?"

With that atypical hint of annoyance, I began trembling. Using my left hand to steady my right arm so I'd not drop the receiver, I said, "Just checking in."

"Well, everything's cool here. You?"

"Cool."

"That's splendid." Seconds elapsed and then he asked, "Anything else?"

"No."

"Well, see you next week," and the line went dead.

So he and Morgan were lovers. Sheets had rustled. Yet, what if I'd heard sheets of paper, not linen? Morgan had dictated terms, *Now's not a good time.* But suppose it wasn't a good time because they were discussing the nursing home? It was what—8:00 P.M. Pacific Time? They could have been going over records. But why did Seth sound so curt? Distracted? Was he showing off his business persona to Morgan? Why would they discuss staffing or finances at the apartment? Files normally stayed in Seth's office. They must be lovers. "But you have no proof," Em once argued.

"Suspicions can bother as much as evidence."

"If you let them. You have a choice, Ann, and I'm not trying to give you pop psychology, but everything boils down to choice."

"All right, say I choose to go with suspicions, assume they're having an affair."

"Then," she raised and lowered her shoulders in an exaggerated shrug, "choose to keep on living the compartmentalized life you'd led with Seth. You've got a good deal. Forget Morgan."

Easier said than done, as the old saying goes. Morgan left a lasting impression—an impression that began before I met him on an April night. I remember that on the classical music station the San Francisco Symphony played "The New World Symphony," and the desk lamp cast a honey-tinged puddle across the report due tomorrow to my department chair. A parents' group and a few classroom teachers supported a policy change to stop the satisfactory/unsatisfactory designation in art and music and return to traditional letter grades. Em, I, and other enrichment teachers opposed this. How to grade the clumsy child with willing spirit but undeveloped artistic bent? How to grade the student without imagination, but with perfect small muscle control so he/she can produce beautiful copies? How, in fact, is it possible to assign a letter to creativity, to the child who envisions a new concept but lacks the means to express the same?

As my pen scratched out my arguments, Seth let himself into the apartment, planted a kiss on the back of my neck, and apologized about being late.

"Your dinner's on the stove," I said, and with the additional accompaniment of serving spoon against pan, and plate against table, I signed and dated my reasons.

"Will you convince them?" Seth asked as he cut the asparagus spears.

"Did my best, but I imagine Em's will swing the most weight. She writes with passion."

He patted the chair beside him—a sign for me to join him—and after I brewed our tea, I took my usual spot on his right. "Delayed tonight because I've been on the phone. I've hired a medical director for the Santa Barbara facility."

"Really." I was pleased. Dr. Gilborn, the former director, had died in January. Seth had approached most physicians in the community with no results.

"If I believed in miracles…" he grinned. "This doctor, Morgan Warner, is relocating to Santa Barbara. He specializes in geriatrics and has had a private practice in San Diego with a partner. They split. I think he and the other doctor were partners, professionally and personally. Anyway, the partner kept the practice and Dr. Warner's not going to build a new one. He plans to be house doctor at several nursing homes and serve as medical director where he can."

"That's legal? To be at more than one?"

Seth stirred sugar into his tea. "Sure, and Warner's a pilot and has a plane, so he can serve quite a wide region as medical director. We just need him for monthly UR meetings. He's flying in tomorrow because he's also talking to Jake over at Rosewood and Tiffany at Bayside."

"You wouldn't hire him for here, as well?"

"No, not unless Dr. Sacamori resigns. Warner's seeing me about 5:00 tomorrow, his last appointment."

"Bring him to dinner?"

Seth did, and immediately I liked Morgan. Tall with fine features, he was captivating, an adept conversationalist, and I thought—as many women probably have—*a shame he's gay*, for he'd be ideal for Em. Thus, initial impressions were favorable, and Seth's response continued to be positive. By early summer, Morgan's name appeared often in Seth's comments after he came home from Santa Barbara.

His clever statements and insightful quips delighted me, as well as Seth. My husband, virtually friendless, had a friend. Aware of how large a role friendship played in my life, I was thrilled. At last, Seth could enjoy such rewards.

When did I first wonder about their friendship? Certainly the ever-increasing references to Morgan, some extended weekends, but definitely I pinpoint a weekend the following spring when I attended a three-day seminar, "Teaching Techniques for the Elementary School Art Teacher" (dismal title) in Santa Barbara and stayed at Seth's apartment.

Later I reminded myself that nothing in those three rooms and bath revealed anything out of the ordinary. But on Sunday afternoon, after the final teacher's workshop, I drove to Seth's hospital office where he typed a letter.

"Inspired?" he asked as I flopped into a chair.

"Exhausted," I answered and rested my feet on the coffee table.

"Read one of my sexy magazines," and he waved his hand at the pallid assortment. "I'll finish this, and we'll go out for dinner."

I closed my eyes, listened to his uneven typing, amused myself by trying to describe how his office smelled and had selected "neutral" when Morgan strolled in. For fifteen minutes or so, we bantered back and forth. Then, Morgan stretched across the desk and straightened Seth's tie. "Don't want you to look like a slovenly administrator. What if the state inspector came in," he joked, "or a private pay family hoping to place their wealthy matriarch?" While they kidded, I sat rigid. That gesture, that realigning the tie. How intimate.

"Ann," Chris walked along the hallway toward me. "Are you done with the phone?" Behind her came the contented interplay of Cammy and Savannah's exchange as they cleared the table.

The house was oppressive. "Sure, all done. I'm off for a walk." As she dialed, she nodded to me, then spoke into the receiver, "Evan, sorry. Not a chance to call earlier."

Not knowing nor caring who Evan was, I stepped into the August night. At the end of the sidewalk that united the curb with Cammy's house, I stopped. Suddenly light-headed, suddenly hearing, "Seth," "Morgan," "Seth," "Morgan" echoing in my brain, I bent over, cupped my palms on my knees and inhaled. As my heart rate evened out, I stood upright and inspected the heavens. Lots of stars.

"Paper said there's a meteor shower tonight," a male voice said in the darkness, but it didn't startle me. It was Dirk.

"I didn't know. Haven't read a paper today or heard any news."

"A good spot's on the rise south of town. Want to take a look? I'm Dirk."

"Why not?" I answered.

"My truck's parked a block away."

Our matching strides were companionable. "Why'd you park at a distance? Spying on us?"

He chuckled, and I warmed at its sound, deep and infectious, similar to Em's.

"Naw, just got this idea to walk where she and I used to walk. Often, I'd park somewhere else, so Cammy wouldn't get upset, turn on the porch light and stand like a guard at the door."

I stumbled on a break in the concrete, and he clutched my upper arm with a tight grip. The heat of his hand lingered for minutes. To divert myself from that sensation, I concentrated on a lighted window, a rectangular box into a living room, where a man with graying hair and a woman with glasses lounged in recliners before a TV screen. Had they known Em? Had they—

"So what's going on at Cammy's? Some kind of touchy-feely thing?"

"Hardly." I recapped our day.

"Doesn't sound too exciting for a California girl." He opened the truck's passenger door, and a shaft of weak light from the ceiling fixture splashed across our profiles. Partly because of his attractiveness, partly because of his answer, and partly because of his broad smile, I laughed. As I climbed into the cab, his hand again etched a pattern of heat across my back, and as I waited for him to pass before the hood, I breathed in his clean, masculine aroma that infused the cab.

As we cruised down the street, I avoided looking at him and directed my question to the windshield. "What do you know about this California girl?"

As lighted houses, interrupted by dark lots, shrank behind us, he said, "Emily Jane said I'd like you, that you were great, fun, put together, and had one hell of a body." Once more he chuckled, and I felt the *frisson* of sexual attraction. "She told me about the time you were out running and met those teenage boys, walking three abreast toward you down a street. One said, 'Hey, baby, you be old, but you be good.'"

Joined laughter's a kind of aphrodisiac, I thought, *a type of foreplay.* Em would have liked exploring that idea.

"What about me?" he asked as he accelerated. "She tell you I was the bad boy?"

Now we made eye contact, and an instant, nearly-forgotten desire spread from the pit of my stomach to between my legs. It prevented me from saying that she'd forever loved him, that her memories of him were ever new. "Sure. That, and that you were fun and—"

"Had a hell of a body," he finished. Again we laughed. Everything we said, no matter how slight or banal, caused laughter. As we sped over a back road, hearing gravel when it pinged against the undercarriage, I felt giddy, wild, and young. Perhaps we traveled for five miles before Dirk braked and pulled down a country lane. We bumped over ruts, climbed to a level pasture, and he doused the lights and the engine. Stillness greeted us, astonishing stillness that reinforced my sense that we were marooned, like castaways. On this island, inhabited by basic man and basic woman, I wanted him with an overpowering urgency I'd not felt since my early intense days with David. Surely he felt this and would reach for me. I anticipated the solid impact of his lips, the crush of his chest that would imprint shirt button indentations upon my skin. Instead, Dirk took his time peering through the windshield at the sky. "Come on. Let's try it in the back. Can't see much from here."

He *was* interested in a meteor shower. I'd invented this chemistry. Disturbed by Em, Robin, Seth, and Morgan, I'd imagined some magnetism. Was I so needy that I read dual meanings into his words, his motions?

When he unlatched his door, the ceiling light further shattered whatever sexual fantasy I'd created as it stripped away the night's romance to reveal a middle-aged man and a middle-aged woman bound solely by their association with one dead woman. Thus, when he guided me from the cab and over the tailgate, I disregarded the pressure of his hand and didn't attempt any repartee when he said, "I'll unroll my sleeping bag. We'll sit on that."

I studied the stars—brilliant and mysterious—as he spread the sleeping bag across part of the truck bed and handed me a cold beer. "Doubt you're a beer drinker, but for tonight, pretend."

On the sleeping bag, using the cab as a head rest, we searched the skies. Both of us were equally poor at identifying constellations, and I laughed when Dirk invented names. "There on the left, that's Old

Crone and Her Twin Ducks." He jabbed a forefinger directly over our heads. "Those are the Seven Midgets."

Like companions or drinking buddies, we shared the night. Yet once more, passion built, spurred by the nudge of a breeze that combed the tiny hairs on the back of our hands, the awesome blackness, the overarching canopy where we spotted a shooting star, and even by the yeasty smell of beer that drifted from the opened bottles.

"You think there's a heaven?" His question, his seriousness surprised me.

"Don't know." I ran my thumb over the bottle's label. "Would like to think there's something after death."

He took a hearty swallow and rested his bottle along a jeaned thigh. "Only deaths I've dealt with until now are my parents. Dad said there's nothing more. Mom believed the opposite. She promised to contact me from the other side."

"And?" I prompted.

Beside me his arm moved in some dismissive motion. "Mom loved hummingbirds. Shortly after she died, a hummingbird suddenly began darting around outside my trailer. Hadn't seen one there before, but who can say. Might have been a coincidence."

"I searched for signs when Robin," my throat closed on her name, and I sipped my beer, "my daughter died. About three weeks after her death I swore her fingers pressed against the soles of my feet. As a very little child she'd dip a cotton ball in rubbing alcohol and wash each of my toes. I was sure she was destined for podiatry." I told him about Robin's death and my divorce from her father, about Em's accompanying me to Robin's grave, about the uncanny experience earlier this evening when Em's childhood photo reminded me of Robin. And then I cried.

He laid his arm over my shoulder and brought me close. The stubble of his whiskers brushed my cheek. Stiff bristles, thrusting bristles. My tears stopped.

When his chest pressed against mine, I smelled his need, and I licked the salty patch of skin at the hollow of his neck just above the opened shirt collar. Our beer bottles clattered against the floor of the truck bed.

As our lips met, as his tongue parted my ready lips, his fingers along the back of my blouse outlined my bra. Our bodies fit against each other so snugly that I felt each muscle, each straining tendon, each hard, aching inch of him.

Then Dirk pulled his head back and smiled. With that smile, with his hand now on my breast, I tugged at his shirt. How many years had it been since I'd been caught by lust as pure as grief, the kind that drives you mad, that demands you tear off clothing, that begrudges every second until a man's inside you? I'd forgotten, or accepted as extinct, that drive and the indescribable wonder of perfect lovemaking, when nerve endings throb.

Afterward we lay on our backs, hip pressed against hip on the one-person bed roll and allowed an infant wind to dry our sweat.

"One of the Seven Midgets just winked," he said, "cause that was some of the best sex he'd ever seen."

"Even Old Crone forgot about her twin ducks and gaped," I answered, then rested my ear against his chest to savor his rumbled laughter.

"Hell, I'm too spent to get us another beer."

I knew that he watched me as I moved to the tailgate, that he admired my body. His reaction, the seductive night caressing my skin, combined to make my every move mystically agile. As I climbed down to the ground, I didn't step on a bur, didn't cut my bare feet en route to the driver's side where I snagged a beer from the cooler wedged behind the seat. When I stood over him in the truck bed, his teeth flashed white in a cocky grin, so I inched the side of the cold bottle along his skin, from his navel downward. He grabbed my arm, tossed me down on my back. "If I were younger, we'd do it again. Require a tad more recovery time now."

As he drank, he talked about his experiments with brewing beer and graded beers he'd tasted (a Mexican brand got an "A") . When he'd drained the bottle, he aimed it at the shape of a tree and a second later, when it hit its target, we yelled, "All right," at the rewarding clunk.

But with that clunk, the mood shifted and we fumbled for our clothes. The metallic whisper of zippers and the scratch of fabric intruded on the night, erasing my lithe ability. Dirk helped me from the truck bed. On solid ground, his kiss held a mixture of sweetness, admiration, appreciation, and banked desire.

Too soon, we jounced down the lane; too soon, were before Cammy's house where a light blazed from only one window. Em's room. It shocked me. Even though I realized Chris was there, it still seemed odd that light should shine from that location. It brought Em, brought the lovemaking with Dirk, into a sharp reality. What had I done? How could I so easily have had sex with him? Em loved Dirk. Thus, I could barely ask, "Have we somehow betrayed her?"

"Naw," he shook his head. "We were talking of signs from the other side. That's what that is. She approves."

Although I didn't feel completely convinced, when he leaned toward me and whispered, "Tomorrow night?" I was unable to answer, "No."

Quiet controlled the house, and I tested each stair for a noisy board before putting weight on it. I mastered the top step and furtively continued toward "my" room, but the bathroom door swung wide, revealing Chris. "Was that Dirk's truck?" she asked. Then she neared me. "Oh, my god, Ann. You have The Glow."

CHRIS

Sunday, about 5:00 A.M.

Once when I started talking and got sidetracked by an entire raft of ideas, Emily Jane said, "Make a mental list. Then when you've completed a topic, draw a line through it and proceed to the next one." Didn't work. I could never imagine a list of what I wanted to say. So non-spontaneous. But I'll try the list suggestion in this book because otherwise I may never get anything written that I want to write. My list includes: Tell About

—talk with Evan

—thoughts when walking by my house last night (oops that must go first in chronological order)

—Ann and Dirk

I hate to write their names together like that. It's like they are a couple. Weird. Too weird.

All right, to the list. I walked out of Cammy's last night after Ann took off and after I called Evan, who told me to come on over to Grant's apartment. I took the longer route, going down Bonner Street, so I could pass my house. Todd's shadow fell across the window pane and out into the square of light that splattered across the lawn. The shadow changed. Todd must be moving back and forth from stove to table, fixing a late meal. He'd be warming a can of chili and chopping an onion to mix into the soup bowl. It felt almost indecent to pause and watch his shadow, knowing so well what he was doing when he didn't know I was there on the sidewalk. I wished I could send me into the house. Conscious of the concrete, like a tether, I freed my ghostly form. It ran up the steps. Its voice spoke Todd's name. Its body nestled against him as he welcomed a figure wonderfully trim and pre-four-pregnancies thin.

The shortened shadow stopped. Todd was sitting. A car magazine would lay on the table to the left of his chili bowl. If he were drinking milk, he'd position the carton on his right, its paper pitcher-shaped spout facing him. But since today was Saturday, and he could sleep in tomorrow, likely he had a beer.

If my ghostly-self drifted over his head and peered inside his skull, what would it find? Thoughts of a beloved wife? Worries about the shop? Plans to trade the van for a passenger car now that the kids are grown?

That made me feel even stranger, because as well as I knew Todd, I couldn't guess his thoughts. Maybe he had secrets—as I suddenly did. Maybe since childhood he'd stored secrets. I was the talking one. Todd used to laugh, "Chris, you could never have an affair. You'd come right home and tell me every detail." But he didn't go over details with me. Never had I doubted him, but what if all these years he'd kept things hidden, the way I intended to keep Evan's trouble and Candi's confession locked out of his sight? If Todd discovered that Evan had taken the car, he'd give up on him completely. It would be the proverbial last straw. He'd never believe that Evan could be saved. Maybe he'd forbid him from coming to our house. And Candi? Todd already had issues with her. If he knew of her affair, could he keep from acting hostile? Wouldn't that alert Scott to a problem? No, I'd keep this a secret.

I left the shadow and the man behind it and headed toward Evan. He's second on my list. As I walked along streets empty of traffic, I began out of habit to write Emily Jane an internal letter. "I feel so not myself tonight," I said as the introductory line.

(This morning it dawned on me that perhaps everything I've written in this journal so far really adds up to a letter to her.)

Sentences spoken only in my mind poured out to Emily Jane as I mounted the enclosed staircase to Grant's apartment. "Look at the paint curling from these wooden steps, and look how candy wrappers and leaves clear from last autumn are stuck in corners. And the light bulb," (which I mentioned when I stubbed my toe) "must be twenty-five watts."

Since the broken screen door didn't shut tightly, a miniature stream of trash extended into the hallway. Depressing. Evan must have heard my feet clumping up the steps, because he emerged from the murky interior before I called his name.

The living room was worse than the last time I'd been here, which was probably six months ago. A table lamp's shattered glass shade washed half the room in a reddish tint and trained harsh light on the other half. It showed cobwebs and a torn couch with one of the three cushions gone. Food stains—had someone heaved a pizza?—marked the wall above the couch.

Evan dragged a kitchen chair over beside a bar stool with a missing rung so that we could form a party of two in the reddish light. He perched above me on the stool, but that seemed awkward. We should be level, but I couldn't very well say, "Let's change places." Then I'd appear like a judge, so I just dove in. "When I first called you, Heather was eating in the kitchen, so I couldn't tell you that Buck Nolan will drop the charges and that you can go back to work."

"Why?"

That stopped me. I'd never considered that he might question me. "Well, it's private."

"You paid him." I heard his disappointed surprise.

"No," but, of course, I had paid with my promise.

"What did you do? How did you fix it?"

"Evan, let's leave it that everything's okay, and no one in the family—not Todd, Heather, Julie, Greg, or Scott—knows about this trouble, and that it's taken care of." While my mouth, as if on automatic, spit out words, my brain taunted, "Liar, liar. Todd knew Evan had some kind of problem. That means if Todd ever says, 'Hey, what was the deal when Evan showed up here on Sunday morning?' you'll have to lie."

As if mulling over what I might have done, Evan wrinkled his forehead and remained still, except for his right foot. The heel in the scuffed tennis shoe rapidly knocked against the wooden stool leg. Something more needed to be said. "This is the only time I'm going to do this. I'm not going to bail you out ever again."

"You don't need to do it this time. I don't want that stupid job. I'm not going back."

My heart thudded against my rib cage and my tongue twisted with too many things to say. "That's… You… No."

"I'll take my chances with juvenile court. They won't lock me up. First offense." Yet, the nervous, jerky movement of his foot contradicted his confidence.

I tried taking some deep breaths, but my lungs refused to behave, so when I spoke, my voice came out high and tinny. "You're talking wildly. Why cause everyone grief when you don't have to?"

"Everyone?" He snorted. "Dad'll be mad for about ten seconds, then he'll give a laugh, shake his head, and say, 'Whatever. You handle it, Evan.' Todd already has me pegged as a loser. Heather, Scott, and Greg *might* be embarrassed, but they already are. And that's all. Grandma? She's not alert, doesn't know anything. Friends?"

"I'm *everyone*," I said. "When you're in trouble, I—" How to explain my feelings, describe how completely I love him? "Hurt."

The jerking foot ceased. He looked away at the food-stained wall. His voice was low. "I'll go to Buck Nolan in the morning."

"Apologize," I whispered. Although my legs quivered, I stood. He didn't. I walked to the screen door, but as I pushed on its frame I felt his hand on my back, as light and quick as if a bird in flight had grazed it.

"Night." I started down the stairs.

"See you," he answered.

Number three on the list: Ann and Dirk. I dread writing that "and" because of what it implies. In school—was it first grade when we learned about addition?—our teacher said, "The plus sign means 'and.' One and one or one plus one equals two." Often the names or initials of a boy and a girl chalked on a wall were joined by the plus sign. It means "and." It means "love," a twosome.

There I am off the list. Okay, from Evan's I headed directly to Cammy's house, relieved that I saw no one and didn't have to talk and act cheerful. I crawled into Emily Jane's bed, ready to lie stiff and tense with worry about Candi, Scott, Evan, and maybe how to pick up Mom's laundry. But sleep won.

When I awoke needing to use the bathroom, I lay in bed a while, hoping that the urge would pass. It never does. I don't know why I don't get up and go immediately. Usually I snuggle beside Todd and lecture myself. "You're more than your bladder. You don't have to cave in to its demands." Or I'll scare myself. "If you give in and go, you're not strengthening that muscle and the doctor will do a bladder tuck before you're sixty." Or I'll say, "Distract your mind. Think of other things, pleasant things like dainty butterflies." I can invent thousands of butterflies and still have to pee.

At last, fully awake, I hurried down the hall and into the bathroom. Then I heard something, a sneaking-in-after-hours sound, followed by a truck's motor. I opened the bathroom door as Ann topped the stairs. Because it had sounded like his truck, I asked about Dirk, and that's when I noticed The Glow, evident even in the poorly-lighted hallway.

Amazingly, she hugged me. As my face collided with her blouse, I smelled sex. "Thank you," she said and turned into her room.

Thank you? For saying she had The Glow? For being here?

Re-entering the bathroom, I sat on the toilet. What should I think? Scraps of thoughts swirled like tiny tornadoes until one thought finally triumphed, *Oh, Emily Jane, why did you have to die when I so need you?*

I grabbed the closest wash cloth from the towel rack to trap my tears. Damp. Someone had recently used my wash cloth. *Damn it!* I switched on the overhead light, then sighed. Not my cloth, at all.

ANN

Sunday morning, around 8:30

If I had thought to give each journal entry a title, I could head this one, "Men," because Dirk was on my mind when Savannah knocked on my bedroom door early this morning and called out, "Phone call." It must be Dirk. Not bothering with a robe, I ran downstairs in my T-shirt and bikini panties. My body, supple and flexible, was young. My "good morning" into the receiver carried hope, joy, and sex.

"You sound happy. I presumed you were furious with me," Seth said.

I blinked away images of Dirk and worked to back pedal into a world before him, but on demand I couldn't bring Seth's face to the forefront. His features were veiled beneath the features of last night.

"Ann, I'm sorry, deeply sorry about being so abrupt. There's no excuse. Morgan was here; we had some business. There's a potential lawsuit, and we're upset."

"Forget it," I said.

"I can't, won't. You—our life—I don't want anything to disturb that. You never call me unless it's important, and I didn't respect that."

Why had I called him? Oh, that unnerving childhood pose of Em's. "I simply wanted to hear your voice, sort of a grounding device."

"See, it was important, and I failed you." Suddenly I could visualize Seth. Frowning, the line between his eyes over the bridge of his nose would deepen with intensity. *He is sincere,* I reminded myself. Instinctively I knew that in his way he loved me. And in his way did he love Morgan? Was this the time to introduce that issue? Deliver some ultimatum? Demand either Morgan or me?

"It's rough back there," he said. "You need support, and I wasn't there for you."

Undisputedly, Seth is a "there for you" type of person, but were these sentiments due to guilt? I toyed with that word as I wiped dust from the base of Cammy's phone. Should I feel guilt? If asked that question on a survey, most people would vote "yes" after learning about my extra curricular activity. But whatever guilt I felt took second place this morning to my desire for one Dirk Hawkins.

Employing my school teacher tone—an objective tone so students couldn't gain hints as to any churning feelings—I said, "I appreciate your call, Seth. Really, I'm fine. We'll see each other next weekend. We have lots to go over then."

Back upstairs, I felt as fine as I'd declared I was. I didn't make my bed, didn't pause for any introspection, just put on shorts and top, laced my shoes, and hustled back down those stairs. This time I tread lightly to prevent Cammy from materializing from the kitchen with a breakfast announcement.

Fast advancing clouds disguised the sun. Grouped in a mass, they confined the humidity, so perspiration beaded before I'd run half a block. My stride was off, but doggedly I kept on, hoping that at any instant a black pickup would appear on the street.

I curved wide semi-circles around families streaming toward the Methodist Church. I varied my route, taking a path that angled across a vacant weed-infested lot. No truck. I made five blocks before turning onto Polk Street and admitting defeat. But what did I expect? Dirk should be so blown away by our animal passion that unable to sleep he'd post himself outside Cammy's? Did I even want that? Wasn't I behaving like a hormonal adolescent? What did this imply about me? Starved for physical attention?

The final one hundred yards to the house I covered in a walk, shaking my arms and legs, not so much for cool down, but to shake away those clinging questions.

Christine sat on the front steps. Tired and forlorn, she mustered but a half-wave as I approached her. At a loss for words, we uneasily regarded each other,. I fanned my face and muttered, "Muggy."

She nodded. "Probably will rain by afternoon."

I pulled the front of my top away from my chest, then let the material fall back in place.

"Cammy wants to treat us to brunch at eleven, at a new restaurant north of town where she and Emily Jane planned to eat but never did."

But Chris, message delivered, didn't budge so I could step onto the porch. "Have a favor. I don't have a car here. Could you drive me to the Care Center, so I can pick up Mom's laundry?"

"Sure. I'll take a fast shower." She swung her legs to the side, and as I passed I realized that Chris could go home for her car. This was an excuse for us to be alone out of the house, for her to travel the Dirk and Em path, which she did as soon as we shut the rental car doors.

"It's none of my business," she began.

I didn't disagree.

"Part of me doesn't care. I mean, Dirk's been married several times, has slept with lots of women, but, see, I haven't known them. They've not been friends of Emily Jane. Turn right at the corner and go to the stop sign. About half a mile ahead is the center. It'll be on your right. Anyway, I just feel peculiar about it. Like you were her last close friend, and he was her first love, only love."

"I feel peculiar, too. I didn't plan for it to happen."

We rode in uncomfortable silence until the stop sign, where we stared at the tractor that crawled across the intersection as if we'd never witnessed anything so interesting. "I did worry about betraying Em, but by the time I went to bed, I believed she'd approve. Wishful thinking?"

When we looked at each other, Chris smiled. "Maybe not. I like to think that something of Emily Jane is hanging around. Could be she wanted you to be together. Never thought of that. Just thought of betrayal, which has been on my mind."

She didn't elaborate, and I didn't inquire. When I parked before the rambling bungalow-style Care Center, Chris grasped the door handle before asking, "You going to see him again?"

I stared through the windshield at the nondescript building and debated. Should I admit the wonder of last night, how I'd felt beautiful, desired, and more alive than I'd ever expected to feel again? But that would necessitate explaining my non-traditional marriage, which works due to my minimal emotional investment, and that would lead to Robin and David. So I opted for the simple truth, "Would like to."

She clicked the door handle, and I followed her inside the lobby, not to meet her mother, but, out of habit or out of affection for Seth, I'd inspect the center. I'd toured many rest homes and had gained recommendations—an employee of the month parking stall; a dining area bright with red-checked oilcloth table covers that were easy to clean; costume jewelry instead of coins for Bingo prizes; a red stop sign by exits that most residents automatically obeyed, which eliminated the necessity for locked doors.

Green was the dominant shade in the lobby and the twin hallways that extended from it. Each hallway depicted a garden theme. The south hall represented vegetables with prints of corn, beans, peas, tomatoes. The north hall had painting of roses, lilies, peonies, zinnias, expressive of local flower gardens. Might this work for us—for Seth? From my purse I took out a notebook and jotted down, "Garden theme?"

SAVANNAH

Sunday, before brunch

How did authors write for hours with pens, particularly with quill pens? Didn't their hands cramp? My fingers wouldn't write any more last night, and I'm unsure how much time I'll have this morning. Against an unexpected coolness, I've lowered the window, except for a crack to let smoke escape from my cigarette that smolders in its tea cup on the ledge. I've slipped on the aqua blouse that I bought at My Lady's Boutique in honor of Emily before I drove to Centerville. "That's your color," Emily told me one rainy evening as I debated among a red, a yellow, and an aqua sweater that I'd found at the Tuesday's half-price sale at the thrift store, back when Tyler figured prominently in my life and looking nice was imperative.

I've put on a pair of ivory slacks, a virtually new pair of brown sandals, and earrings of twisted gold. Aware that I didn't like the weight of earrings, Emily would say, "Must be something important if you're wearing earrings." This morning is important. When Chris and Ann return from wherever they've gone, we'll drive to the town's latest restaurant for brunch, where Cammy said she'd promised to take Emily.

The four of us will see it for her, so while I wait for this occasion, I'll continue with My Story.

I don't recall what I did after Cora Lee left on that long ago evening. Surely, I returned to the hospital for visiting hours. Undoubtedly I called Emily after Tyler didn't answer, because, of course, he was entertaining Mother's guest.

Mechanically, I conquered subsequent days, studied for upcoming finals, and joked with Tyler during phone calls about Leatha, the woman his mother had selected. I laughed at her name, asking, "Is she lethal?" unaware of how prophetic I was. I sat by Mama's bed and squelched growing anger over the fact that I had a white father.

How could I attack this worn, frail woman? How even carry on any personal conversation when lonely patients in nearby beds strained to hear everything Mama and I said? The closest we ventured to The Subject was when Mama begged me, "Please go back to college. I'll heal better and faster if I know you're in class. You're so close to the end. Nothing must interfere with graduation."

"Cora Lee came by. Offered to help."

Mama's expression remained impassive. "May take her up on that."

With Mama's release from the hospital, and with the story of my father still unresolved, I caught the bus to Monroe. As miles gathered, a stoniness grew and a determination. I could do this: pass my finals, graduate, spill out my everlasting love to Tyler and, suggest we run away. With my business degree and with his background, we could launch a company. Full of plans, thrilled with hopes for tomorrow, sure that Tyler could abandon Mommy and take off with me, I walked into our dorm room where Emily met me with the news—actually a rumor that Chris wrote her—that Dirk had married.

Distraught, Emily rambled on for hours about teaching in California. Finally she decided that night, a night in which Tyler inexplicably didn't call, that over the weekend she'd go home and find out the truth.

"Is that necessary?"

In her oversized orange nightgown she sat cross-legged on her single bed, her black hair tousled around her face. Notes from Literature of Major Instruments class were flung on each side of her, and I thought *she could be a character, Catherine in* Wuthering Heights. In some unique fashion, this attachment to Dirk formed the ballast in her life. Of course, I could pour out the accumulated fears and worries that had ballooned in Hampton, and Emily would listen. But she'd not hear.

"Yes," she said. "Want to come along?"

Now I answered, "Yes." I could be with Cammy. During the remainder of the week, Tyler never called. Whenever I stopped cramming for finals or completing back assignments, tiny shafts of fear shot into my stomach and lodged against my spine.

The night before Emily and I left on the bus, I swallowed my pride and called him. Falsely jovial, he apologized. "Have been at a conference in Omaha and just got home." He inquired about Mama, and as we talked his false cheer vanished. "I've missed you," he said.

"This weekend I'm going with Emily to Centerville."

Quiet consumed the phone line, before he said softly, "Whatever happens, Savannah, never doubt that I love you."

On Saturday morning, she and I boarded the bus. Emily's near-hysterical state rippled through the air in the bus and through the air in Cammy's house, so I had few chances to be alone with Cammy or to speak with her at any length about Tyler, Mama, Cora Lee, and a father with an increasingly more obvious skeleton. But in itself her calmness soothed me, if not Emily.

Saturday afternoon, Emily learned that Dirk had eloped, so that evening she and I wandered around town. Block after block, Emily talked, talked, talked in a dispassionate manner. "Dirk and I could never have married, so it's good, it's actually good that he's found the right woman and that she's not from this part of the country. She can offer him a life removed from what he's known. They can spend decades exploring the years before they met." But then she cried and beat her fists against her thighs.

"This is a good thing," she repeated. "It frees me to go anywhere. I can go to California, get involved with exciting, well-educated people."

"Be chased by handsome, sexy men." It wasn't a funny remark, but we both laughed. Emily hugged me, we bumped hips and clumsily continued our trek around Centerville.

Sunday morning, Emily's angst remained on center stage. That was all right. It eclipsed mine, but at dusk when we arrived at the bus terminal a mile from campus, I spotted Tyler. Though the bus window I studied him, resting against the fender of his Buick. Because of fledgling lamp light, I couldn't distinguish his features, but his solid silhouette, the set of his shoulders spoke of a man and a life I wanted.

As she stepped into the narrow bus aisle, Emily gave me a bittersweet smile. "Well, one of us has a man waiting."

I reached beneath the seat for a paper shopping bag in which I'd stuffed clothes. "I doubt for long," I muttered, but Emily apparently didn't hear, because she moved ahead.

When I stepped onto the pavement, spring air washed cleanly over my face, and I dreamed that it carried the promise of a new life for me.

"Thought you wouldn't turn down a lift," Tyler said. Close to him, I saw conflict, distress, and love.

"You're right," I answered.

"How'd you know we'd be on this bus?" Emily asked.

"Didn't, but I've checked every arrival today."

Knowledge that he'd haunted the station affected me, but I said nothing. In fact, nothing much was said on the ride to the dorm. Emily left the back seat, thanked Tyler, said she'd see me later, and picked up my shopping bag. Its side had ripped. As she walked away, she struggled to overlap jagged brown sides as if over a scar impossible to mend.

He didn't start the car, nor did he reach for me. "I'm sorry I didn't call. The conference—"

Intermittently lights appeared in dorm windows. In less than two weeks, I'd no longer live here. College would be over. Never again would I see this view and a melancholy gripped me.

"It's okay." In our room, the light flicked on. Emily would dump the torn bag atop my blue and white plaid spread. She'd deposit her case on her bed, would step to the mirror, examine her face, lick her right forefinger and smooth each eyebrow. A standard gesture. Why she did this, I had no idea, but it was her habit, one I'd deeply miss.

Tyler's laugh held no humor. "I'm sure it's not okay, but I had to see you."

"Yes."

Awaiting a longer response, he drummed his fingers on the steering wheel spokes. I rolled down my window, hearing spring chant its message of newness, a balance to the ending that loomed in this car.

"I've experimented with lots of speeches," he said. A slight breeze swept through the opened windows. "Whether they've been long or short, they've concluded the same way. I love you, want you to be my wife, but—

"Mother Bradford has other plans," I said.

His outstretched fingers stiffened against the spokes. "Maybe if my family hadn't battled so hard for this success. Maybe if Dad hadn't died. Maybe if Donald had children." As he offered excuses, I felt angry. At least he'd had a father, a brother, and success. Additionally, no one was forcing him to knuckle under to Mother, but if he couldn't pull free by himself, I wouldn't plead.

"I completely understand. Marry Leatha. Twenty years from now you'll thank me."

"No." But in the headlight glare of an oncoming car, I watched expressions remold his face, reminding me of a child I'd once observed playing in a yard with a garden hose. Delighted, she giggled as water sprayed from the nozzle. Behind her, an adult at the faucet turned the handle, and as the pressure gradually decreased, the child frowned at the trickle. In stages, she comprehended that for whatever reason the fun was over. She'd laid the hose on the grass and walked away for another toy, a sturdy tricycle, that doubtless wouldn't disappoint.

"Savannah," he tried to grasp my arm. "We can't end this."

So, I thought, *you want me as a mistress?* Then I heard the spring night whisper, newness, and I could say, "Tyler, we could talk for hours and the outcome would be the same. It's rather like removing a bandage. Peel the tape slowly or rip it at once." My right foot touched the concrete.

"Hate to compare us to bandages," he tried to joke.

Free of the car, I looked at him over my shoulder. "You'll never know how sorry I am, how much I wanted to marry you."

In the empty Sunday-evening dorm lobby, I sank into a wing chair, and for the only time I can recall, I made no effort to stop the tears. At last, when I entered our room, I found Emily desultorily stacking and restacking piles of note cards for her History of Western Music course. She swung her chair around. "So?"

I kicked off my shoes and crawled into bed, curving my body into what Mama called a "hunkered down position." "It's over."

"Thought he was the right one."

"He was."

"Want to talk?"

"Thanks, but no."

The chair moaned as her body resettled. When she returned to the cards on her desk, I was grateful for her silence.

During our final days, Emily didn't probe. We studied for tests, often surfacing at the same moment for food. She had bought a gigantic sack of outdated doughnuts, which were edible when dunked in coffee. Of course she talked of Dirk, but mostly she dwelt on dreams of California. "Interviews with school recruiters have gone well, so I'm pretty confident." She submerged half a cake doughnut into her mug. "Should be offered at least one job. I can teach on a provisional and at night and next summer pick up additional units for my credential."

She rescued the soggy half from the brown depths of her mug and popped it into her mouth. "Since you and the apparel king are no longer on the marriage track, why not come with me?"

Postcard pictures of palm trees, sandy beaches, orange groves flitted before my eyes. "You're serious?"

She handed me the doughnut sack with its Rorschach grease spots. "We could share an apartment or a house."

My chocolate doughnut reluctantly broke into unequal sections, and I drowned one portion in my Santa Claus mug. "Well, I've no job possibility, no money to move, no money for a rental deposit, let alone—"

As if these were gossamer threads, Emily batted away such obstacles, spinning instead graphic scenes in which we dashed into shimmering waves and swam in the Pacific, or partied until dawn in an upscale San Francisco apartment. In one version, she concocted a rental house that for some reason came with a caged bird and a mixed breed dog with a backyard dog house. He completely loved us and never barked. "Soon we'll each be able to afford new cars, driving them to jobs we adore."

"And these jobs are a snap to find?"

"You see yourself employed at a bank?" she countered, and as I attempted to thread that movie into my inner projector, she went on. "Just suppose you were hired as a loan officer, and I taught music at an elementary school where we never have to put boots on kids or locate mittens. The classroom windows are open and the gorgeous harmony of their voices soars? Wafts?"

"Wafts is good."

"Wafts out the windows, and I stage a musical."

"Original musical."

"Why not? There'll be standing room only."

We created elaborate scripts until Cora Lee's letter arrived. In short, Mama's recovery had halted. Prognosis? Surgery. The next mail delivery brought a letter from Mr. Hendricks. He'd scrawled across a half sheet of paper, "Come on home, and we'll talk. I've big plans for the variety store." My future was sealed. And even though Emily tried to convince me that we could indeed go to the West Coast, I surrendered that fantasy. I'd work in Hampton and take care of Mama.

Mama called the day before graduation, and in the tone reserved for the unaccustomed long-distance call, she apologized. "I've stalled until the last minute, hoping I could come. I can't make the ceremony, honey."

"It's all right."

"It's not." I heard her tears. "I've counted on seeing you walk across that stage, counted on seeing your dorm room, the campus."

"I'll get plenty of pictures. We'll come some day, you and I, and take a tour."

As I spoke, I wondered exactly who would take these photos, for I would have no one in the audience.

However, I was wrong. When our class marched onto the football field to the traditional "Pomp and Circumstance," I glimpsed Tyler in the stadium bleachers. Then I picked out Cammy. Sunlight reflected from the camera that partly obscured her face. In the post graduation chaos, Tyler wove his way to me through the crowd. As he neared, I knew I loved him, knew that in the future these seconds would reappear, defining him. Tall, purposeful, and coming to me.

"Congratulations," he extended a small gift wrapped in silver paper. Our hands touched and stayed together. "I've missed you."

"And I, you," I answered, but where could we go from there? Like a scene in a movie, we stared at each other until Emily called out. "Meet you back at the dorm."

"Write me?" he asked.

But I never did. He would marry Leatha, I would be Mama's caregiver, and I boarded the bus for Hampton

So, I didn't thank Tyler for the starkly beautiful silver chain and dewdrop pendant. Occasionally I still snap the clasp at the back of my neck and treasure its delicate strength against my breasts.

Cammy calls. We're off for brunch.

CHRIS

Sunday, after 2:30 P.M.

This morning while Ann waited in the Care Center lobby, I waited in Mom's room for those brain cells that retain an imprint of my face and my name to activate. Didn't happen. On a folding chair beside her bed, I babbled along. "Mom, it's me, Christine, your daughter, here for your laundry. It's a Sunday, and it's going to rain soon. Remember that summer when Grant (and I stressed his name) peeled off his underpants, stuck them on his head and danced on the lawn hoping that that grouchy neighbor—what was her name?—would yell that he was an embarrassment parading around nude."

No use. Wherever Mom was, it wasn't with me. Her eyes were blank. I stroked her hand. Skin incredibly thin. I squeezed slightly. Maybe she'd return the squeeze, but her hand was as unresponsive as her mouth.

My sister Margaret periodically has one of these "pre-planning" fits, demanding that we "nail down"—her phrase—Mom's funeral service.

I protest, saying, "Don't rush things," but on this grayish morning, with only Mom's body on the bed, I wondered how many more weeks the heart would go on pumping. If I agreed that we should plan the service, would it help me to better accept the inevitable?

I smelled urine. Mom needed changing. If I knew where they kept the diapers, in which supply closet, I'd do it myself. Instead I yanked together the strings of her laundry bag, kissed her goodbye, and at the nurses' station told Mrs. Cruz, "Please send an aide to Mom's room."

She sighed. "As soon as possible. We're short this morning. We're doing the best we can."

Too disheartened to give my usual response that I knew they did well, that I appreciated the care, that I realized it was hard to keep good employees, I dragged the laundry bag into the lobby. Strangely, Ann supplied comfort; that is, after she explained that she'd written down ideas that her husband might adopt in either of his two nursing homes.

"Does he have patients who don't talk, who do nothing but stare?"

As we drove away from the Care Center, she said, "Seth thinks they *are* doing something. He believes their minds are in another dimension. Maybe they're reliving the past, rewriting events as they wished they'd been. Maybe they're having conversations with people dead or not visible to us. Naturally, he has no proof. It's just a feeling, but he doesn't see them as unhappy, distressed, or in pain. Some choose not to participate in activities or to go with their families. They appear to be choosing themselves or some inner source as a companion."

I liked that.

Ann dropped me and the laundry at my house, where I intended to shower, change clothes, and get back to Cammy's after I saw Todd. But he was gone. He'd left the bed unmade, and I stooped over his side and smelled his sweaty, greasy, elusive essence.

Heather's door was closed, but with a safety pin she'd stabbed a note to a cereal box on the kitchen ledge. "Julie called. Baby sick."

What did that mean? Crying? Hospitalized? Fussy? Double pneumonia?

As soon as I dialed the last digit, Julie answered and burst into tears, "Oh, Mom."

It's remarkable how often your body can go into the wild-heart-beat-dry-mouth syndrome, and then bounce back to "normal." Sometime I'd count the number of times I'd put the old bod through the panic/relax dynamic recently.

"I was so scared," she sobbed. "Jason's okay, he's home. Had a high fever. Andrew and I rushed him to emergency. I called you last night." The last three words were a wail.

"I'm staying at Cammy's."

She hiccupped. "I forgot, and honestly, Mom, Heather's no help. She told me to trust the doctor, and that she'd have you call me. Then you didn't."

Oh boy, I'd have to scold Heather. "But how's Jason?"

"He has an ear infection. The doctor prescribed antibiotics and sent us home, but I was frantic."

"You sound tired."

"I'm exhausted, too tired to sleep. Andrew's sleeping though."

"Well, hon, fix yourself some hot cocoa, and—"

"Mom, it's nearly one hundred degrees."

"I was simply trying to think of some comfort food."

She laughed, and I lessened my steel grip on the receiver to stretch toward the sink. I snared the dish rag and wiped up blots of chili in dried puddles on the stove top. "Do you see your pediatrician?"

"Tomorrow." On a roll now, she gave every detail from Jason's dull eyes and irritability, to her rising fear, to what Andrew said and read aloud from the medical book, to how her heart hammered as she punched in Dr. Sorel's number.

Hands of the kitchen clock jumped to 10:46. Impossible to shower. Assuring Julie of my pride in how well she and Andrew had handled this emergency, I promised to call tomorrow evening after their appointment with Dr. Sorel. I dashed to the bedroom and pawed through clothes in my closet. What about my gray-flower figured blouse? A pink skirt? There wasn't time to press it. Maybe the diners would credit the seat belt with causing all the wrinkles. I aimed the nozzle of the deodorant can beneath my armpits and liberally sprayed the blouse material before wiggling into pantyhose and my best white sandals.

When I arrived, Savannah and Ann stood in the yard as Cammy cautiously backed her car from the garage. How much longer would she be able to drive? What would her life be like without a car? Having no, or few, friends, would she be house bound? Become a total recluse?

With fingers glued to the upper fourth of the steering wheel, Cammy maintained a steady twenty-two miles per hour along residential streets. Hundreds of feet before each corner, she signaled a turn, and once for an entire block, we listened to the insistent click of the signal after she forgot to flip the lever to off.

When Savannah said, "Ah, the signal?" Cammy nodded primly, adjusted it, and as an apology told us, "I don't drive much. The last time was to Emily's grave."

Grave? Ann and I shared puzzled glances.

"Emily's buried?" Savannah asked, but Cammy said no more. I decided she can't talk and drive. At the restaurant, she took three swings at a straight-in parking space, and with each swing narrowly missed a sports car.

Spencer's is nice. White tablecloths, lacy napkins, silverware that gleams, fresh-cut flowers in Candlewick bud vases. Cammy ordered champagne, and we toasted Emily Jane. As we ate our eggs Benedict, Cammy said, "I'll drive us to the Elmwood Cemetery. Elmwood's the next town," she informed the others. "In fact, Chris's son is the Elmwood High School coach."

Where his wife is getting it on with another man, I thought.

"Em's buried in Elmwood?" Ann asked.

"Yes, beside her father and her mother." *Fake mother*, I corrected. *Emily Jane knew you were her mother.*

From the windows in Spencer's, we could see mist, light as the first snowfall, unhurriedly coat the parking lot, so with windshield wipers clacking, we returned at twenty-two miles per hour to Cammy's house to change clothes and get umbrellas.

In the house, I drew on my sweats, and while waiting for the others, began writing in this journal. I hear their voices, so I'll write more later.

Here it is later on Sunday

Emily Jane, do you remember our rating system? Was it in seventh or eighth grade? We became such experts, we could just look at someone and whisper, "A five." Or, I'd hand you a book and say, "Not bad, about an eight." Although we mostly rated people, we did rate food. Peas received a weak one. We refined the system and added minus and plus signs.

I bring this up because I wonder what number we'd attach to today, at least this far into today. I first considered that while I stood by the washing machine. That was after our Elmwood Cemetery adventure in the rain, and after we'd driven back to Centerville. By then the rain had again decided to be a mist, so I walked home from Cammy's to start Mom's laundry.

As I walked, I didn't use my umbrella, but simply let the tiny rain drops do whatever they wanted to do to my hair. The rain didn't help the relaxer that Heather insisted I apply after I flew back from Chicago and Jason's birth. The cool weather produced goose bumps on my arms, so when I set the machine for the permanent press cycle, I sought its warmth and rested against the agitating washer. I like the feel of its bumping action, and that's when I debated how Emily Jane would rate the day. Not high, that's for sure. A four-plus? A four? I mean, what had been accomplished?

At Spencer's, we didn't say anything with any depth. After that, we were petrified by Cammy's driving. Next, the cemetery proved dismal in the rain, and the grave looked pathetically raw, as if Emily Jane couldn't possibly be under that piled soil, and if she were, she deserved better. And then, we did nothing at the grave. Nothing at all. No speech, no readings. It would have been appropriate if Dirk had been there to sing, but Cammy never accepted him, so forget that. Plus, if he'd sung I would have sobbed uncontrollably, and Ann would have searched for a dry spot behind a headstone so she and Dirk could have had a quick roll in the grass. Then—

The front door of our house opened and Todd called, "Hey, Chris, you here?"

Damp and frizzy headed, I charged from the laundry room into his arms. He laughed into my neck. "I'm greasy, been at the shop and finished Millard's jeep."

I didn't care. As I clung to him, my invisible interior reservoir began refilling.

"How goes it at Cammy's?"

"Not so hot today, but by this time tomorrow, when I'm finally home for good, maybe everything will have evened out, and I'll have a different perspective."

From his coveralls, he dug out a phone bill. "I intended to write a check for the phone when I was at the shop, but then I noticed this forty-eight dollar charge to a number in Kentucky."

"I know nothing about it."

He raked his hand across the top of his head so tufts of hair resembled matted blades of grass. "What about your boy Evan?"

Not wanting to wade into that stormy sea, I said, "Come, tell me what you've been doing while I take a bath." Yet as I adjusted the hot and cold faucets, we heard the phone ring. Todd left to answer, and I climbed into the tub, stretched out, and rested my head on the rear rim. Bliss. Absolute bliss. "Now this is a ten, Emily Jane."

As Todd's returning footsteps grew louder, I yelled, "Why not take off your old dirty clothes and join me?"

He kneeled by the tub and tweaked my nipple, then lowered the toilet lid to sit down. "That was Greg on the phone."

Since our second son rarely communicates, I tensed. "And?"

Greg, our quiet child, had quit college. This summer, he was in one of those isolated towers in Montana searching for fires through binoculars. On the three post cards he'd sent that I'd anchored with magnets to the refrigerator side, he'd repeated that he loved this job.

"Never better. He'll be home in three weeks, but he's bringing someone. Said he'd kind of gotten married."

Bath water turned into a tidal wave as I jerked upright. "Kind of?"

Todd grinned. "My words exactly. So then he said, 'Well, I did get married, but not in a fancy ceremony or anything, just at the county clerk's office.' "

"Married," I stammered. "Married?" I banged my toes against the tub's soap dish as I floundered toward the bath mat. "Can't be. Impossible." My hands shook as I toweled myself, and my voice shook as I asked, "Who?"

"A Celia someone. Greg said she's also a fire watcher and is older."

Todd handed me my frayed bathrobe that hangs on the door hook, and I wrapped the comforting terry cloth tight around me. "What was the hurry?"

He assumed his "don't know" stance.

"I'm going right out and call him."

"He's sending a letter and pictures." Todd positioned a hand on each of my shoulders. "What will you say if you call? I told him congratulations. Said if he liked her, we'd like her."

Although I had big doubts about that, Todd's logic and kindness slowed me down. "I can't imagine him married. He's never really dated. What are they going to do? Live where?"

Gently, Todd kissed me—a baby kiss, a make-your-finger-stop-hurting kiss. "We did all right, Chris. Everyone said we were too young, just out of high school. We had no money, had no jobs. Our families were sure it wouldn't last. Well, we showed them, didn't we? We've done fine. And, look, Julie has a good marriage and so does Scott."

I bit my lips to keep from disputing the latter and nestled close against him, burying my face into his stinky blue coveralls

"We made some great love in this bathroom," he murmured into my damp hair. The bathroom is the sexiest room in the house, or it can be when the air is steamy, when dwarf-sized rivers chart courses down foggy mirrors, when bodies are soft and pliable.

"If I didn't have to get back to Cammy's," I said. Then the screen door slammed and Heather's quick steps pounded along the hallway. We grinned, our minds on the mutual subject of recalling some of the countless times we've been interrupted.

"Think of it this way." Todd clutched the doorknob. "If we'd not been stopped or deterred so often, we'd have a dozen kids today."

As I wiped steam from the mirror with the arm of my bathrobe, I thought about Greg, the child I knew least well. He'd never played sports nor joined clubs, had never made the honor roll. "He's like the faceless child," I told Emily Jane. "He doesn't stand out. Maybe he'll have a career as a spy."

"Greg hasn't found himself yet," she answered. "Bet he'll be a middle America type, one of those who helps hold the country together."

"Hmm. Julie thinks he's gay, but I think he's a slow starter, with less testosterone than Todd or Scott."

Greg had minimal drive. "Sleep," he once announced, "is my hobby." When Greg was in high school, Todd demanded that he find an after-school job. He had several, one after the other, and to each he arrived tardy and to each, as Neil Anderson put it after firing Greg as a grocery carry-out clerk, "he failed to give his all."

"Well, Emily Jane," I brushed my hair. "Could be an older woman is what he needs. Could be she'll take care of him."

"Mom?" Heather's voice through the porous door seemed right at my ear. "Is it true? Greg?"

"Guess so." I stepped into the hall. "Your dad took the message."

She followed me to the bedroom and as I dressed asked questions to which I had no answers: How long's he known her? What's her problem? Why did they get married and not just live together?

Suddenly, I felt worn-out and boxed-in. "I have no idea, Heather, but I do know that Julie called last night and you didn't let me know immediately."

"Oh, God." She slapped a hand to her forehead and dramatically flopped on my still unmade bed. "I forgot, totally forgot. That's why I left the note before I took off for work this morning." She peeked at me through spread fingers. "You mad? Is Jason okay?"

"Ear infection, and, no, I'm not mad." Which I wasn't, simply dispirited. As I buckled on scuffed sandals, I longed to collapse on the bed where Heather was moaning, "Sorry, sorry, sorry."

Instead, I confronted the mirror and its dumpy, middle-aged woman with kinky hair, with slacks too tight across thighs, stomach, and hips, and a peach blouse worn so many times that the original sheen that had once flattered her complexion had now faded into nothingness.

No time to change or to experiment with eye makeup. I patted Heather's calf. "When you get through lolling around on my bed, please make it."

In the living room, Todd sprawled on the couch before a televised baseball game. I picked up his beer can on the coffee table and chugged a major swallow.

"You'll be home tomorrow, babe. Things will be better." Tears were darned close. Why is it that kindness or sympathy, as in Todd's voice, can send me for the Kleenex box?

With a nod, I replaced the can, waved to him, and went out the front door. In the cool grayness, the rain had ceased. "Now that's something to be thankful for." On my inner sound system I heard that standard positive comment, which Mom must have said a million times while we were growing up. Mom. Laundry. If Heather used the machine, I hoped she'd not dump Mom's clothes into the dryer on high heat. The red cardigan, for instance, would shrink into a child-sized garment.

At Cammy's, I dialed our number to tell Heather about the clothes, but since the line was busy, and since Cammy asked us to come into the parlor, I didn't try home again.

SAVANNAH

Sunday, 4:30 P.M.

What tableau best represents today? The four of us riding to the restaurant bound by the confines of Cammy's car? The four of us bound by the confines of our space at Spencer's and by a certain consciousness that this was the one spot we'd gone this weekend untouched by Emily—the only place new to everyone? Thus I'll not forget how rigidly we sat around the square table, how superficial and strained our dialogue.

Again, enclosed in the car, we returned to Cammy's for different clothes before seating ourselves in the same seats in the car to go to the graveyard. On my left: Cammy behind the steering wheel, her white hair secured by a silver barrette in an elderly version of a pony tail. Behind her: Chris in droopy, navy blue sweats. To her right, out of my view, was Ann in jeans that accented shapely legs and butt—in a separate league from my "mature" jeans with elastic waistband inserts. Yet unease at Cammy's driving linked us as did the surprise at Emily's burial.

Some years back in one of her letters, Emily wrote about death. She favored cremation. I replied that the black community did not highly regard cremation, that this was but one concept I'd learned in my constant reading about African-American history. Reading, as I did, helped fill the void I'd experienced for far too long.

About thirty miles from Centerville, after a speed likened to the flow of molasses, we approached the Elmwood Cemetery entrance with its grilled iron arch. The trip had consumed almost an hour, during which Cammy squinted through a windshield where wipers battled water tossed by oncoming traffic and by water flung by every vehicle that passed us. Everything passed us until we turned onto a lonely country road that ended at a cemetery as lonely as its approach.

NOTES WHEN SUMMER ENDS

We crawled down the main gravel road from which narrow lanes branched, as if the cemetery itself conformed to the square plat of Midwestern maps. At the fourth lane, she signaled and inched by a dozen or so long-established tombstones before she braked.

Even through the rain-streaked windows, we could see denuded earth in the second row. Cammy's breathing was labored and she looked waxen. How painful this was for her. Despite the overpowering feeling I had that she wanted to drive us, perhaps I should have offered. Now, as I reached out for her hand, I heard a gasp from Ann. And when Cammy killed the motor, when Chris and I opened doors, Ann didn't move.

"Come on." Chris took Ann by the arm as I hurried to the driver's side to escort Cammy.

Graveyards are deceptive. Ground appears level, but I've never walked through one where the ground doesn't dip or stones don't impair straight forward movement. Elmwood was no exception. Cammy and I lurched ahead. The other two followed.

In abbreviated rows, we lined up across from each other at Emily's grave. "I've ordered a stone," Cammy said. "Just her name with birth and death dates."

Rain thudded against the black soil, and Chris raised an umbrella over her and Ann. A bent rib poked from one side, and I smiled. Somehow typical of Chris, I decided. Cammy tightened her raincoat sash and pinched her coat panels together, so that they rose like a ruff around her neck. Unlike the others, I welcomed rain upon my face and on my knit top.

"I'd not counted on this weather. I'd hoped we'd say a few remarks, but now it seems a poor idea."

Thunder rolled in the distance.

"It's not a poor idea," Chris argued. "You've shown us Emily Jane's grave."

"Yes, right beside her parents."

Sure enough. Through slanting rain I read "Amelia Kerrington" and by turning farther to the right saw "Jared Kerrington."

"Were those her wishes, to be buried?" Ann sounded testy.

"On one of her lucid days, when she was grateful to suck on chipped ice, she said, 'It doesn't matter what you do after I die, but promise people won't gawk at this wrecked body, and promise me no service. I want those who cared about me to keep an alive memory of who I was, not a sanitized memory. And that happens at a service because people always make the deceased sound close to sainthood.' So because I own the plot, I made the decision. A good friend, Ralston Hamilton, paid for Amy and Jared's funeral. He bought several adjacent plots, which—"

"Was he somehow," Chris paused as if testing the correct word, "involved with Amelia?"

Cammy smiled. "Emily told you that I was her mother, didn't she? I knew that she developed some romantic story. But my sister Amelia was Emily's mother. Jared was her father, and they died in a car wreck exactly as I told her many times. However, I concluded that if, when she was young, she needed to believe that I was her mother, what harm was there? Everyone should have a mother."

Thunder again, and I checked the sky for lightning. A gust of wind slanted rain with a stronger force. Ann drew in upon herself and moved closer to Chris beneath the crippled umbrella.

"You'll be buried here, too?" I asked

"Yes, by Ralston Hamilton." Cammy pointed to a granite marker and then caught my eye. I understood that later she'd explain. She took a step backward, her heels sinking into soil that had strayed from Emily's grave. "I'll go back to the car. Stay, though, as long as you like."

But why stay? As Cammy walked away, I turned attention to the imposing gray Hamilton marker with its inscription of "Loving Husband." Yet there was no accompanying monument to any loving wife.

Under the broken umbrella, Chris and Ann inspected the Kerrington headstones, and then returned to Emily's barren plot, where Ann bent, picked something up, and slipped it into her jeans' pocket.

NOTES WHEN SUMMER ENDS

As I strolled behind them toward the car, I revived a Sunday when Emily and I left the dorm, headed for the day-old bakery. An unexpected shower deposited raindrops on her black hair. They streaked her jacket so that, to my eyes, she appeared dewy, similar to a painting with a halo. That's the image I've stored, my first choice of how she'll forever inhabit my memory. Leaving the concave mound, I felt an additional solace, a tie between that picture and the rain pummeling us today.

In the car, as if separated by invisible fences, we sat apart, our breaths steaming the window glass. We were as divided as we'd been on Friday night. On some level visiting the grave hadn't worked for the others. Did it renew grief? Make Emily's death more vivid? Seem an ignoble end to her vitality? For me, the visit had introduced a name, Ralston Hamilton, which obviously figured largely in Cammy's past.

She put the car in gear, fiddled with the defroster knob, and with hands clenched atop the steering wheel, guided the car underneath the cemetery's arch. The lengthy trip to Centerville was marked not by our remarks, but by the metronomic swipe of wipers, the hiss of tires on wet pavement, and the erratic splat when tires bisected puddles.

As she pulled into her driveway, Cammy said, "Supper at six."

Ann made some token counter offer. "Let me treat at a restaurant." But Cammy refused. "No. The meal's planned."

In my/her room, I draped my wet shirt and damp jeans over the back of a chair and snuggled into my robe before lighting a welcome cigarette.

Perhaps supper would be a unifying source. Until then, I'd once more, enter another chapter of My Story.

After graduation and moving into our cottage, I claimed the lumpy couch as my bed. In pain, Mama required the bedroom. Mr. Hendricks gave me the assistant manager title, and I relished the job. Less than a week later, he summoned me into his cluttered office on the second floor to reveal plans for a second variety store in Jackson, the next town to the east. "When it's ready, I want you to run it."

For the first time in months, I felt enthused. As he unrolled blueprints, I daydreamed about displays and the staff I'd hire. Each morning I'd walk briskly to the entrance with my key extended. It would rasp in the lock before the door opened. For a moment I'd indulge myself with merchandise on the shelves and the fragrance of pristine products, then head for my office. I even visualized the car I'd buy, the apartment I'd rent. That dream world was my reality as Mama declined.

In early July, the doctor hospitalized her because of an infection, but she insisted upon leaving before he discharged her. "I've not worked in months. I'm in debt," she said.

I reminded her, "You're a county patient. It doesn't cost you anything to stay, to get well so you can walk."

"In Hampton General is where I picked up this infection when they operated on my leg. Who's to guarantee they can cure it? Then I'll never be back to work. Chances of healing are better at home. Cora Lee can look in on me."

Cora Lee again. Partly due to Mama's protests and partly due to my job—the inconvenience of scheduling hospital visits around my store hours—I agreed to bring her home.

Yet, during that oppressive summer unrelieved by rain or a cooling trend, Mama failed to improve. Nightly, at 5:30, I locked up at Hendricks' Variety unless a shopper lingered or someone rushed in at 5:29 for a plunger or a greeting card, a floor fan, a stick of deodorant, or candy that a clerk must scoop from the bin, measure into the silver scale, and pour into a small white sack. I'd take slow strides home as hurrying through the Missouri evening defeated me. As I advanced against the heat, I'd plan the supper menu, gauging what might tempt Mama's appetite. Occasionally Cora Lee was at the cottage, where heat had set up permanent quarters. She'd report on Mama's day, shake her head, or in an undertone mutter, "Not looking good." She never referred to our conversation in the spring, but it teased my thoughts.

In August, Mama was hospitalized with a high fever. I'd tally the variety store receipts, eat a sandwich at Dora's Café, and go to the hospital and stay until an official voice boomed over the public address system, "It's 8:30. Visiting hours are over."

NOTES WHEN SUMMER ENDS

With the cottage packed by the day's high temperatures, I'd throw open windows and doors, then retreat outside to think about Tyler and Emily, about how I should question Cora Lee, and how I could lead a life without Mama, my linchpin. Clearly she was dying, and for some reason had given up. Was she, who'd never been sick, without patience after nearly three months? Was she tired of an invalid's life? Depressed? Had her entire goal been to see me graduate? With that accomplished, did she think I'd build a more successful future on my own without her? And what was her future? House cleaning? Living with me in my apartment? No, Mama's style was independence. I was convinced that Mama, if not willing herself to die, no longer cared to cooperate with life.

Days dragged by. On Sundays, I'd mow the lawn with the rusty push mower and clean the three-room cabin. Nights expanded, and on one of them, when I rested on the stoop, I heard footsteps along the narrow pathway to our house. They preceded Cora Lee.

"How's she doing?"

With a sigh as my answer, I scooted over so she could join me. The wood flooring groaned beneath her weight, but I found her size consoling.

"Thanks for your help," I said.

"Wish I could do more, but..." She let the sentence drift away on the night air.

"You think, as I do, that Mama's given up?"

Her silence was confirmation.

"Why? I'm at home, working. She can cut back or quit cleaning houses entirely. Eventually, we'll move into a nicer place."

"With your degree, you're going to be content with Hampton?"

"No," and I told about Mr. Hendricks' plans. "Instead of building, he's remodeling a former hardware store. Wants it open by Thanksgiving. Mama and I can live in Jackson."

She expelled a deep breath. "Not sure why, but Emmaline's not fighting this infection." Cora Lee stirred slightly, and I thought, *Put your arms around me; hug me.* She didn't. Probably if she had done so I would have cried, for I ached with the strain of withheld tears.

Abruptly she announced, "Your father's name was Leif."

Leif. Leif. A car drove past, and I thought, *It's an unusually quiet evening. No traffic. No children playing.*

"Was?"

"Died maybe ten years ago." *The night she came to our cottage, the night she hugged Mama.*

Questions wove into such a tight ball that I couldn't untangle an end with which to begin. I inched my right palm along the porch floor across paint bubbles and mottled patches.

"He and I grew up in Minnesota. Leif's father, Helmer, farmed down the road from our one hundred and sixty acres. My father, Eric, was Helmer's brother. Since I was closest in age to my cousin Leif, and maybe because he had no sister, he treated me as special." Her laugh was harsh. "Maybe because I was female, he found me special, because from infancy, it seems, Leif had an eye for the girls. Sharp and handsome, he had, as well, a rich voice. I remember when he stood alone on the stage, reciting some old English poetry in a grade school program. I was awed at how he pronounced the words."

Cora Lee's low, nearly hypnotic tone indicated that she wasn't with me, that she was back in that Minnesota school, enchanted by poetry delivered by a young man denied to me.

"I have a couple photos of him," she said as she boosted herself upright.

"But what about him and Mama?"

"They met at college. The Midwest was too confining for Leif, so after high school he went to New York. I stayed in Minnesota and married, so I'm unsure what Leif did for a couple years. This was war time. With rationing and crowded trains, you didn't travel, didn't have constant communication." She shook her head. "My father, on the draft board, kept Leif and others from being inducted. Nothing that I'm proud of."

"Mama and him?" I reminded her.

"When Emmaline arrived on campus, Leif was a college senior. I don't know how they met, how long they 'dated,' but he called home, must have been in late winter, to announce that he was marrying a beautiful black girl. Our families were horrified. Since I'd always been closest to him, they dispatched me to 'try and talk some sense into him.'" As she spoke, Cora Lee retreated into the dark.

"So Mama and Leif (how heavily his name lay on my tongue) married?"

"Said they did, but who would have married them? There were miscegenation laws, you know. All I can tell you is that Emmaline's family said that she was dead to them."

Obscured by night, Cora Lee said, "I really must go."

"Pictures of my father?"

"Come by my house and see them. Over on Butler Avenue. Keep me informed about Emmaline."

Since I couldn't sleep, I tried imagining Minnesota and Swedish-owned farms. But mostly images dominated of a Nordic-looking man and an innocent black girl, who decided to be together, to defy families and society....

After midnight—

In a college creative writing class, taken as part of my English requirement, the professor strutted across the front of the room like a banty rooster and in a shrill crow scolded us for "being too literal. Don't be a slave to chronology. Start your story with the most dramatic incident, with what stands out."

That advice popped into my head as I sat near Cammy's dresser, enjoying a cigarette and pondering what to write about this evening. What "stands out" pertains not only to Emily—that I'll sort out later—but to what I learned about Cammy. And that included more than information about Ralston Hamilton. In telling me what she'd not shared with others—not even with Emily—Cammy supplied a lack in my life. Mama never told me her story. All I ever learned about her came through Cora Lee. When Cammy chose to tell about Ralston, I knew a privileged inclusion.

Should I repeat Cammy's story in these pages? If she collects our journals, isn't it redundant to write what she already knows? But what if she's interested in how it sounded to me? Maybe she'd value what I took away, maybe like to know that when I retreated to her/my room, I deleted doubts she'd admitted about raising Emily, that I disregarded all language devoted to emotions that troubled her concerning the characters in Her Story. I bet she'll smile when I confess that I concentrated exclusively on her; that I honored her recital enough to write out my version in long hand, rather like the biographical versions she commits to paper.

In the basement this evening I first experienced a clarity. As her narrative proceeded (yes, in chronological order) I saw a youthful Cammy and felt a thanksgiving that her tale encompassed a timelessness.

"My older sister Amelia and I grew up on a farm north of Centerville," she said. "Until eighth grade, we attended country school. In good weather we could walk, but in winter months Papa drove us or saddled up horses for us to ride.

"Amelia was four years older, so she went on to town school and graduated before I entered my sophomore year. Back then, grades ten to twelve made up high school. Papa and Mama arranged for Amy to board at the vet's home when weather was bad or when she needed to stay in town to sing at night for programs. She had a beautiful voice, a talent that Emily inherited."

I turned to Cammy seated beside me and wondered, not for the first time, if I'd inherited anything from my father.

"The Kerringtons lived in a rental next door to the vet's family. Jared was their oldest son, and that's where the romance started.

"After high school, the two eloped. Mama and Papa were upset because Amy and Jared moved to Denver, another country in my parents' eyes. They never regretted that Amy didn't develop her musical potential, only that she left them.

"I suppose that Papa elected not to board me with the vet's because the Kerringtons had younger sons, so I ended up at the Methodist parsonage with the minister and his wife, Ralston and Florence Hamilton, a kind couple." Cammy rose and from the top file drawer withdrew a photo which she studied. "Florence was older than Ralston, and a few months after they'd married, she'd fallen from a wagon on a church hay ride. Damaged her spine and was confined to a wheelchair.

"During my sophomore year, the winter was mild, so I spent only an occasional night at the Hamilton's." She handed me the photo. Devoid of people, it showed a plain clapboard manse. "They included me in their supper conversation. Florence was hungry for any details about classes, friends, parties. They asked my opinions on politics and religion, listened to my replies and never corrected any ridiculous statement nor imposed their theology. I admired how well she managed from her wheelchair, and I admired the Reverend's consideration. Consideration was never Papa's strong suit." She gave a short laugh. "Each night, the Reverend lifted her from the wheelchair and carried her into the downstairs study that he'd converted into a bedroom for her. He tucked her in, prayed with her, and retired to an office he'd constructed from a supply closet at the church next door. He'd spend hours there, then carefully climb the stairs and ease his bedroom door closed. It was the one other room upstairs under the eaves across from mine."

I examined the picture. Probably the house no longer stood, just as the cottage in which I'd grown up was no more. When Benjamin and I drove to Hampton, we found a brilliant yellow two-story residence and a yard landscaped with rock, where our cottage should have been. I regret I have no picture of where I grew up.

"That summer, when my parents could spare me, I worked for the Hamiltons, did some of the hard cleaning. Hung rugs on the clothes-lines—beat them with the carpet beater—waxed floors, starched curtains. I looked forward to meals with them and talking, no, discussing, because Mrs. Hamilton would smile, 'Now, Camellia, you can't sit there and not enter in. It's not permitted. Speak up. Give us your views.' She read widely, loaned me books, and in her quiet, courteous manner expected me to read them. Biographies particularly intrigued her.

"Florence Hamilton taught me amenities and exposed me to culture. Farm life wasn't easy. There wasn't time or energy to debate Machiavelli, try unusual recipes, create flower arrangements, or set out salad forks.

"Gradually I learned that she was the only child of a wealthy eastern family. I don't mean to imply that's why Ralston married her, but it did mean in that functional parsonage, she could add beauty and quality. She wallpapered rooms with light colors, and she transformed their solemn dining room. To me, the pattern of faint green ferns that wound themselves around slightly darker columns against an off-white background suggested Grecian ruins and English gardens. In the middle of winter, the wallpaper promised summer.

"By my junior year, I was convinced that Florence was brave, brilliant, and cosmopolitan. I spent time with her even when snow plows kept country roads clear, even when weather was nice. Naturally, sometimes I stayed because of a school activity, but usually I simply wanted to be in her house. Determined to be a minister's wife, she'd entertain women's groups or Sunday School classes. I'd serve refreshments, take coats, clean up afterwards. From her, and from Ralston, I also slowly learned about church politics.

"Sometimes I attended service. If I were with them over a weekend, I'd push her wheelchair through a side door and join her in the front pew. She'd beam as Ralston preached. I've said little about him," and she switched to her rocker, as if in this her favorite chair, Cammy could safely venture into a deeper confession, "because initially he was on the periphery. My conversations, interests, and sympathies, meshed with Florence. He was in his late twenties, but to a sixteen-year-old, Ralston seemed an old man, an authority on God. I didn't find him particularly handsome, but I'll grant you that he radiated a certain aura from the pulpit.

"Yet high school boys were much more interesting, and whenever I dated, I spent the night at the parsonage. No matter how quietly I crept in, Florence would call out in a stage whisper, 'Cammy, come tell about your evening.' Taking the chair beside her single bed, I'd reconstruct the date.'"

I closed my eyes remembering Mama's interest in Franklin Waverly. While omitting how I'd removed my blouse, I did describe to her movies we'd seen. I don't think Mama and I ever saw a movie.

"When I was a senior, Florence embarked on a college campaign. No one in my family had gone to college. 'It's a waste of money for women,' Papa said. 'They'll just get married anyway.' But Florence said, 'Money's not an issue. I'll pay.' She helped me apply to a Methodist liberal arts school, and as part of her intellectual stimulation program, proposed that I 'assist' Ralston with his sermons."

Cammy altered her voice, as if trying to copy Florence's. "'You can edit them, check quotations, examine their structure. Now, dear, I'm not hinting that you need it,' she smiled at Ralston, 'but it would be highly instructive for Cammy.'

"That spring I worked beside Ralston in the tiny church study, and that spring we fell in love." She gazed at the distant wall, avoiding my eyes. "I didn't realize it, or more accurately, didn't admit it, nor did he. Later, before we faced it, I attributed the chemistry to spring air that poured through the open window combating the musty sanctuary odor. I blamed my unsettled emotions—sorrow at upcoming graduation and excitement about college. I blamed our close proximity in that crowded room, blamed our talks, and the attention he gave me.

"I wanted to spend every day at the parsonage," and she smoothed her hand over the face of the picture, "wanted to move in, but I had obligations at the farm. When I received my acceptance letter from college, Mama said, 'That's it. I've lost both of my daughters.' They rarely heard from Amy, and the Kerrington family had left town in the middle of the night with the rent unpaid, so my parents had no chance of contact with Amy through them.

"'We lost both of them because of town living,' Papa said, adding rude comments about the Hamiltons. Therefore, throughout the next two years, while I attended college, I generally stayed at the parsonage during vacations and merely paid day visits to the farm.

"At the Hamiltons', I memorized Ralston's motions, the way his lips turned a bit at the right when he smiled, the way he invariably crossed his right leg over his left…so that in my bedroom at night— directly above Florence's room—I could bask in them."

Well I remembered memorizing Tyler's motions. For an instant, I saw him anew, walking tall and straight toward me after graduation, but the image faded as I recalled Benjamin, a streak of gray in his hair. Bent over the light table in the print shop, he cocked his head at my approach. His face brightened, and he abandoned the negative he was examining. Carefully, he unrolled his shirt sleeves that exposed firm forearms and carefully buttoned his cuffs. Then, as if presentable, he walked to where I waited.

"I searched his phrases for hidden implications. When he handed me *Ethan Frome* and said, 'You might like this,' did he mean that he felt toward me as Ethan felt toward Mattie, or did he simply believe that the novel warranted discussion as much as did Florence's biographies?

"Before sleep, I'd scold myself, 'Camellia, this is wrong. Ralston loves Florence and that's absolutely right. No woman's ever been as kind, as instructional as she's been. Why she nicknamed you "Cammy." You can't hurt her.

"I existed in this limbo land until the summer before my junior year at college. It was the end of June, the twenty-ninth, and I'd just helped Florence to bed so she could nap after she'd led an afternoon Bible study in the living room. I'd served pineapple upside down cake, so I washed the clear dessert plates. Elongated ovals, they had depressions where delicate tinted cups could fit (designed, I'm sure, for tea, they held coffee regardless of the season).

"The phone rang. I wiped my hands and lifted the wall receiver." Apparently unaware that her right hand rose as if reaching for the phone, Cammy continued talking. "Because of the muffled words, as if someone pressed a Rainbow Bread wrapper to his or her mouth, I thought it was a prank call; then I heard 'Camellia?'

"In an incoherent stream, Mother—for it was she with the strangled voice—finally made me understand that Amy and Jared were dead. Their car had smashed into a bridge abutment, but their baby Emily was unhurt.

"I scooted a chair across the kitchen floor, sat down, and inspected the dull daubs in the linoleum. If I blinked my eyes, they flashed like minnows. I don't remember getting up, running to the church, or beating on Ralston's study door.

"I do recall fragments." Now she turned to me, as if I should be included, "Sitting beside Ralston as he drove us to the farm, the stark kitchen light bulb that revealed Papa without teeth. Either he'd forgotten his dentures or had decided against wearing them. In some frenzy, Mama peeled potato after potato and, as if reciting a litany, chanted, 'Camellia, you take the baby. We can't raise it. You take the baby.'

"Ralston handled the practical aspects, the funeral, purchasing burial plots in the Elmwood Cemetery because they were cheaper than in Centerville. To my knowledge, my parents never paid him.

"Florence brightened at the idea of a baby in the house." Cammy stopped.

Baby in the house. After Benjamin and I married, I, too, longed for a baby in the house, but it never happened. Some nights when I told him how desperately I wanted a child, he held me, saying that his three sons were mine. And so they have become.

"'We'll put a crib in your room. The women's circle can give, if not a shower, then a "Welcome Emily" party. Oh, I did so want a child. Emily's presence will enrich all our lives.'

"Amy and Jared's bodies traveled by train from Denver, but I needed to go for my niece. Whether Florence suggested that Ralston drive me to Denver or whether he convinced her, I'll never know. But he and I set out in his black Ford after Minnie Scully, a church member, arrived to stay with Florence.

"I could make a case that Emily determined my life, but I could also argue that the trip transformed everything. Alone with Ralston." Cammy sat straighter, but still she couldn't form complete sentences. "...the freedom that traveling gives...it seemed we weren't account-able...we could be...together.

"I carried Emily into the parsonage." She laid the picture face down on the library table. "Florence beamed from her wheelchair, but as we neared, her smile faltered. I knew she knew. She said nothing then nor later, but a barrier had snapped in place between us.

"Florence cradled Emily, called her 'precious,' raised her cheek for Ralston's kiss, complimented Minnie on her expert care, and without resorting to a list, recited Ralston's phone messages. All appeared nor-mal, but it wasn't.

"Guilt, seasoned with grief, shrouded me like a black cloak, impairing my speech and my actions. We got through the funerals, and then Florence announced at the supper table that the Benekee house, over on Polk Street, was for sale. 'I'll buy it for you, Cammy. It's selfish of me to hold you and Emily here in one upstairs bedroom. Soon the child will need her own room, more space, a house with a yard.'"

"However, she wasn't thinking of Emily, but of removing me from Ralston. I have no idea why she chose this house. Why she didn't rent an apartment or kick me out, remains a mystery. I like to think that she still cared for me. I'd been her closest woman friend."

I let that phrase, woman friend, wrap around me. Emily had been my closest woman friend, and suddenly I ached for her.

"Often Florence had repeated, 'You're the younger sister I never had.' Despite my affair with her husband, perhaps those original feel-ings for me still counted.

"Although I protested the generosity, it was a hollow protest. Within a month, Emily and I were in 731 Polk with the bedroom fur-nishings I'd used at the Hamiltons'. From church women, Florence amassed the basics, augmented by items from the farm. I'm confident that my parents or that church members suspected nothing at that time. They praised Florence for caring and for planning for our future.

"Where was Ralston in all this?" Her shrug was one of defeat. "As distressed, as in conflict, as I. We avoided each other. While awaiting my move to this house, I'd lie in that parsonage bed with Emily beside me and would listen as his door shut at night. Floorboards would sway, and I'd battle the urge to cross that narrow hallway.

"After I was installed here, with assurances from Florence and my parents that I shouldn't get a job, should devote all my energies to Emily so she'd outgrow any possible trauma from her parents' death, I realized how long and empty my days would be. College was over."

College was over. I'd felt the same finality as Cammy had. In the few months that Mama had been a student, had she treasured classes? Had she hoped someday to go back?

"Weeks passed. I took Emily to visit Florence, who was cordial. She'd hired Minnie, so didn't 'require any further services from you.' I slipped into church on Sunday mornings to see Ralston in the pulpit and to hear his voice.

"One September night so hot I couldn't sleep, I rested on the front porch and thought so strongly about him that my thoughts must have invaded the church study where he was writing his sermon. Instead of going home, he walked here.

"Afterward...we vowed not to do this again, but it was an empty promise. However, over the next few years, someone spotted Ralston as he left in the middle of the night. Rumors spread. I'd like to think that they never reached Florence. And people shunned me."

I nearly interrupted Cammy's speech, nearly said, "Shunning is similar to being ignored."

"On Christmas Eve night, before the congregation could accuse Ralston or take any action, part of the church burned. Apparently, after the service, some worshipper hadn't completely extinguished a candle. Ralston dashed into his study for his books and was overcome by smoke.

"After his funeral, Florence invited me to stop by. *This is it,* I thought. *She'll denounce me.* Instead, she told of her move to a Methodist nursing facility in Wisconsin. 'Take any of the household furniture you'd like,' she said. 'I'll continue sending your monthly stipend.'

"As before, I objected, but she stared at me. Finally I offered my help with her move, and then I gushed, telling her, quite truthfully, that she'd done more for me than anyone. 'I'll never forget you,' I said. 'I'll be forever indebted.' From her wheelchair she maintained her stare, and it went through me. Ashamed, I faltered. Florence extended her hand, and I shook it, acutely conscious of its warmth and softness as if over the years the bones had melted.

"That impression remained, and I wondered if it signaled that Ralston and my relationship had sapped her strength, or if it showed that her softness disguised strength, or if the softness implied that she'd assimilated her hurt and had forgiven me.

"I asked for this library table upon which Ralston wrote his sermons. Miraculously it survived the fire. On the leg, to your left, is a scorch mark."

As I traced my fingers over the blistered mark, I thought about the precious few possessions of Mama's that I had and the one necklace from Tyler. Such limited tangible pieces to hold. Yet, Benjamin declared that in such scarcity lay value, for it allowed me to build a life with him.

"The dining room table and chairs belonged to Florence, as did the desk in my parlor. My bed, the one you're sleeping on, is the one I slept in at the Hamilton's. Some of the other furniture—that I didn't buy— is from the farm. When my parents died, I inherited that property. For a while I rented it, then sold it for a fair price. I invested the money, and that income, plus money from Florence, provided for Emily and me.

"After she left Centerville, I never saw Florence, never heard from her. She died at the nursing home, leaving me as her beneficiary. There she was buried, so I'll be buried beside Ralston in the last of the plots he purchased."

From her story I extract many parallels: growing up without resources: realizing that Mama and Cammy had both been estranged from their parents: understanding that Emily and I, as only children, had known mother figures, never fathers; identifying with Cammy's sense of isolation; of being the other, of loving an unobtainable man—

Well, I'm tired, so my organization and rationale is likely unclear. In the morning I'll complete My Story, or the completion to this point of a story I didn't conclude in the basement, for after her lengthy account Cammy was altered. I felt what she told me was something she'd not examined from beginning to end in decades— maybe never. When she finished, her voice was throaty from hour after hour of explaining. She was withdrawn, physically changed

I walked to the rocker (was it Ralston's?) and kissed her forehead. Contrary to the softness she'd mentioned in regard to Florence, I met firmness when I rested my cheek against her temple.

ANN

Monday—3:30 A.M.

I'm not re-reading any of this. If I did, undoubtedly, I'd cross out portions or tear up the entire journal. Then later today, I'd face Cammy with false arrogance. "I've nothing to hand you," I'd say if she asked for my "memory book."

By not re-reading, I'm not sure exactly where I stopped writing, but think it was almost twenty-four hours ago after I left Chris at her home—a square "modest" house, as the euphemism goes—where I can't imagine raising four children. It reminds me of the tract houses near Crawford School, occupied primarily by Latino families. Em enrolled in Spanish classes at night school, so she could communicate and correctly pronounce words in the Spanish songs she introduced to her students. She hunted information about Mexican composers. Will her replacement be that dedicated?

When we filed into Spencer's on Sunday morning, I was glad that Em had never been there. It's a restaurant attempting to be more than it is, like a posturing actor unaware he's delivered a melodramatic performance. Em should be remembered as a Rosie's Diner woman. But to Cammy, and apparently to Chris, Spencer's spelled quality.

In that artifical atmosphere, we four assumed another coloration. Perhaps that fakery contributed to the problem on those interminable rides to and from the cemetery. God, I hate cemeteries. All of us were lost there. No epiphanies. No "closure"—a preposterous concept I hate as much as cemeteries. My one "good" moment occurred as we left. On the exposed hill of dirt that concealed Em's coffin, I noticed a triangular rock, shiny with moisture. Black, it matched Em's hair. It belongs in California on Robin's grave.

Back at Cammy's, I lay on "my" bed, as Chris took off and Savannah headed downstairs, I presume into the basement with Cammy. I tried to think about Em, about Seth, about Dirk, but as if mirroring the day, my thoughts resisted honesty and no revelations emerged.

When I woke up, silvered light streamed through the window panes, and as I lay appreciating oblongs that glittered on the floor, I felt better, heard friendly noises below.

In the dining room, Savannah and Cammy set a table gentled by the chandelier's glow. "Nice," I said in greeting.

"Emily installed a dimmer switch one Christmas." Ah, Cammy, too, seemed more relaxed and wasn't distributing photos by each plate. I could get through this evening. Apparently we three guests shared that goal and tried to compensate for a less-than-satisfactory day. (I could imagine Em's laugh as she said, "A C+ day, Ann.") We were conscious that this time tomorrow, we'd be back in other lives where other concerns would reduce this weekend into a smaller and smaller package.

Around the table, we made an extra effort to laugh at any half-humorous remarks, to nod supportively at any vignette, to prompt Cammy in recounting Em's childhood—experiences universal and yet specific. We willed good will.

After strawberry shortcake topped with whipping cream so rich that with every bite my waistband tightened, and globs of fat spread through every artery, Cammy invited us into the parlor.

Along that wall, Em's hospital bed had stood. Was the window the last thing she saw? The desk? The piano? I'd choose the latter, its keys encased by the wooden fall board. In her apartment, Em's piano was always open. "Keys should be exposed," she said, "should act as magnets so you'll touch them. A closed piano keyboard says, 'hands off.'"

On this cool evening, the coffee Cammy poured tasted good. We formed a rough semi-circle of chairs around Cammy's desk chair. In the ensuing silence, as we awaited direction from her, I said, "I'm not sure if this is the right moment or not, but what should I do about Em's apartment?"

China cups stayed flat against china saucers. Eyes regarded me without expression. "I mean, I have a key, her other key. Rent's due September one, so everything must be out in another ten days or so."

With no response, I struggled ahead. "Should I put everything into storage? Hold a yard sale? Would any of you come help me? Cammy?"

Sitting tall, affecting that patrician manner, she slowly ran her palms along her skirt, from hip to knees. "You knew Emily best at the end. What would she like?"

You knew her best. With such an admission, I blinked away tears.

"It'll be hard for you," Chris said. "If only to give moral support, I suppose I could come help you with the apartment, but I have my hands full with family problems."

"Savannah?"

"I could," she answered, but her tone said, "*I don't want to.*" "Benjamin's inspired about possibly buying a print shop, but he certainly can get along without me for a couple days."

"Cammy?"

"It would…be interesting…Emily's apartment…where she taught, but I have my own mental pictures…I…

As if on cue, we drank our coffee. "We don't have to decide tonight. I—"

"But we do," Cammy interrupted me. "I was indecisive a second ago. Today was indecisive, and I feel bad about it. I don't want to travel to California unless it's necessary. I don't need, or really want, to see her surroundings. With your words and your animation, you three have given me what I need. So, Ann, why not select one item for each of us. Something of Emily's that you think she'd like us to have and send it. I'll pay the expenses."

One thing for each. Alone, then, I'd sort through all her belongings, closets, and drawers. I'd rummage through her desk, but I didn't have to be alone. I could count on Seth to go into those closed-up rooms with me. Probably he'd say, "Like me to start on the desk?" I flashed onto it and the office chair beside it. Usually her orange cardigan—she'd bought an extra large size because it was the only one in stock—hung from its back, nearly grazing the rug. It might fit Savannah, complement her lovely complexion.

Again, Cammy rubbed palms the length of her thighs. "Tonight I'll play us a tape of Emily's." She brought a cheap recorder from the room's closet, centered it on the desk, and inserted a cassette. "It's from a high school concert." She depressed the play button and the tape whirred, introducing audience sounds: rustles, coughs, throat clearings. A pianist hit beginning chords to "Go, Tell It on the Mountain." The speaker spilled out tinny, metallic piano and choral notes. But when the solo commenced, Em's youthful richness cancelled technical limitations. With careful enunciation, she sang, "When I was a seeker, I sought both night and day." She had something. She really did, some enchantment.

To my right, Chris masked her face with her hands. "*Ignore her sobs,*" I told myself. "*Fill your mind with Em's voice. Re-create times you've heard her sing.*" Beyond that initial encounter at school when she redefined "Barbara Allan," there'd been a faculty talent show and her "Autumn Leaves" charged with poignancy. In an East Bay piano bar, she'd sung along with a pianist, entertaining customers for part of an evening with show tunes. When she performed a medley of Christmas songs for a women's group, she asked if I'd like to come along. When she finished "I'll Be Home for Christmas," the audience, washed by nostalgia, couldn't clap for several seconds. Cammy found a handkerchief in her pants' pocket, but Savannah, as if resolved not to cry, stared at a Grant Wood reproduction on the opposite wall.

Applause burst from the recorder; then Em sang once more, joined by Dirk. As my mouth dried, I stared at the floral carpeting so no one could detect the naked heat that must be evident on my face. Even on this gospel number, his teenage voice transmitted a sexuality. Then their voices merged. How natural they sounded together. His voice wrapped around hers, and hers broke free to urge his on before he teased a sustained note from Em.

If on this inexpensive recorder, if on an unprofessionally produced cassette they sounded this outstanding, they must have thrilled

Centerville audiences. Dirk's voice, though, stemmed Cammy's sorrow, for when he followed with a solo, she tucked the hanky back in her pocket. "He couldn't even read music. He never practiced or studied like she did."

"It shows," Chris loyally agreed. "Emily Jane was superior."

Savannah muttered some truism backing Cammy's statement, but I kept quiet. He sounded damned fine to me. The two were equals. As the remainder of the tape wound around its spindle, I thought, *This is similar to watching old movies.* I can enjoy a Clark Gable or a Judy Garland film and never brood over the fact that they're no longer alive. I don't feel sad that if they were living they'd be aged, removed from the youthful bodies on the screen. The tape represented yesterday. The Dirk on that stage had evolved into the Dirk of last night.

How had he spent his day? Driven back roads? Lain on the bed in the motel?

If so, he'd not have worn a shirt. Jeans slack around his waist would show skin, because he'd not have bothered with underwear after his morning shower. Had he strummed his guitar? Been by himself?

When the phone rang, the women started. I didn't. I'd been expecting his call.

"When can you get away?" he asked.

"Not sure," I whispered into the mouthpiece.

"About midnight, I'll park in the next block, where I was last night, and wait."

As exhilarated as one who gets news that her painting's sold, as one who hears she's won a contest or doesn't have a feared disease, I had to struggle to compose myself. In the hall's half-light, items around me were clear; extra clear. The newel post jutted out prominently, lines and angles distinct. The cove mold on the stairs poked through the gloom. From the front door, I saw a yellow fan from the streetlight stain the curb. With such acute vision, I surveyed the women in the parlor who seemed raised from the background, superimposed against the desk, the wall, the Grant Wood print.

NOTES WHEN SUMMER ENDS

As if posed for a still life, they did not move while the high school chorus concluded, "Give Me Your Tired, Your Poor." Carefully I sat and checked the wall clock on my left. Almost 9:00. I must corral my desire, must be in this moment, so I studied the black recorder with its one final choral arrangement. Long applause; yet the recorder's wheels revolved. Of course, an encore. Em and Dirk sang "Autumn Leaves." Their plaintive duet resonated and in many respects surpassed her solo at the faculty talent show.

The sobs I swallowed felt rock-like, but I mustn't cry. Like a champagne bottle when the cork's released, my sobs would rush out. And like an open champagne bottle, the cork wouldn't easily be reinserted. I would become as distraught as I had at Robin's death, a period so dark and dreadful that I could not go there again. I groped for something neutral with which to distract myself. What about classroom projects? Maybe the first one should be a cartoon series based on the kids' summer experiences? What about sand painting or twig weaving? A calendar? With balmy September weather, we could go outdoors, draw the school building and trees in the foreground for a lesson in perspective.

Mercifully the tape ended. Tiredness and defeat crept into the room. "Once more," Cammy said, "I've done the wrong thing. I imagined that the tape would generate more memories, that each of you might contribute something, well, insightful, so that on this final night, we'd take away something unforgettable. Instead we're depressed."

"Perhaps a shared depression is necessary," Savannah said. "At black funerals, people mourn and wail, while most white people believe in stoicism. They'll do anything to avoid breaking down, to keep emotions at bay."

Chris nodded. "You're right. We all miss her, miss her dreadfully." She blew her nose. "It's stupid to try and fool ourselves by recalling only moments with Emily Jane about which we can laugh."

"For me," Cammy tapped her fingers on the recorder, "the tape was more distressing because of Dirk. I'd not listened to it since I bought it, had forgotten that he had as many numbers as she did."

"Why didn't you ever like him?" I asked.

Her eyes sparked. I'd hit a nerve. "It wasn't a question of like. He was, probably still is, a likeable fellow. Considering the family he came from, guess he's done well, but he turned her head. He charmed her so completely that she wouldn't even look at another boy, wouldn't develop her talent. She chose Monroe, a college not noted for music, with an inferior program, because it was the campus closest to Centerville and him. She could have been so much more.... The kindest thing Dirk did for her was to marry someone else. At least, the marriage pushed her out of the state and into teaching."

"Emily retained a blind spot for him, that's for sure. She didn't date much when we were in college and when she did, the guy failed to measure up."

"I resented, as well, that Dirk influenced our relationship," Cammy said. "Since Emily knew how I felt about him, she blocked off that part of her life from me. She'd slip away to meet him, or not tell me of events where he was." Cammy pulled at the knob on the narrow middle desk drawer. High school yearbooks fit inside. Grouped behind her, we scanned pictures as she flipped the pages to a collage of candid shots in the choral section. Em and Dirk. Usually her lips were parted as if on the verge of laughter. Usually he wore that defiant smile, and I couldn't refrain from smiling back.

The annuals unleashed Chris's stories, ones so freshly told that they might have happened yesterday: of Em's bid for class secretary, of Em fainting in biology class at a cat dissection, of Em missing a music festival due to laryngitis. We loved them, and I was amazed at her vivid recollections. For me, high school memories are misty.

With Chris's exuberance, with Cammy obviously pleased at this upbeat turn, a luster settled over the evening. Granted the word "nice" is overused, but it summed up the atmosphere. It *was* nice, probably what Cammy had desired for the entire weekend.

When the phone rang for a second time, I jumped. Dirk couldn't make it? Had changed his mind? I ran to the hallway. The receiver was cold against my ear.

"Can I please speak to Mom?"

Mom? This wasn't a Mom house. None of us had living children—except for Chris. When she left the room to answer the phone, the stories ended in the parlor. As Cammy closed the drawer on the yearbooks, Savannah and I reiterated how we'd benefited from the dip into a past so vibrantly alive to Chris.

"We each have a section of Emily's life," Savannah said.

"That's all we ever have of anyone, isn't it?" I answered. "Even if you live with someone, you never share everything. Even if you raise a child from birth and are close for years, you see only what you want to see or what that person allows you to see." And Robin. What would she now withhold? What would I forever withhold from her?

When Chris came back into the room, she looked tired and instantly agreed when Cammy yawned and said, "It's growing late."

I climbed the stairs with Chris, and out of range of the others, she asked, "You're meeting Dirk?"

"In about an hour. It still bothers you?"

She sighed. "I don't know. Guess not. Don't really know what bothers me. Mom used to say when upset that things were at sixes and sevens."

"There's more then than Dirk and me."

As if trying to relax tense muscles, she hunched her shoulders, rotated her head. "Yep. The latest, that call from my daughter Heather, was to let me know that she'd come in from work determined to call her brother Greg. He's in Montana and phoned today with news that he's married, a total shocker. Heather talked to new wife, who asked her to close her eyes, bow her head, and after a 'rambling' prayer, quoted Bible verses, ones that Heather insists were 'threatening.' 'She's unbalanced, Mom,' Heather said. 'We've got to get Greg away from her.'"

"You've not talked to his new wife?"

"Not yet, but I assured Heather that I'll call tomorrow."

"Maybe new wife's joking or drunk or—"

"Celia, that's the new wife's name. Knowing Greg the little that I do—he's my most unknowable child—he's likely gotten involved with some religious nut." Unexpectedly, Chris patted my upper arm, imprinting a tenderness. *She must be a great mother,* I thought, *in whose lap a child could cuddle, protected temporarily against the world.*

"Emily Jane would assure me that it will all work out," she said. "I'll cling to that belief and go on to bed."

As water filled the bathtub, I laid out fresh underwear, rejected a pair of snug jeans because they'd not easily slide off my hips, and settled for a full skirt, a blue short-sleeved blouse with buttons conveniently down the front, and sandals with but a single clasp on their thin straps.

In the medicine cabinet, I found a vial of bath salts to use instead of the practical generic soap bar. As lavender crystals foamed beneath the faucet's pressure I realized that they must be Em's. I would carry her scent with me tonight. *Em,* I thought, *I hope you'd relish this, me immersed in your fragrance, preparing for your old lover, a man for whom I pure and simply lust.* But as the bath bubbles dissolved, and as the water slowly cooled, I wondered why I was going tonight, wondered what I was really doing. Abruptly, I pulled the chain attached to the tub's plug. I'd not get into analyzing or justifying. Sex, like an opiate, could supplant worry, alleviate grief. Reason enough.

Quickly I dressed and walking as quietly as possible, I descended to the front hallway. A dim light shone from an empty kitchen. Savannah and Cammy must be in the basement. I stepped onto the porch. Although rain had moved on, it had left coolness as remembrance. For warmth I hugged my arms as I hurried along the sidewalk.

Did he sense my movement? Spot my light blouse? The parking lights flashed on, and I climbed into the black truck. He scooted over from behind the steering wheel. In his arms, I sought his mouth. With a smile he raised his head and asked, "What's the latest back there?" motioning in the direction of Cammy's house. So Em was uppermost on his mind. My body calmed and I recapped the evening, the tape, and Chris's memories.

"Yah, those were good times."

I appreciated the fact that he kept his arm around me, that in that fashion Dirk included me while he entered the stories I could merely repeat.

"What else did you do today?"

I described the brunch, but when I began on the cemetery trip, his arm tightened on my shoulder. "Emily Jane's buried? In Elmwood?"

"By her parents, and yes," I said as he started to interrupt, "Cammy vowed that she's Em's aunt and not her mother."

"Hold on." He stretched over the seat back for a bottle of beer and surprised me with an individual-sized bottle of wine. "It's chilled," he grinned, "but forget about a glass."

As Dirk opened his beer, I broke the seal, unscrewed the cap. We drank, our swallows the lone sound, until he asked, "Why Elmwood?"

"A family friend, a Ralston Hamilton, apparently paid for the plots."

He pursed his lips in a beats-me attitude. "Must be a friend of Cammy's. Know nothing about her. She and me aren't exactly buddies."

As I colored in the graveyard picture, Dirk listened in cursory fashion, but he was elsewhere. Back in teenaged days? Re-creating the last time he'd seen Em? Had she sat in this truck in this same spot? My words came more slowly, and when I paused mid-sentence, he arched his right eyebrow. "Let's go."

"To Elmwood?"

"Yah, show me her grave."

"At 12:30! Hey, I'm no fan of cemeteries. I—"

"You're leaving tomorrow, and I'm taking off at daybreak. This is my one chance."

Under the steering wheel, he stuck the beer between his thighs and turned the ignition key. Town streets were empty as was the road to Elmwood. We could have been the only people awake in the entire area, and what people we were. I smiled as I thought, *What about this, Em? Me in the Heartland, driving at seventy-five per to your grave in the middle of the night.*

The truck headlights played across the grilled gate secured with a padlock. "Out of luck," I said, but he killed the lights and the motor.

"We'll climb over. You can do it. You've great strong legs. Some twenty-four hours later I still have sore ribs."

Just that line, just that glance, rekindled desire. I finished the wine and followed him in blackness broken by the bobbing shaft of light from his flashlight. He shook the gates and judged their height before we eased along the perimeter. Every three feet or so, a pointed iron stake supported the fence. But near the back, he spotted a bent stake. "I'll boost you."

Had I foreseen breaking into a graveyard and not making love in a pickup, I'd have chosen jeans, but with Dirk guiding my legs, with my left hand clutching my skirt and with my right tugging on the stake, I cleared the top of the fence. With one fluid jump, he landed beside me. From here, I had no idea the location of Em's grave, so we worked our way toward the gate, where I hoped I could retrace Cammy's route.

My sandals squished against the wet, and spears of grass flecked droplets across my instep in a curiously erotic sensation, similar to what I felt when David used to blow lightly across my cheek, exciting a nerve. As if wired to sensual circuitry, that touch aroused me. The moisture released the loamy scent of earth. Among these tombstones, it spoke of fecundity.

As if attuned to my reactions, Dirk pulled me close. We collided with each other as we tried to walk, so he laughed and kissed my forehead. "You're a real sport, Ann. No wonder Emily Jane loved you."

Loved me. Strange, I'd never affixed that label to our friendship, but, of course, I had loved her. Aiming the flashlight along the road, he moved ahead of me. Did Em have any wild premonition that Dirk and I would be together? Incidents abound of a dying person, usually a spouse, selecting the future partner for their wife/husband. Yet Dirk and I would not be together. He certainly had a woman somewhere, and I had Seth—I think.

When the roving beam homed in on the brown/black mound, he stopped. My ankles and calves were completely soaked, and beside him

173

NOTES WHEN SUMMER ENDS

I thought not of Em or even of passion, but of dry feet. He flicked off the flashlight and with a skilled sure-footedness walked away. To cry? I moved to the left, to Amy's tombstone, and backed against it. In this environment I should think profoundly, I instructed myself, should imagine Em's mother who had been denied her daughter, should feel some kinship with her, or I should experience some transcendental moment. Instead, I experienced dampness, a certain discomfort, and an increasing sensitivity to night music—moisture leaking from pine boughs, crickets serenading, a cow bawling in some pasture, an owl answering another, and my pulse humming an undercurrent of desire.

Minutes later I heard the crinkle of Dirk's jeans as he approached. He switched on the flashlight and laid a plastic floral arrangement at one end of Em's grave.

"Did you steal that?"

He laughed. "Just relieved a grave that was burdened with far too many."

I stepped closer. "Are the flowers pink?"

"Nearest I could come to orange."

"Always her favorite color?"

"Yah." He chuckled. "You ever known anyone who had orange as a favorite color?"

He glided the light over Jared Kerrington's gravestone, Amy Kerrington's gravestone, and Ralston Hamilton's granite marker before inching it along Em's unmarked plot. "She'd have laughed at my being here at night," he said. He didn't sound sad or wistful. Taking my hand, he knitted his fingers with mine. That's how we stood beside her grave. Once I thought he was about to speak, but apparently changing his mind, he nodded. Quite simply that was it. We retreated to the bent stake, where Dirk helped me over the fence.

In the truck he rummaged behind the seat, bringing forward crumpled fabric. A jacket? towel? sweatshirt? He reached for my left foot, brought my leg toward him, yanked off the sandal without bothering with the buckle and enfolded my bare foot with the cloth—a sweatshirt. Through the layer I felt his thumb and forefinger encompass my little toe. Gently, he dried it. Then his thumb and forefinger selected the fourth toe. They rubbed the cloth up and down the top of my toe, over the knuckle; up and down the base of the toe. On to the next one. Leisurely, rhythmically, he slid his fingers up, down in an insistent beat.

My breathing corresponded to the tempo of his motion, and my body warmed, relaxed. I pressed my head against the passenger side window, hoping that my hair might paste a slight oily stain upon the glass so that tomorrow when he drove further and further from Centerville, he could glance to his right and notice a tangible clue that I'd been in his life.

My left foot rested in his lap as he caressed my big toe. I raised my right leg so he could toss that sandal onto the floor mat. Again he swaddled my foot before massaging each toe. Dirk moved the sweatshirt to my ankles, rubbing them in his deliberate cadence.

I slipped down on the seat. His hands gloved in the sweatshirt advanced to my calves. Stroke, stroke. He nudged my skirt upward, and the sweatshirt brushed my inner thighs. Stroking, climbing, the material met the silk of my panties. Through two layers of cloth, his heat met mine. He tossed the sweatshirt behind the seat and unzipped his fly. For hard, fast minutes, Em, cemeteries, Seth, Morgan, and the group at Cammy's did not exist, never had. This, the finale of the evening, sang just for me in clear, fine notes.

He lay on top me, my left arm pinned against the seat back. With my right I stroked his hair, wiry to the touch, and traced the whorls of his ear. "Thank you," I said.

"Thank you?" I treasured how the vibration of his question rumbled from his chest into mine.

"For drying my feet, for the fantastic sex."

"We're not half bad for beginners, are we?" he kidded as he sat up. For a second I feared he'd launch into some revelation about Em, such as "Emily Jane and I had great sex," or "You and I are almost as finely tuned as Emily Jane and I were."

Instead, he asked, "Beer?"

"Why not." When I sat up, smelling the aftermath of love making, he tugged my feet back into his lap. We clinked our bottles in some unspoken toast before he asked, "When do you take off tomorrow?"

"Plane's supposed to leave at 1:30."

"Then?"

I told him of my marriage, about Seth and Morgan, about returning to the classroom, about cleaning out Em's apartment. "And you?" I asked.

"Am heading back to Houston."

"And a wife?"

"Well, let's say I have papers that prove I'm married, but it's debatable if she's exactly a wife." The explanation stopped there, but he mentioned assorted children, his job at a pesticide company, occasional gigs. "Normally I play alone at some down and out bars." It was an ideal moment for him to recall Em, but he didn't say her name again during the ride to Centerville. But before Cammy's darkened rectangle of a house, he pulled a dog-eared business card from his wallet. "When you go through Emily Jane's stuff, if you find anything I should have, here's my address."

"Okay." My fingers searched for the door handle, but he caught my wrist.

"Not sure what to say, Ann, but you and I surely did ignite a few fires. In some way we're on the same wavelength. Wish—" he shrugged. "Doesn't do much good to wish."

At that, I kissed him, thinking, *Dirk Hawkins, you made a wish of mine come true, one I didn't even know I had.*

On the porch I was tempted to turn around, watch the black truck roll on down the street, watch the tail lights disappear. I didn't. I went into Cammy's house.

CHRIS

Monday afternoon

It seems strange to be writing in this journal at my kitchen table. I should write in Emily Jane's room, but our whatever-it-was is over. Three hours ago, Ann left for the airport. She surprised me—think she surprised all of us—with goodbye hugs. When she hugged Cammy, at the last, Cammy cried. This astonished me/us as Cammy has been composed.

Quickly Ann said, "Why not reconsider? Fly out to California and help me with Em's (Emily Jane's—my interpretation) apartment."

"No, I'm too old for that. I haven't traveled before, and I don't intend to now. I'll stay put. You just send me something." That reminded Savannah and me to give our addresses, which Ann entered in one of those pocket organizers. We started to leave the room with her, to go with her to the rental car, but Ann, with a let-me-alone attitude picked up her bag. How can she pack everything in a carry-on? I needed two trunk-sized suitcases when I went to Chicago. "Don't come outside. Waving goodbye is rather anti-climactic." She walked briskly away. Actually, she marched because her heels tapped out a meaning against the front hallway floor, and the screen snapped shut behind her.

We listened for her car engine. Minutes passed before we heard it and before she drove off. Now the atmosphere was different, and although Cammy said, "More coffee, Chris?" I declined. Ann's word, "anti-climactic," summed it up. The weekend was over, and today's demands had invaded this house.

"I'll get my stuff." I climbed the stairs. Would this be the final time? Probably. No one had suggested another meeting, no yearly "let's remember Emily Jane" reunion, and that was okay.

NOTES WHEN SUMMER ENDS

I hesitated at the doorway into Emily Jane's bedroom. As Cammy had asked, I'd removed the sheets and wadded them into a ball at the foot of the bed. But I wished I hadn't, because the stripped bed reminded me of a hospital bed after a patient's death. Like a sharp, painful symbol, it said, "Don't kid yourself. Regardless of this weekend, regardless of the laughs, Emily Jane is dead, and this room is dead." I hurried to cram my things into a plastic bag and stuck the journal on top, because at breakfast Cammy had said, "Keep your journals. At first I intended to ask for them when you left, but they're yours—your thoughts, your stories. I have to write my own version of her. I can't borrow yours."

That statement freed us, I guess, because almost immediately, our sentences overlapped one another as if we had too much to say about Emily Jane and were out of time. We echoed how much we'd miss her, how much she'd influenced our lives. We didn't struggle for amusing anecdotes, but sat there and were sad.

With a last glance at the room, I slung the bag in Santa Claus style over my shoulder. At the bottom of the stairs, I detoured into the parlor. Last night, when we'd been in here, I'd spotted a booklet on family home safety tips lying on a shelf. In thick black lines, as if using a felt marker, the artist had sketched a man directing a fire extinguisher at a blazing barbecue grill. The sketch practically cried, "Cut me out," as did the drawing of a child dialing the operator. I could taste the pleasure of directing scissor blades around each figure. Outdated and overlooked, the book was one Cammy didn't use and wouldn't miss. Before I could reconsider, I jammed it in the bag under my dirty sweats.

I said goodbye to Savannah and Cammy. In parting, she politely inquired about Mom. As I ambled along the alley shaded by hollyhocks, I wished Mom were lucid, so that I could ask what rumors had once circulated about Cammy. After all these years, I was genuinely curious about her past. Sure, she'd never had friends in the house when Emily Jane and I were young, but I was only hazily aware of that. In the self-centeredness of a kid, I didn't care. I believed that adults didn't really have lives, not like Todd, Dirk, Emily Jane, and I had.

My quiet house smelled of sausage. Todd had fried patties, obviously over high heat as scorched meat particles clung like barnacles to the skillet. I put it to soak in the sink. Yeah, no messages on the machine unless Heather had mistakenly erased them. I dropped my plastic sack in the bedroom, took car keys from the odds and ends tray and drove to Grant's apartment. I banged on the door. "Evan. E-van."

With no answer, I breathed relief. Maybe he had gone to work, so the van and I went to the dry cleaner's where the sign posted on the lawn read "Roofing by Nolan." On the dry cleaner's roof, Evan juggled a bundle of shingles. Those outsized knee pads made him look ungainly, but, oh, so beautiful. He was working! I swung the car into an immediate U-turn praying he didn't see me. He'd think, *She's spying on me.* Well, I was.

For now, for this morning, he was okay, and hope flooded me. Suddenly, I longed for Todd, wanted to say, "It's over. I'm home. Let's celebrate and go to Maverick Hamburgers for supper," so I parked before his shop.

Marvelous, he stood by his desk in the office, wasn't peering down at a motor or up at a car on the lift. I wouldn't have to invent small talk with Mary Beth, his office manager.

Three years older than Todd and me, she'd worked for her father after she graduated. He owned the automotive shop. When he retired and Todd bought the business, Mary Beth came along, like part of the package. Her books always balance, she understands almost as much about parts as do the mechanics, but she's mighty territorial. If, for instance, I phone and say, "May I please speak to Todd," she'll give this impatient sigh—implying is this *really* necessary?—before she agrees to get him or to deliver a message. And if I drop in, she'll roll her eyes and drum her pencil—ticky, ticky, ticky—against her desk (it's bigger than Todd's) as I act friendly. I compliment a bit of clothing or a piece of jewelry or praise her on neatness. "I'll hire you to organize my house," I say in a sweet, admiring tone.

"Anyone can organize if she *really* cares to," she answers, and I think, *With an attitude like that, no wonder you live alone with an arthritic dog.*

When I entered the shop, Todd grinned hello and said, "Mary Beth, carry on. My wife and I are off for coffee." Wonderful. He and I walked half-a-block to Chick's Doughnuts.

"It's like a date," I said.

"That means expensive jelly doughnuts then."

We sort of hunched over at one of those dinky plastic tables with molded seats as part of the unit, drank coffee from Styrofoam cups, and I told of my morning (excluding joy at finding Evan on the job).

"So the 'thing' was a success?"

"Think so. Think somehow Cammy feels better."

"What will she do?"

I tunneled the tip of my tongue into the center of the doughnut that was packed with filling and lapped at the raspberry jelly. "Do? Don't know. What she's always done, I guess. Stay in that house. Maybe I'll visit her sometime."

Contentedly we ate, licked frosting and crumbs from our lips, and sipped coffee, the bottom of the pot kind. Todd talked about a mechanic who'd applied for a job this morning. "He walked in, just as Dirk walked out."

Briefly I'd forgotten Dirk, hadn't heard Ann creep in from being with him last night, and this morning she'd been the last at the breakfast table (after tying up the bathroom for quite a long time), so there'd been no opportunity to speak with her alone.

"Invite him to go with us tonight to Maverick Hamburgers?"

"He's already taken off. He apologized that he'd not dropped by, that he'd not spent time with me. Said 'stuff' had come up."

I'm not sure why I didn't tell Todd about Ann. He wouldn't have been shocked. In fact, he likely knew more about Dirk's women than I'd ever suspected, but some kind of reticence (must check the dictionary, but think that's the word I mean) stopped me. "Say when he'll be back?"

As Todd laughed, I studied how his face reshaped itself. Born in his eyes, laughter traveled to his lips (well, whatever you call that part of the mouth that's on each side of the lips, where laugh lines form), and then radiated outward. I've never tired of watching that. "Nope. Bet he has no idea either. Whenever." As if a switch had been thrown, laughter vanished. Traces didn't linger as they do on some faces. "Said he'd been to Emily Jane's grave."

From Todd's eyes, I probably looked as if a light switch of amazement had been flicked on. "When? How'd he find it?"

In answer, Todd frowned. "He just said he was glad he'd gone. Could accept that Emily Jane is—how did he put it?—'out of songs.'"

Tiredness, sadness, nibbled at my joy. Todd covered my hand with his before he checked the wall clock. "Better get back before Mary Beth fires me."

We strolled toward the shop, speaking of Greg and wife, of Julie and sick baby. At my van in full view of Mary Beth, Todd kissed me, a passionate kiss. "Tonight," he whispered.

"After hamburgers with onions and beer," I promised.

At home I unpacked, tucked the family home safety booklet that I lifted from Cammy's into my hidden stash. I have a strong hunch that I'll soon need to cut out pictures. In the laundry room, I discovered that Heather had dried Mom's clothes, had neatly folded the "old lady dusters," and had piled items in the bag marked with Mom's name and room number. I must remember to thank her. Before delivering the bag to the Care Center, though, and before calling Greg, I decided to bring this journal up to date. With my thumb, I fan the pages I've filled. They're puffy, as if my entries have given the pages life. Impressive. I've never kept a journal, a diary, but I like it.

Okay, Emily Jane, I'm hooked. Sure, I realize future comments will be for me, but they'll be a continuation, at least in my mind, of what we've had, and what we might have had.

ANN

Monday afternoon

My flight to Denver's been delayed, which means I may miss the connecting flight to San Francisco, so seated in the Des Moines terminal I'll complete these last few pages. Easier here than writing on the plane's jiggling tray table. In Denver, if I must take a later plane, I'll phone Seth. His call this morning both surprised and alarmed me.

"I flew in from Santa Barbara last night," he said, "so I'll meet your plane." His voice was as taut as Cammy's screen door spring when stretched to the extreme.

"You have something to tell me that can't wait?"

"No," and the voice uncoiled. "Over this weekend I realized that not only do I miss you but that I need you in my life. I like our marriage. I don't want change."

Silently, I concurred. Could I picture the future without Seth? Definitely. Did I want a future without him? No. We'd built a firm, solid friendship. Em once said, "If Seth were an animal, he'd be an English sheep dog. Big, easy, companionable." True. He and I had created an easy, companionable marriage, sufficient for most of our needs. He and Em had been my dearest friends. Without her, I would depend exclusively on Seth's friendship.

"I've not done, or won't do anything to jeopardize what we have," he went on.

Could I translate that into he'd never care for Morgan in the same way he did for me? Or was he intimating that I'd fabricated more between Morgan and him than there actually was? Could he be referring to protected sex, that he'd never expose me to the possibility of disease, of AIDS....

After giving Seth my flight schedule, I replaced the receiver and let my heart rate stabilize. For the third time in less than eight hours, I stood in Cammy's hallway with a pounding heart beat. The first took place before dawn, while I listened to the sound of Dirk's truck as it stole away from the curb, away from me.

After hours of lying awake, of wrestling with a spectrum of thoughts and emotions, of posing questions without solutions, of poking forgotten images back inside caverns in my mind, I decided to run.

New sun streaked the east as I hit the streets of Centerville. With no humidity, I moved well. My body flowed and quickly I established a rare, but extraordinary pace in which I merged with the elements. As if I were buoyed or propelled ahead on wings, I didn't rip through the air, nor fight a nearly palpable presence as sometimes occurred.

A teenager tossing newspapers onto lawns from his car waved to me. I called, "Hi, boy," to an Irish setter, who thumped his tail against a front fence post at my approach. On the cusp of waking, the town smelled clean, looked pristine. Do towns everywhere look their best at sunrise? Does promise of another day cancel, for short minutes, the errors of yesterday?

Purposefully, I didn't search for Dirk's truck, did not allow the dim notion of spotting his truck to develop into a theme for this run. What if I did meet him? What else could we say?

Better to place him miles down the road, steering with his left hand, seeking with the other for his coffee mug balanced near the tape deck. He'd catch sight of the faint smudge, like a fingerprint on the passenger window. I painted a smile across his lips and inserted a thought—*I'll never forget her*—into his brain before I circled a mini-park across from the courthouse and without breaking stride, returned to 731 Polk Street. Here, I laid my hand on the stair's newel post, grateful for the cool wood as my breathing grew more regular.

After sleeping a couple hours, I took an unhurried shower, thoroughly rinsing away the sweet, sour residue of the night. Although I was late for breakfast, no one commented on my tardiness.

NOTES WHEN SUMMER ENDS

The morning achieved a close, but not intimate, stage necessary for Cammy, and for us, as well. When she unexpectedly declined the journals, I almost insisted, "Take mine. Read about Dirk, possibly understand his importance, his long-term effect on Em and how he's enriched my life." Subconsciously, perhaps, I wanted to introduce Robin, my suffering. Wanted her to understand my marriage and revise her image of a narcissistic California woman who was likely unworthy of Em's friendship.

While Cammy's tears unsettled me, her reminder that I should select something of Em's, coupled with her decision about the journals, apparently planted a fledgling idea. As I left the room, mindful in my concluding survey of the difference between this childhood house and Em's last residence, I resurrected her apartment living room. On her desk in the corner, I'd seen her write in notebooks. Were these diaries? If so, I'd not read them, would send them to Cammy. She, and only she, could share that confidential Em, permanently off limits to Savannah, Chris, and me.

I stowed my bag in the trunk, and as I unlocked the driver's side, saw a glossy paper stuck beneath the wiper blade. A page, torn from a magazine, folded into quarters, opened onto a color photo of a star-packed sky, a near duplicate of the one Saturday night. Across the top, he'd printed "The Old Crone and Her Twin Ducks" and "The Seven Midgets." He'd drawn arrows to constellations. Below the picture the logo of the advertised beer ran at an angle. Em would laugh at this and toss her black hair. "How fitting that Dirk could find a photo of dual loves: beer and a sky that spells out sex."

Next I wondered, did he hunt for such a picture? Stumble across it? No matter. He'd thought of me....

Now people in surrounding seats gather purses, papers, bags, for an announcement over the loud speaker directs Denver passengers to Gate Eight.

I double check that the star advertisement is securely tucked inside my journal. Yes, I'm ready then, for home.

SAVANNAH

Monday afternoon

My cases, lined to the right of Cammy's dresser, are packed and eager, it seems, to fit into the car's trunk, but I'm not quite ready to carry them downstairs. They probably think I should be ready to go, as Ann left hours ago with Chris not far behind her.

Cammy and I stayed at the kitchen table, gradually emptying the pot of coffee and gradually reviewing the weekend. When the noon whistle blew, I jumped. Not only had I forgotten that many small towns signal week day lunch hours with a whistle, but I was astonished that it was already twelve.

I agreed to eat cottage cheese and fruit with Cammy, as I didn't want to go just yet and leave her restful company. On the other hand, this sharply illustrated that I have no woman in my life with whom I can be me, no woman with whom I can sit in easy silence, no woman with whom I needn't pretend. But I do have Benjamin.

During one of our midnight dorm conversations about marriage— long before Dirk married that out-of-state woman—Emily said, "To be a wife you must sacrifice some of yourself. I've lived too many independent years with Cammy. That's spoiled me. I haven't had to share with others."

I countered with, "But if you deeply love someone you don't actually give away anything. The reward of an apparent sacrifice or compromise is a better life for both of you."

Rustling from the opposite side of the room told me that Emily was shaking her head no against the pillow case. "I truly love Dirk, but if I married him, in order for us to achieve any unity, I'd conform to his demands, or at least many of them, and I'd either give up a portion of myself or deny it. Then I'd be guilty of living falsely."

NOTES WHEN SUMMER ENDS

In Cammy's kitchen, I wished once again that I could talk to Emily, tell her that with Benjamin I'd not relinquished a portion of myself, and in this marriage I'd not been guilty of living falsely.

At one o'clock, after drying lunch and breakfast dishes, I packed. Now, I light one more cigarette and pick up the pen to finish My Story in the journal.

Working for Mr. Hendricks and taking care of Mama consumed my days, so it was the last week in August before I chiseled out an hour one evening in which to walk across the tracks and search for Cora Lee's house.

Nervous at what I'd learn and at going alone into the upscale white section, I was acutely conscious of signs warning that I was crossing into a new country. The road in this nice area was smoothly paved, so no little clusters of dust generated behind my shoes as I moved through the twilight. White people on their porches stared at me, and when I passed houses with no one around, I felt that blue eyes peered through shuttered windows to register my progress.

It dawned on me that I didn't know Cora Lee's address, only Butler Avenue, so I asked a child polishing his bicycle.

"Sure, I'll show you," and on his bike, peddling slowly, he turned often to ensure I stayed behind.

The yard before her house was perfect. Roses cascaded over the fence, and the lush lawn spoke of care. I realized I had no idea if she were still married, lived alone, or had a family. Would I meet relatives inside?

I knocked on the screen door, and a huge white man appeared. His animosity poured through the fine mesh, so when I asked, "Is Cora Lee here?" my voice shook.

"We're not hiring any help," he said, and his assumption angered me.

"I'm not applying for a job. I'm looking for my second cousin, Cora Lee Hanson."

The man snorted, but from another room Cora Lee called out, "Who is it, Martin?" Then, an end table light brightened the living room, so I could see her by a back wall. She neared the man, released the screen door hook, and he stepped aside. He appeared to be about Cora Lee's age, but not introducing us, she gestured for me to step into the next room, an Old World room filled with heavy hand-carved furniture, pewter pitchers, and art work from Sweden that decorated the walls.

"Emmaline?"

"She's—she's still alive," I answered. "Mr. Hendricks knew of a practical nurse, and I've hired her."

Cora Lee nodded, then swung around to the scowling man. "Go along, Martin, I have business here."

Unsure who he was, of the role he played in her life, I felt uncomfortably out-of-place. "If this isn't a good time," I said.

"Good as any," she answered and nodded for me to sit. From a wall cabinet, she picked out a black scrapbook. Beside me she flipped pages of photographs, each locked into position by triangular black corners. At last, she paused at a page and passed me the album. In the faint end table light it was hard to see. I brought the page close to my face and examined the top photo. A broad-shouldered white man, well over six feet tall, posed beside a 1940-something Ford sedan and grinned at the camera. So this, this was my father. Yes, definitely good looking. My damp hands stuck to the scrapbook pages as my mouth dried. I squinted, hunting any resemblance to me. I tipped the book, to focus on the next picture of Mama and him. Seated at a table, they leaned toward each other. She was lovely.

"That's Leif and his family." Cora Lee pointed to a third picture, but with the light reflecting, I could distinguish little. By tilting the album another five degrees I had better luck with the final photograph on the page, one slightly out of focus. A tall teenaged boy and a heavy teenaged girl nearly blended into dense background foliage.

"Taken at a picnic over by Sawyer's Creek," Cora Lee said. She tapped her fingernail against the young woman. "That's me. It's the only picture I have of Leif and me, so I won't give you that one. Take the others," and she freed the picture of my father by the car, the one of my parents at the table, and the group shot.

In the future, when Cora Lee opened the album, would she recreate the missing pictures that once carved out this territory? Tonight, however, those darker black squares represented for me the foundations of a demolished house.

Thanking her, I tucked them in my shirt pocket where they wouldn't wrinkle as I went home. "What else can you tell me about my father?"

"Very little. When I arrived in New York, he and Emmaline told me they were married. They had a studio apartment, a sad place really, in a bad neighborhood. Poorly furnished. Depressing. He had some kind of job, in a war plant, I believe. Emmaline was pregnant and scared. Told me that her parents had disowned her, and that aside from Leif, she had no one. And she didn't have him for long. He took off with another woman or women. I'm not sure if he hung around until you were born or not."

"Did he ever come to see me later?"

"Wish I could answer yes, but—"

I glanced around the room. Had my father ever seen these furnishings? Obviously they were antiques. Had they come from that distant Minnesota farm?

"In the meantime," Cora Lee continued, "my husband and I moved here to Hampton." She smiled slightly, and as if offering an aside, as if allowing one splinter of her internal world to show, she said, "After we divorced, I reclaimed my maiden name, Hanson."

"How did Mama get here?"

"Somehow she got my name and contacted me. Broke, and a single parent, Emmaline had nowhere to turn. I sent her some money so she could bring you here, She began cleaning houses, and kept to herself. But there's an invisible grapevine in this world. Seems she was always the subject of gossip, and apparently gossip always centered around a relationship with a white man. Emmaline was tainted."

"You said my father was dead."

As if delaying, as if determining what next to say, she brushed at some non-existent spots across the skirt of her dress. "Was shot," she said.

My heartbeat quickened, and I felt as if my lungs couldn't extract enough oxygen from the oppressive room.

"I'm assuming some jealous husband pulled the trigger, but Minnesota relatives hushed it up, just as they hushed up my divorce. Good, salt-of-the-earth people don't admit to problems." Although I heard her bitterness, I ignored it. I wanted facts.

"But where? How?"

She gave a massive sigh. "I don't know. The family sent me the briefest of details, and an obituary that said Leif had met an accidental death in Florida. That's all I could tell Emmaline. That's all I know. Anything else you must ask your mother. Let her fill in the blanks."

Floorboards sighed behind the door. Lowered voices. Insistent words. Cora Lee stiffened. Were any of my relatives just beyond the wall? Cora Lee rose. I knew she wanted to go into that kitchen, I knew she was going to reveal no more, and I needed to get back to Mama.

I stood beside Cora Lee, hoping she'd answer another question. "Do you know if Mama's relatives are still alive?"

"Imagine so. She came from Georgia, assume that's why she named you Savannah."

She escorted me onto the porch, where I pushed my luck, tried for one more answer. "My father's family is still in Minnesota?"

"Don't even think of it." Her expression and voice hardened. "You want to hurt them? They don't want souvenirs of Leif's past, especially a black girl who shows up saying, 'I'm your niece' or 'I'm your cousin.' And that goes for your mother's family, as well. Do they want some reminder of their pain? Oh, it's highly romantic to contemplate reconnecting with family. Stories have been written about the successful reuniting, but for every happy experience, there are countless miserable ones. Your mother's done the right thing. She's raised you well. You make your own history, Savannah." Behind me she hooked the screen.

I took a few steps along the pristine walkway, then heard her voice, low and caring, "Keep me informed about Emmaline."

With a nod, I hurried over the tracks to relieve the nurse and to search through our kitchen junk drawer for a magnifying glass. Micro-centimeter by micro-centimeter, I went over the pictures, concluding finally that maybe I'd inherited my father's smile and that, undoubtedly, I'd inherited my bosom from this white grandmother.

In the group scene, she and Grandfather Eric sat on straight kitchen chairs in a side yard of firm packed dirt. Assorted men ranged behind, and I picked out Leif. Possibly he was sixteen or seventeen. Were the others brothers? Uncles? My nameless grandmother more than filled her white shirtwaist, just as I did. Decades later, I could feel how the fabric strained over her chest, how the buttons tensed in their holes.

Memory is cloudy, tricky, so perhaps it wasn't the day after I'd been to Cora Lee's that Mama worsened and the nurse summoned the ambulance, but it seemed like the next day. And it seems that Mama died within hours, but maybe it took longer. Whatever human time elapsed isn't important for this journal. Of importance for My Story is that Mama revealed nothing more. I never learned when or how my father left her, or if they'd ever had any contact. Never learned of relatives in Georgia. I never learned her narrative.

Minutes after she died, I dialed Emily. "I'll get the first flight back," she said. But in a rare moment of sensibility at that time I said, "No." I wanted to call Tyler, dreamed of his embrace, his support as I planned a simple service, but, naturally, that was impossible. At one point Emily had been to Monroe, learned that Tyler and Leatha were married, had produced baby boy Bradford, and that another Bradford store was opening in Shelby, Iowa.

Alone in our cottage, eyes sore from crying, I hunted for scraps of Mama's past. Although I knew each room intimately, although hiding places were nonexistent, I re-inspected back closet corners, shoved the mattress from the bed, dumped Mama's handkerchief drawer, and searched through the cigar box she'd labeled, "Due Bills." I pawed through the cardboard box in which she'd filed my letters. I even descended into the partially-dug root cellar where she stored beans, tomatoes, relish, and fruit that she canned. Shoving aside dusty bottles, I trained a flashlight beam under the sloping wall. At last in a crawl space over the kitchen, I located a battered suitcase with my birth certificate, vaccination records, report cards, a construction paper Valentine ("I love you, Mama. Be Mine"), a crayoned drawing of our house signed "Savannah Hanson Second Grade," with popsicle sticks pasted into a frame. The suitcase contained but an outline of my life. It held even less of Mama's.

Mr. Hendricks and Mama's main employers, the Simontons, paid the undertaker's bill and attended the graveside service. Cora Lee didn't come, but I'd not expected her to, for when I'd phoned with news of Mama's death, she'd not asked about funeral arrangements. "I'm sorry," she said. "I'll pray for her soul." Before disconnecting she added, "Take care, Savannah. Make a life for yourself that will make Emmaline proud."

And mostly I have. I never traveled to Georgia in search of maternal relatives, never tried to contact my father's family, never attempted to learn the particulars of his life or of his death, or where he's buried. But that hasn't stopped my mind from wondering about him and all my missing ancestors. I've come to see that's the beauty of My Story. I can write and rewrite it however I choose.

I can do the same for Tyler, for Emily, for Cora Lee, for….

Well, here I'll stop. I'll put my purse over my shoulder, promise Cammy that I'll visit her in the fall, and then I'll drive away. As I do, I'll watch in my mind's eye as Cammy climbs the stairs to reclaim her room. She'll find it as neat as when she ushered me in on Friday, except beside the hand mirror with its primrose decoration that rests on the dresser, she'll discover one addition—this journal waiting for her.

ABOUT THE AUTHOR

Beverly Lauderdale's articles and short fiction have appeared in numerous publications. A graduate of Simpson College and Holy Names University, she lives in northern California.

Excerpt from

CRICKET'S SERENADE

BY

CAROLITA BLYTHE

Release Date: May 2006

-1-

I had spent the first twenty-five years of my life in the country-side of Jamaica – in a village that disappeared behind a shroud of total and complete blackness once the sun went down. And the wailing of the wind and the crying of the night owls made it seem as if there was something other-worldly laying in wait around every corner. And yet in all that time, I never once crossed paths with a ghost. That might not seem like much of an admission, but of the one hundred or so people who called Stepney home, only two ever laid claim to such a statement. One was Matilda Alexander, my aunt. The other was me. You see, seeing ghosts in Stepney was about as commonplace as thunderstorms during the rainy season. Mavis Parker had seen her neighbor, Farmer Warren, drinking water outside her front gate one night. That would have been all right, had the man not passed on twenty years before. Effie Blackshire came upon her dead brother nestled between the branches of an old cotton tree, whistling the melody to Jimmy Cliff's "Wonderful World, Beautiful People." Even preacher man, as great a believer in the word of the bible as ever there was, once admitted to observing "some funny business of the other worldly kind." But as far as I could tell, these duppy sightings only ever seemed to take place after a night of too much white rum and Red Stripe or a long day out in the fields under the glare of the sun. Duppies did not exist in the past. Duppies do not exist in the present – or so I thought. I had managed to hold on to this belief the entire twenty-five years I spent in Stepney and the eighteen years I'd been away. I had managed to hold on until today.

There was this old woman who lived in the village who could sense life-changing events before they took place. She had these strange eyes. They looked as if they were made of glass and I was always afraid that if I looked into them too deeply, I would have been able to see how I was going to die or when, so I always passed her by with my head down. The old woman believed that everyone had these powers of prophecy. It was just that most people didn't know how to read the signs. I never quite believed her, but when my phone rang last night, a strange feeling came over me. The ring wasn't louder or more shrill than usual. The person wasn't calling at a strange time. It was maybe six in the evening, just before sunset. I can't really explain it, but for some reason, I felt a little apprehensive in picking up the receiver.

"Is this Souci, the former Souci Alexander?" the voice on the other end asked.

"Yes," I said. I didn't have that many callers so it wasn't usually very difficult to place a voice.

"This is Agnes. Agnes Gooding."

I guess I didn't say anything because the next thing I remember was her repeating my name over and over and over again. I wasn't trying to be rude. I didn't mean to not answer her, but Agnes Gooding was a name that lived only in my past. Even then, no one would have mistaken us for friends. In fact, if I had been asked to describe my feelings for her in one word, I would have said dislike. In two words, I would have said strong dislike. Truth is, I once thought I hated her, but being older and wiser now, I realized it was probably more jealousy than anything else. Jamaicans have always been so consumed with race and class, and I suppose I'm no different. Agnes was lighter skinned, like so many of those who had all the money on the island, and she could even trace her ancestry back beyond the days of slavery. She could trace it back to her great-great-great grandfather's family in northern England. I was a simple country girl, just an insignificant member of the masses. There were no British officers or landowners I could trace my roots back to. There were only mountain people and former slaves. I can't even say with any certainty what date I was born. My birth certificate states November eleventh, but I recall Aunt Mattie once telling me that the eleventh was actually the date someone from our village happened to be going into the town —which is where the registry office was located. I had actually come into the word several weeks before. I didn't discount this, considering I had also been mistakenly listed as a male child on that same birth certificate and had to go through many pains to get that changed. (The particular "someone" who registered me was known to have a weakness for Wincarnes Wine and there's no telling how sober he might or might not have been on that trip into town.) But in the country, being a day or a week or even a month off on dates isn't that big a deal — unlike in Agnes' world where everything has to be so precise. I hadn't seen or spoken to her in a very long time, so I really couldn't think of any reason why she would be on the other end of the telephone line.

"I'm in St. Ann," she said, "and I have to see you. What I have to say shouldn't be said over the phone."

I quickly added up the years. It had been fourteen. What could someone possibly have to say after fourteen years? Agnes guessed it would take her about half-hour to get to me, and my heart started beating just a little bit faster. There was only one thing Agnes Gooding and I had in common, and that thing…that person, was part of the reason I had left Jamaica fourteen years before and had not returned until three weeks ago.

After I hung up the phone, I moved out onto the verandah where I could look off at the quiet street that curved down the hill. Mango and orange trees grew on both sides. From where I was standing, I could see some of the activity taking place in the outdoor marketplace at the bottom of the hill. The busiest market day in Brown's Town was drawing to a close, and people who had come from various surrounding areas were trying to make their final purchases. They could get fresh honey loaded into empty rum bottles, ripe scotch bonnet peppers for their Sunday rice and peas, pig's tail to add a little flavor to stew peas or crates of Craven A's for their after dinner smoke.

I had gotten lost in thought about returning to Jamaica and about Agnes' strange call when I noticed a white Camry slowly winding it's way up the hill. I took a long, deep breath and held it for a while. The car continued along the incline, then slowed a bit as it reached my gate. It stopped, but nothing further happened for several moments. I waited with anticipation as the driver's side window eased down. A small, white hand appeared and waved.

"Drive up," I said, hoping I wouldn't come to regret my hospitality. Aunt Mattie used to always warn against unannounced visitors arriving with the fall of night. "Dem is here only to destroy de peace of de soul," she would say. Aunt Mattie had a different saying for every occasion. After she died, I would always try to remember them, but I never could. This evening, her words seemed to just come alive in my mind.

The car made its way up the dirt drive and came to a stop just in front of my house. I held my breath as I waited for Agnes to step from the driver's seat. To be honest, a part of me was hoping to see someone that time had not been kind to. I was hoping for someone ten dress sizes larger with a head full of grays and a couple of warts to round out the package. That would prove that everything eventually evened out in life. But as Agnes got out of the car, I was disappointed to see how little she had changed. She was still so tall and thin and graceful – like a ballet dancer. Her hair was still as black as a country night and she even wore it in the same style – pulled back in a loose bun just above her neck. She even dressed in the same style. She was wearing a pretty blue linen sleeveless dress with strappy matching sandals. The only thing different was her jewelry. The gemstone bracelets and earrings were gone – replaced by a large silver cross that dangled from a silver necklace.

I showed her to the set of stairs that led up to the verandah. When she reached the second level, she stood still for a few seconds, as if someone had fastened her ankles to the tiles. Her eyes were fixed on my face. Those wide, all seeing eyes now seemed a little smaller, a little worn down. I'm not sure how long we stood there without saying a word. I was trying to feel her out. The Agnes Gooding I remembered had not been the sweetest person. What did she have in store for me now? Finally, she began moving towards me. But she was very hesitant, which made it seem as if she was moving in slow motion. She settled about a foot away from me, then brought her hands forward and latched onto mine. Every muscle in my body tensed up. I swallowed hard, blinked slowly and waited for those sharp Agnes Gooding-like words to come hurtling at me like a dagger.

"It's been so long. God has obviously kept you in his hands."

Kindness from Agnes Gooding? Now I was really sure she was up to no good.

"You look the same, Agnes. But then you have always looked good," I had to admit. "But I heard you were off the island, living in London or some such far away place.'

"It was time to come back. I've just been here eight weeks now. And then I found out you had returned to the island yourself."

"Three weeks. I don't think it was in the paper…"

"Oh, it doesn't have to be. You know how upper Kingston is. We have our own gossip news corps that circulate the happenings around town faster than JBC or CNN." She proceeded to stare at me as a strange, sad smile formed on her face. "Oh Souci, I'm so sorry. I'm sure you thought the devil had long prepared a spot for me in his house."

I had to pause for a few moments, try to figure out her strategy. What was all this talk of God and the devil? Agnes had never been religious.

"It was a long time ago, I guess."

"Says Cinderella to the wicked step-sister. But time does not excuse my behavior. I wish I could say I was only a child then, that I could blame it on immaturity. But I was a full grown woman getting over my second husband. This is probably little consolation, but I had my reasons." She bit her bottom lip and shifted her eyes over to a nearby guava tree. "Souci, why did you come back to Jamaica? It's been so long."

"I guess when Lewis died and all that business went down…So

much of what I knew of Jamaica outside of Stepney was based on Lewis, so I just had to get away from it. But this island is my island. It's my home. I needed to deal with everything that happened and to move on. Besides, my daughter wanted to know the place where her mom was born, where she was born."

Neither of us said anything for a while. I was waiting for Agnes to tell me what prompted her visit.

"Souci, if I could trouble you…" she began. I leaned in. "For some tea."

"Tea?"

"Yes. But if it's too much trouble…"

"No, no, no," I said. I don't know if she sensed the puzzlement in my voice. "I have mint."

"Fresh mint? Oh, that would be a nice change."

After showing Agnes to a seat at the patio table in the corner of the verandah, I left for the kitchen. I was completely confused.

"Maybe I'm dreaming this," I said to myself. "I always used to dream things as a child and swear they really happened when they really didn't. What does my husband say? You live amongst the what-ifs and the why-nots. Maybe this is a what-if."

"Did you say something?" Agnes called out.

"No. Just singing."

I tried to tell myself not to anticipate anything. I thought of the words to "Michael Row the Boat Ashore" as I boiled the tea, sliced up the rum cake I had made the day before and arranged everything neatly on a serving tray.

When I returned to the verandah, Agnes was sitting quietly, wringing her hands together.

"Thank you," she said softly as I put the tea on the table. I tried not to stare as she took a small bite of the cake. I had always been fascinated by her lips. They were the deepest cherry red – naturally. She never needed to use lipstick or gloss. I just couldn't believe how good time had been to her. When I was a little girl, my aunt used to tell me that mean people grew old and shriveled long before their time. Looking at Agnes, I decided this wasn't true. Agnes looked over at me and I quickly looked away. I looked off into the heavens. The sun had turned in for the night and Blackbirds flew off into the small trace of light remaining. I tried to take in all the air my lungs would allow, but it was just so warm. The air was so thick, I had to put a little extra effort into breathing. The usual evening breezes were nowhere to be found. The leaves of the giant palms stood still. Agnes took a few sips of tea, and let out a small sigh. She then eased back into her chair and looked straight ahead. As the sunset cast a rusty glow against her face, she seemed locked in a long forgotten memory.

"You've done so well for yourself, Souci. A line of books."

"Nothing important. Just fluffy romance stories you can read on the beach."

"Sometimes it's the fluff that makes life bearable. And you've been married for a while now. Did your husband not return to the island with you?"

"I wanted to come down and try and get things together before he got here. Plus, we planned to have Charlotte spend the summer with relatives in Atlanta anyway, so things worked out well."

"When I first met you, you were this young country girl who could hardly get through a sentence without stumbling."

Here we go, I thought. Welcome back Agnes Gooding of old.

"Now you're so accomplished."

I was caught off guard. Agnes shook her head slowly, then parted her lips

as if she were about to say something else, but suddenly stopped. I just couldn't take it anymore.

"Agnes, I'm not surprised you knew how or where to find me, but I don't understand why you would even want to," I said finally.

"I had some business to take care of in Ocho Rios, and since it's not that far…"

"It's not really that close either."

Agnes sighed deeply. Tears gathered in the corners of her eyes.

"No, I guess it's not. The truth is, I was going to do this through a phone call, but it just didn't seem right…"

"But what's so important that you would need to talk to me about."

"You have to come to Kingston."

"Why?"

Silence came in the way of an answer.

"The way I see it, I'll get to Kingston in my own time. Brown's Town's been a big step for me. Kingston I'll have to ease into."

"The time is right for you to come now…"

"Agnes, you're not the one who can determine that. I'm not ready…"

"Souci, Lewis is in Kingston."

"Lewis who?" was all I could muster, because up until this point, I still held no belief in ghosts.

"Lewis Montrose…"

"…is dead," I finished.

Agnes shook her head. "Not all together."

"How can you be not all together dead? You're either dead or you're not."

"It means he's not dead…yet."

"Lewis not dead yet is almost as hard to understand as Lewis not all

together dead, Agnes. It's hard to understand because he is dead."

"That's just it, Souci. He's not dead at all. He's alive."

How do you respond to being told that someone who you knew for a fact had died years before wasn't really dead? You don't. I didn't. I just looked at Agnes for some time, trying to figure out exactly what she was up to. I was waiting for her to say, "gotcha." But her eyes were still and her face was calm. Just then, I realized she wasn't half-mad or on prescription drugs. She was telling the truth. My head started whizzing around, but I couldn't speak. I remember the articles in the Caribbean papers in New York detailing Lewis' life. I remember the sinking feeling in my stomach when I heard the news. In history books, there was a date of death following his date of birth. And now this person sitting before me was saying that all I had known to be true was not true after all.

"How can he not be…"

"Think about it, Souci. How many things in Lewis' life were not as they seemed? Well, the same can be said of his death."

"But why are you telling me this?"

"We've been gone for so long. That's how we were able to keep this thing going. But now Lewis is really coming close to his end and he needs to see you."

"I don't understand this. Where has he been? How did you fool everyone…"

"I can't say. Just come to Kingston. Tomorrow, the next day, but you must come soon. We don't have very long, and you must not tell a soul."

"I've known many people who have died…once. My whole family in the country really. But I've never known anyone who was about to die a second time." That was meant to be a thought, but I must have said it out loud because I heard Agnes asking me to repeat myself.

"Lewis asked for me?" I said instead.

"He doesn't know I'm here," Agnes admitted.

"Then why are you telling me this?"

"Because I know what he needs, what he needs to do before he's gone. I know the peace he needs to make, and you're it."

Agnes was in her car before I had a chance to get hold of my thoughts. Actually, I don't even remember her leaving the verandah.

"You can stay here 'till morning," I called out to her when I finally came to my senses. "The mountain roads around here aren't lit at night and it's dangerous for someone who doesn't know the way."

"I don't like spending too much time away from Kingston," she said. "Besides, I have faith in the lord to guide me." And with that, she was gone.

I climbed into bed at about one in the morning, but was back up and pacing across the verandah by two. I couldn't figure out what I was feeling. I was scared. I was relieved. I was in disbelief. The front gate was still open, so I wrapped a robe around my shoulders and walked along the path leading to it. It had finally cooled down some, and the fronds of the coconut trees were once again swaying in the breeze. I could make out a light flickering in the distance. Pooh Harvey was closing up his bar. Saturday nights were always a hot time there and he usually had to threaten people to get them out. Before I could reach the gate, a small goat belonging to Mack Shakespeare, who lived up the hill, wandered into the yard. There were two bells about his neck, and they made a hollow dinging noise whenever he moved. I tried shooing, even pushing, but he held his ground. I didn't have the energy to fight with him, so I closed the gate behind him. I made my way back up to the verandah where I sat and watched him nibbling at the grass.

The shrill ring of the telephone woke me up. I had fallen asleep on the verandah, and as I sat up in the patio chair, I could feel a stiffness in my neck. The sun felt warm and alive against my face. The phone rang again and I ran into the living room to pick up the receiver.

"Just checking in," came George's friendly voice. When I had first met him I thought, no one can possibly sound this happy. "Checking in on sunny Jamaica," he continued. He reminded me of a chirping bird.

I can't remember exactly what I told my husband, something about not sleeping much the night before and needing to curl up in bed the rest of the morning. There was still so much I had never and probably would never share with George about my past, so I couldn't even begin to explain Agnes Gooding's visit the night before.

I showered and dressed in much of a daze. Don't even remember the water hitting my skin or putting on my white button down shirt. Mack Shakespeare's goat stumbled out of the yard when I opened the gate to drive my small Blue Volkswagen through. I don't recall much of the scenery that unfolded those first few miles. It was almost as if there was someone else driving the car - some invisible person. The hands squeezing the steering wheel and the feet working the clutch, the gas and the brakes didn't belong to me. It wasn't until I reached Bamboo, some eight miles away, that I realized I hadn't eaten anything since the slice of cake the night before. But there was no room in my belly for food – only nervous tension. Still, when I neared a group of higglers, I stopped to buy some oranges and bananas, in case I became hungry during the drive. I didn't haggle with the market woman, just paid the requested amount, which seemed to upset her quite a bit. After all, she had been denied an opportunity at showcasing her prime bargaining skills. But I just wanted to start back on the road. I had a date with my past. I had a date with a ghost.

With two hours to go until Kingston, all that lay before me was the green of the valleys and the early morning mist. Suddenly, I couldn't stop my mind from drifting back to the day my life strayed from the course I believe God had truly meant for me.

2006 Publication Schedule

January

A Lover's Legacy
Veronica Parker
1-58571-167-5
$9.95

Love Lasts Forever
Dominiqua Douglas
1-58571-187-X
$9.95

Under the Cherry
  Moon
Christal Jordan-Mims
1-58571-169-1
$12.95

February

Second Chances at Love
Cheris Hodges
1-58571-188-8
$9.95

Enchanted Desire
Wanda Y. Thomas
1-58571-176-4
$9.95

Caught Up
Deatri King Bey
1-58571-178-0
$12.95

March

I'm Gonna Make You
  Love Me
Gwyneth Bolton
1-58571-181-0
$9.95

Through the Fire
Seressia Glass
1-58571-173-X
$9.95

Notes When Summer
  Ends
Beverly Lauderdale
1-58571-180-2
$12.95

April

Sin and Surrender
J.M. Jeffries
1-58571-189-6
$9.95

Unearthing Passions
Elaine Sims
1-58571-184-5
$9.95

Between Tears
Pamela Ridley
1-58571-179-9
$12.95

May

Misty Blue
Dyanne Davis
1-58571-186-1
$9.95

Ironic
Pamela Leigh Starr
1-58571-168-3
$9.95

Cricket's Serenade
Carolita Blythe
1-58571-183-7
$12.95

June

Cupid
Barbara Keaton
1-58571-174-8
$9.95

Havana Sunrise
Kymberly Hunt
1-58571-182-9
$9.95

2006 Publication Schedule (continued)

July

Love Me Carefully
A.C. Arthur
1-58571-177-2
$9.95

No Ordinary Love
Angela Weaver
1-58571-198-5
$9.95

Rehoboth Road
Anita Ballard-Jones
1-58571-196-9
$12.95

August

Scent of Rain
Annetta P. Lee
158571-199-3
$9.95

Love in High Gear
Charlotte Roy
158571-185-3
$9.95

Rise of the Phoenix
Kenneth Whetstone
1-58571-197-7
$12.95

September

The Business of Love
Cheris Hodges
1-58571-193-4
$9.95

Rock Star
Rosyln Hardy Holcomb
1-58571-200-0
$9.95

A Dead Man Speaks
Lisa Jones Johnson
1-58571-203-5
$12.95

October

Rivers of the Soul-Part 1
Leslie Esdaile
1-58571-223-X
$9.95

A Dangerous Woman
J.M. Jeffries
1-58571-195-0
$9.95

Sinful Intentions
Crystal Rhodes
1-58571-201-9
$12.95

November

Only You
Crystal Hubbard
1-58571-208-6
$9.95

Ebony Eyes
Kei Swanson
1-58571-194-2
$9.95

Still Waters Run Deep –
    Part 2
Leslie Esdaile
1-58571-224-8
$9.95

December

Let's Get It On
Dyanne Davis
1-58571-210-8
$9.95

Nights Over Egypt
Barbara Keaton
1-58571-192-6
$9.95

A Pefect Place to Pray
I.L. Goodwin
1-58571-202-7
$12.95

Other Genesis Press, Inc. Titles

A Dangerous Deception	J.M. Jeffries	$8.95
A Dangerous Love	J.M. Jeffries	$8.95
A Dangerous Obsession	J.M. Jeffries	$8.95
A Drummer's Beat to Mend	Kei Swanson	$9.95
A Happy Life	Charlotte Harris	$9.95
A Heart's Awakening	Veronica Parker	$9.95
A Lark on the Wing	Phyliss Hamilton	$9.95
A Love of Her Own	Cheris F. Hodges	$9.95
A Love to Cherish	Beverly Clark	$8.95
A Risk of Rain	Dar Tomlinson	$8.95
A Twist of Fate	Beverly Clark	$8.95
A Will to Love	Angie Daniels	$9.95
Acquisitions	Kimberley White	$8.95
Across	Carol Payne	$12.95
After the Vows	Leslie Esdaile	$10.95
(Summer Anthology)	T.T. Henderson	
	Jacqueline Thomas	
Again My Love	Kayla Perrin	$10.95
Against the Wind	Gwynne Forster	$8.95
All I Ask	Barbara Keaton	$8.95
Ambrosia	T.T. Henderson	$8.95
An Unfinished Love Affair	Barbara Keaton	$8.95
And Then Came You	Dorothy Elizabeth Love	$8.95
Angel's Paradise	Janice Angelique	$9.95
At Last	Lisa G. Riley	$8.95
Best of Friends	Natalie Dunbar	$8.95
Beyond the Rapture	Beverly Clark	$9.95
Blaze	Barbara Keaton	$9.95
Blood Lust	J. M. Jeffries	$9.95
Bodyguard	Andrea Jackson	$9.95
Boss of Me	Diana Nyad	$8.95
Bound by Love	Beverly Clark	$8.95
Breeze	Robin Hampton Allen	$10.95

Other Genesis Press, Inc. Titles (continued)

Broken	Dar Tomlinson	$24.95
By Design	Barbara Keaton	$8.95
Cajun Heat	Charlene Berry	$8.95
Careless Whispers	Rochelle Alers	$8.95
Cats & Other Tales	Marilyn Wagner	$8.95
Caught in a Trap	Andre Michelle	$8.95
Caught Up In the Rapture	Lisa G. Riley	$9.95
Cautious Heart	Cheris F Hodges	$8.95
Chances	Pamela Leigh Starr	$8.95
Cherish the Flame	Beverly Clark	$8.95
Class Reunion	Irma Jenkins/John Brown	$12.95
Code Name: Diva	J.M. Jeffries	$9.95
Conquering Dr. Wexler's Heart	Kimberley White	$9.95
Crossing Paths, Tempting Memories	Dorothy Elizabeth Love	$9.95
Cypress Whisperings	Phyllis Hamilton	$8.95
Dark Embrace	Crystal Wilson Harris	$8.95
Dark Storm Rising	Chinelu Moore	$10.95
Daughter of the Wind	Joan Xian	$8.95
Deadly Sacrifice	Jack Kean	$22.95
Designer Passion	Dar Tomlinson	$8.95
Dreamtective	Liz Swados	$5.95
Ebony Butterfly II	Delilah Dawson	$14.95
Echoes of Yesterday	Beverly Clark	$9.95
Eden's Garden	Elizabeth Rose	$8.95
Everlastin' Love	Gay G. Gunn	$8.95
Everlasting Moments	Dorothy Elizabeth Love	$8.95
Everything and More	Sinclair Lebeau	$8.95
Everything but Love	Natalie Dunbar	$8.95
Eve's Prescription	Edwina Martin Arnold	$8.95
Falling	Natalie Dunbar	$9.95
Fate	Pamela Leigh Starr	$8.95
Finding Isabella	A.J. Garrotto	$8.95

Other Genesis Press, Inc. Titles (continued)

Forbidden Quest	Dar Tomlinson	$10.95
Forever Love	Wanda Thomas	$8.95
From the Ashes	Kathleen Suzanne	$8.95
	Jeanne Sumerix	
Gentle Yearning	Rochelle Alers	$10.95
Glory of Love	Sinclair LeBeau	$10.95
Go Gentle into that Good Night	Malcom Boyd	$12.95
Goldengroove	Mary Beth Craft	$16.95
Groove, Bang, and Jive	Steve Cannon	$8.99
Hand in Glove	Andrea Jackson	$9.95
Hard to Love	Kimberley White	$9.95
Hart & Soul	Angie Daniels	$8.95
Heartbeat	Stephanie Bedwell-Grime	$8.95
Hearts Remember	M. Loui Quezada	$8.95
Hidden Memories	Robin Allen	$10.95
Higher Ground	Leah Latimer	$19.95
Hitler, the War, and the Pope	Ronald Rychiak	$26.95
How to Write a Romance	Kathryn Falk	$18.95
I Married a Reclining Chair	Lisa M. Fuhs	$8.95
Indigo After Dark Vol. I	Nia Dixon/Angelique	$10.95
Indigo After Dark Vol. II	Dolores Bundy/Cole Riley	$10.95
Indigo After Dark Vol. III	Montana Blue/Coco Morena	$10.95
Indigo After Dark Vol. IV	Cassandra Colt/	$14.95
	Diana Richeaux	
Indigo After Dark Vol. V	Delilah Dawson	$14.95
Icie	Pamela Leigh Starr	$8.95
I'll Be Your Shelter	Giselle Carmichael	$8.95
I'll Paint a Sun	A.J. Garrotto	$9.95
Illusions	Pamela Leigh Starr	$8.95
Indiscretions	Donna Hill	$8.95
Intentional Mistakes	Michele Sudler	$9.95
Interlude	Donna Hill	$8.95
Intimate Intentions	Angie Daniels	$8.95

Other Genesis Press, Inc. Titles (continued)

Jolie's Surrender	Edwina Martin-Arnold	$8.95
Kiss or Keep	Debra Phillips	$8.95
Lace	Giselle Carmichael	$9.95
Last Train to Memphis	Elsa Cook	$12.95
Lasting Valor	Ken Olsen	$24.95
Let Us Prey	Hunter Lundy	$25.95
Life Is Never As It Seems	J.J. Michael	$12.95
Lighter Shade of Brown	Vicki Andrews	$8.95
Love Always	Mildred E. Riley	$10.95
Love Doesn't Come Easy	Charlyne Dickerson	$8.95
Love Unveiled	Gloria Greene	$10.95
Love's Deception	Charlene Berry	$10.95
Love's Destiny	M. Loui Quezada	$8.95
Mae's Promise	Melody Walcott	$8.95
Magnolia Sunset	Giselle Carmichael	$8.95
Matters of Life and Death	Lesego Malepe, Ph.D.	$15.95
Meant to Be	Jeanne Sumerix	$8.95
Midnight Clear	Leslie Esdaile	$10.95
(Anthology)	Gwynne Forster	
	Carmen Green	
	Monica Jackson	
Midnight Magic	Gwynne Forster	$8.95
Midnight Peril	Vicki Andrews	$10.95
Misconceptions	Pamela Leigh Starr	$9.95
Montgomery's Children	Richard Perry	$14.95
My Buffalo Soldier	Barbara B. K. Reeves	$8.95
Naked Soul	Gwynne Forster	$8.95
Next to Last Chance	Louisa Dixon	$24.95
No Apologies	Seressia Glass	$8.95
No Commitment Required	Seressia Glass	$8.95
No Regrets	Mildred E. Riley	$8.95
Nowhere to Run	Gay G. Gunn	$10.95
O Bed! O Breakfast!	Rob Kuehnle	$14.95

Other Genesis Press, Inc. Titles (continued)

Object of His Desire	A. C. Arthur	$8.95
Office Policy	A. C. Arthur	$9.95
Once in a Blue Moon	Dorianne Cole	$9.95
One Day at a Time	Bella McFarland	$8.95
Outside Chance	Louisa Dixon	$24.95
Passion	T.T. Henderson	$10.95
Passion's Blood	Cherif Fortin	$22.95
Passion's Journey	Wanda Thomas	$8.95
Past Promises	Jahmel West	$8.95
Path of Fire	T.T. Henderson	$8.95
Path of Thorns	Annetta P. Lee	$9.95
Peace Be Still	Colette Haywood	$12.95
Picture Perfect	Reon Carter	$8.95
Playing for Keeps	Stephanie Salinas	$8.95
Pride & Joi	Gay G. Gunn	$15.95
Pride & Joi	Gay G. Gunn	$8.95
Promises to Keep	Alicia Wiggins	$8.95
Quiet Storm	Donna Hill	$10.95
Reckless Surrender	Rochelle Alers	$6.95
Red Polka Dot in a World of Plaid	Varian Johnson	$12.95
Reluctant Captive	Joyce Jackson	$8.95
Rendezvous with Fate	Jeanne Sumerix	$8.95
Revelations	Cheris F. Hodges	$8.95
Rivers of the Soul	Leslie Esdaile	$8.95
Rocky Mountain Romance	Kathleen Suzanne	$8.95
Rooms of the Heart	Donna Hill	$8.95
Rough on Rats and Tough on Cats	Chris Parker	$12.95
Secret Library Vol. 1	Nina Sheridan	$18.95
Secret Library Vol. 2	Cassandra Colt	$8.95
Shades of Brown	Denise Becker	$8.95
Shades of Desire	Monica White	$8.95

Other Genesis Press, Inc. Titles (continued)

Shadows in the Moonlight	Jeanne Sumerix	$8.95
Sin	Crystal Rhodes	$8.95
So Amazing	Sinclair LeBeau	$8.95
Somebody's Someone	Sinclair LeBeau	$8.95
Someone to Love	Alicia Wiggins	$8.95
Song in the Park	Martin Brant	$15.95
Soul Eyes	Wayne L. Wilson	$12.95
Soul to Soul	Donna Hill	$8.95
Southern Comfort	J.M. Jeffries	$8.95
Still the Storm	Sharon Robinson	$8.95
Still Waters Run Deep	Leslie Esdaile	$8.95
Stories to Excite You	Anna Forrest/Divine	$14.95
Subtle Secrets	Wanda Y. Thomas	$8.95
Suddenly You	Crystal Hubbard	$9.95
Sweet Repercussions	Kimberley White	$9.95
Sweet Tomorrows	Kimberly White	$8.95
Taken by You	Dorothy Elizabeth Love	$9.95
Tattooed Tears	T. T. Henderson	$8.95
The Color Line	Lizzette Grayson Carter	$9.95
The Color of Trouble	Dyanne Davis	$8.95
The Disappearance of Allison Jones	Kayla Perrin	$5.95
The Honey Dipper's Legacy	Pannell-Allen	$14.95
The Joker's Love Tune	Sidney Rickman	$15.95
The Little Pretender	Barbara Cartland	$10.95
The Love We Had	Natalie Dunbar	$8.95
The Man Who Could Fly	Bob & Milana Beamon	$18.95
The Missing Link	Charlyne Dickerson	$8.95
The Price of Love	Sinclair LeBeau	$8.95
The Smoking Life	Ilene Barth	$29.95
The Words of the Pitcher	Kei Swanson	$8.95
Three Wishes	Seressia Glass	$8.95
Ties That Bind	Kathleen Suzanne	$8.95
Tiger Woods	Libby Hughes	$5.95

Other Genesis Press, Inc. Titles (continued)

Time is of the Essence	Angie Daniels	$9.95
Timeless Devotion	Bella McFarland	$9.95
Tomorrow's Promise	Leslie Esdaile	$8.95
Truly Inseparable	Wanda Y. Thomas	$8.95
Unbreak My Heart	Dar Tomlinson	$8.95
Uncommon Prayer	Kenneth Swanson	$9.95
Unconditional	A.C. Arthur	$9.95
Unconditional Love	Alicia Wiggins	$8.95
Until Death Do Us Part	Susan Paul	$8.95
Vows of Passion	Bella McFarland	$9.95
Wedding Gown	Dyanne Davis	$8.95
What's Under Benjamin's Bed	Sandra Schaffer	$8.95
When Dreams Float	Dorothy Elizabeth Love	$8.95
Whispers in the Night	Dorothy Elizabeth Love	$8.95
Whispers in the Sand	LaFlorya Gauthier	$10.95
Wild Ravens	Altonya Washington	$9.95
Yesterday Is Gone	Beverly Clark	$10.95
Yesterday's Dreams, Tomorrow's Promises	Reon Laudat	$8.95
Your Precious Love	Sinclair LeBeau	$8.95

Order Form

Mail to: Genesis Press, Inc.
P.O. Box 101
Columbus, MS 39703

Name _____
Address _____
City/State _____ Zip _____
Telephone _____

Ship to (if different from above)
Name _____
Address _____
City/State _____ Zip _____
Telephone _____

Credit Card Information
Credit Card # _____ ☐ Visa   ☐ Mastercard
Expiration Date (mm/yy) _____ ☐ AmEx   ☐ Discover

Qty.	Author	Title	Price	Total

Use this order

form, or call

1-888-INDIGO-1

Total for books _____
Shipping and handling:
  $5 first two books,
  $1 each additional book _____
Total S & H _____
Total amount enclosed _____

Mississippi residents add 7% sales tax